# The Book of

# Cebagii

I0602060

Kavin Peeples

Cadmus Publishing

www.cadmuspublishing.com

Kavin   Peeples

# THE MAIN TABLE OF THE CONTENTS:

# Volume 1

# Sec. I: The Prologue

There are three sources of human knowledge;

A.  Human experience.

B.  Human instinct & biology.

C.  Spiritual experiences & revelations.

If one destroys physical artifacts then one destroys the physical basis for confirming the validity of the knowledge, were that knowledge comes from human experience in this physical realm.

If one alters human perception of there body, by psychological and pharmaceutical means, then ones destroys the innate evidence of the validity of knowledge which is innate.

If one smashes idols, kills priestesses, and burns sacred text, then one destroys a religion. If one then replaces the native religion with a foreign religion, then one destroys the ability to correctly perceive and comprehend one spiritual experiences. This destroys the ability to acquire knowledge by spiritual means, because it shuts one off from various spiritual sources, and then restricts one to other particular spiritual sources.

This is how organized religion fights all other religion and convinces everyone in this world that there is no truth except for the one religion which that organized religion has allowed physical, biological, and spiritual evidence to continue to exist, in order to validate that particular religion and invalidate all others.

The war amongst religions is a war over the truth. In this war the evidence of inconvenient truths is destroyed, and therefore clearly those fighting this war have no intent to ever allow the truth to ever be known.

Becoming a part of any society requires that we make certain compromises, in order that we can have equality, equity, and extended range of human realization of a life of purpose and meaning. We also abandon the truth, and replace it with a necessary lie upon which society is based.

This is only the beginning of the battle to break free of the religions of deception & lies; to look at history through the eyes of a higher

beings who is unknown to the world, and whose voices are called hallucinations and mental illness; and whose history are called myths.

And so let us hear what the goddesses without a temple have to say of history & mystery, of life & death, and of truths.

- Oba Kavii Led Arah.

Notes:

Kavin   Peeples

1) The Term " Heaven ", shall herein refer to the physical realm, to the regions of outer space within our Local Star Group, and to the Spiritual Communities of Higher Evolved Beings, who live in those places. Heavens are in three locations in our solar system, these locations are the gravitational stable points in the Earth orbital path, or the Lagrangian Points. The Heavens are artificial ring-worlds.

2) The term " Matriarchate ", shall refer to the government of Heaven, which is ran by female Sacred Vessels of the Creator Alpha Omega. It is a system of social organization in which women are the primary authority figures in family, business, school, and government.

3) The term " Demigoddess " shall refer to one of six species of higher evolved beings, who are Isogynic beings, and whose primary physical manifestation is female. Their ancestral birthplace is this earth, and for the last 100,000 years they have lived in the Heavens, where they are the civil servants constituting the government of the Matriarchate.

Narrative:

This Earth is one of many billions of worlds in the universe, it is older then most religions give it credit, and it's history is a complex story of divine intervention, cataclysm, creation & evolution, and a infinite variety of living species which are born and die here on this quiet earth.

The nearest star ( Sun) is many things to the living things on this Earth, indeed the very thins which are essential to life, also can destroy life in our world. The Sun is also the giver of both life and death. The Sun's radiation warms the earth to Goldilocks conditions. But the Sun also overheats our world, and in time would make Earth a dry dead world.

All life would disappear including humanity if the Sun were the only force influencing our world. But however the Creator Alpha Omega has provided the means to maintain this world in a habitable state.

Within the outer reachs of our Solar System is a region called the," Orrt Cloud ". The Orrt Cloud contain all the water the earth will ever need, in the form of enormous Ice Asteroids. These Asteroids leave the Orrt Cloud and colide with earth, delivering water to continually re-plenish our surface water. At times the quantity of water coming to the earth as torrential rains, is so great that its drainage into the seas floods the surface and washes away women, children, cities, and civilization. These are the periodic global floods of antiquity.

The process of replenishment also causes swarms of enormous As-teroids to collide with the surface of he Sun. This temporay cooling of the Suns surface plasma is called , " SolarDark ". SolarDark is a variation in the energy output of the Sun, in which the surface of the Sun temporarily loses its luminescence. This Darking cools the earth, bringing about the Glaciation or Ice Ages. Without these two harmoni-ous processes the earth would burn up and dry out.

What gives life can also take life; SolarDark and Global Floods would produce extinction level if not for divine intervention by the Creator Alpha Omega's proxies.

Heaven is above us, in outer space, in many regions of the inter-planetary and interstellar territories. The Heavens have always been the home of higher evolved species for millions of years. Some still today call these residents of Heaven, "gods", but however like ourselves they are mortal living creatures.

We allow the use of the term, " god ", to indicate any other living species, whose natural qualities, give its capacities far beyond our ordinary human comprehension. "God", does not refer to the Creator Alpha Omega, who is everything, and more, infinite, immortal, and always present everywhere in the universe. The gods can never reach equality with the Creator Alpha Omega.

The Creator Alpha Omega has provided the means to maintain  this earth through intermediaries. In heaven there are presently six (6) higher evolved species. These living creatures are gods. The gods are descended from earthlings. Although they have lived in the Heavens they are tied to the Earth by their natural instincts. The gods are tied to humanity because of their moral conscious.

The gods have intervened to save humanity time and time again. This intervention has also come at a cost to the gods, but we believe that the sacrifices they have made have spiritually progressed the gods in ways we have yet to experience within ourselves. Ways we can not know until our own immortal minds progress to the next higher stage, and we are reborn as gods, then we'll understand what is incomprehensible in the human condition.

100,000 years ago are ancestors watched as the six higher evolved species left this world to live in a place free of the ravages of mother nature. They called their new home Heaven. They would periodically return to earth, and when the came down from heaven it was always a monumental event in the life's of the earthlings. They higher species were called, the 'Pantheon ", but the miracles they performed, earned them the title of " Gods ". They were worshipped by humanity all over the earth.

They continued to walk amongst earthlings, and call earth there home for a little while longer. In time heaven would change the higher evolved species. Heaven gave them the means to devote themselves to higher pursuits, and they changed, spiritually, intellectually, and physically!

The Pantheon developed the science to create artificial planetoids, and small stars. Th ey used the Sun's energy field to transport themselves to the other stars in our local star group. They went in search of those who came before them, the ancient ones, who 250, 000 years ago disappeared into the Milky Way, leaving behind , '' the planet of the children ''. One might say that the Pantheon were in search of their Mothers.

Notes:

(1). The Demigoddesses are three species of higher evolved creatures leaving in heaven for the last 100,000 years. They are descended from species originated on this earth. Their ancestors once lived amongst homo sapiens, Neanderthals, and Cromagnon. They are the closest biological relative to homo sapiens, and are reproductively compatible, capable of producing viable fertile offspring. Their life in outer space has transformed them physically.

Narrative:

At the appointed time and place, the gods would come down from heaven, and be received by the crowds of worshipping humans.

The six species of gods were always impressive, but none were as extraordinary as the Demigoddesses.

The Demigoddesses were three higher species which were Isogynic beings. Isogynic beings have the physical-sexual attributes of '' two human genders '' in one body.

The first species of Demigoddesses are indistinguishable from homo sapiens women, except for their penises. They are the most beautiful wom-en men have ever seen.

The second species of Demigoddesses are mush taller then the first, and they possess Elongated Heads, thus greater cranial volume, this allows them to display exceptional extrasensory perception as well as significantly higher intelligence.

The third species of Demigoddesses are as tall as nine feet, and have the largest cranial elongation of all known species. These are the most evolved of the Demigoddesses.

The one characteristic all Demigoddesses have in common, even the ones with the giant heads, is their extraordinary feminine beauty. By any human standard, they are the most beautiful of the gods in heaven.

The Matriarchate of heaven is governed democratically by the three species of Demigoddesses. This is because the Matriarchate has always a religious society, and the Demigoddesses became the Sacred Vessels of the Creator Alpha Omega after the migration o heaven and the " Great Transformation ". And so the interpreters of the Creator Alpha Omega, also interpret his Divine Laws & Cannon for the entire Pantheon. Rare- ly has their ever been any disagreement within the Pantheon as to their leadership of heaven, because the true leader has always been the Creator Alpha Omega.

The Demigoddesses would come to earth and awe the earthlings with their simple miracles. They would tell of he Creator Alpha Omega, and share wisdom and knowledge. The human were in awe!

One summer when the appointed time had come, the human gathered at the appointed places, and the great ships of the Pantheon landed be-fore their eyes. The ceremonies begun, and at some point things changed forever. The Demigoddesses explained that a great flood The Deluge was

about to occur. They explained that places had been prepared for humans
and their livestock, for the wild animals, and for the agricultural vegeta-
tion at the equator. The Sun would grow dark. The rains would come.
Them!world would flood, then the waters would recess as the world grow
cold, and ice would cover the higher latitudes.

It was a frightening story about to come true, but however, the Creator
Alpha Omega had sent the Pantheon to save all life on earth from extinction.

The communities at the equator would have warmth from inside the
earth, and there would been light in the skies from the thirteen artificial
stars the Pantheon had built in orbit around the earth.

To our ancestors much of this was beyond their understanding. Their
greatest technology was the spear and the flint knife. But it was clear beyond all doubt, that these creatures now standing before them were the
gods. Only the gods could put the Suns in the heavens! No one dared
question the gods except the wicked and the imbeciles. So our ancestors
said goodbye to all they had built, climbed onboard the starships, and were
taken to their new homes in Africa, to start over.

The Demigoddesses assured humans that there would never be another
Flood like the one about to occur. This was they said a Catastrophic Natural Anomaly & Extinction Level Event.

In their hearts the Demigoddesses wish that the could take humanity to
heaven with them. Outer Space was infinite, and there was enough room
for everyone. But they know that could never be.

I the past individual human beings and been taken up to live in heaven
by the gods, and they lived long Happy lives. But however these were rare
cases. There was something about the earth that could not be reproduced
in space. Humanity needed that earth quality or they decayed. They need

to feel the rain on their faces. They needed to walk through tall grass on the planes, and climb trees, listen to the wind blowing trough the leaves, and taste snowflakes. Humanity was a part of earth and could not survive if taken away from earth.

The Pantheon know that they could not be mothers to this planet of children forever. Mankind needed to group and take on responsibility for their welfare. The day would come when mankind would have to take its place and heaven, and assume the role of Guardians Of The Earth. The Demigoddesses turned to the Creator Alpha Omega often in prayer with the question of humanity's future. They waited for the answer which

would come at the appropriate time & place. Till then they had to care for humanity.

The Pantheon was not a population of billions, nor hundreds of millions. They did not reproduce with reckless abandon. Therefore it was a task to decide who and how many of the gods would devote themselves to watching over the equatorial communities during this time of crisis on earth.

Some would say that the decision to appoint the Demigods, as Watchers, was a mistake made in heaven. Others would say that it was a sign that what lies deep within us, reaches out into the world around us, seeking fulfillment.

Even gods have hearts which break!

# Sec. II: Fall Of The Demigods

Narrative:There were many good reasons for leaving earth, and there were many benefits to life in heaven they had built for themselves.

The decision by the Pantheon to leave this earth and build new home in outer space, was a natural progression were their technological growth had lead them. It freed them from the extremes of earth weather, earthquakes, drought, disease, from the natural cataclysms which had driven many species into extinction.

The ancestors of the six species in the Pantheon had originated on this earth, and had evolved next to the various species of hominoids. They had lived amongst homo sapiens, and even had interbreed with homo sapiens on occasion. But however there was a spiritual and intellectual gulf between humanity and the higher evolved species, which humanity at the time could not cross.

Demigoddesses were the species closest to humanity, and they had always felt the strongest attachment to human beings; yet they would leave humanity to continue the struggle with a uncompassionate universe for life on earth. The Demigoddesses in heaven begun the long struggle with their own nature to become higher moral species.

The higher evolved species also had grown into a deeply spiritual community, and needed the freedom from earth's distractions in order to continue their spiritual growth. Heaven was a place of quiet for the practice of ritual, meditation, and contemplation.

Heaven had separated the higher evolved species from hominoids. The Demigoddesses were now part of a select society, and sexual re-production became a highly organized activity. There was no longer the possibility of human & Demigoddesses copulation, and Demigoddesses became a purely endogenous species.

By the use of genetic science, they were able over the thousands of years to eliminate many flaws in their kind, and enhance certain other beneficial qualites. The six species developed into physical distinct forms, and the Demigoddesses became Sacred Vessels to the Creator Alpha Omega.

Higher Evolved Creatures are still only creatures, and subject to the laws of nature, and nature produced disabilities within all living species. Nature had produced three species of Demigoddesses, and within each species, three subspecies.

The Isogynic beings belonged to the primary subspecies, and there were two forms.

The Demigods and the Demigoddess-Special, were the lesser special forms (subspecies ) that occurred in the Demigoddess species(s). While the Demigoddesses were Isogynic beings, the Demigoddesses-Special were the sexually female form, and the Demigods were the sexually male form.

It is not a flaw in nature that creatures descended from earthlings possess a instinctual affinity from the earth. The Demigods did not feel that there was a place for them in heaven. like thee humans the demigods were still instinctively tied to the physical environment of earth.

The Demigods did not have the qualies of the Demigoddesses which made outer space a blessing for the Demigoddesses.

Demigods were not sacred vessels; They were not civil servants (they were males in a matriarchal religion, culture, and society ); they were not teachers & counselors, doctors & healers, or engineers & scientist. They lived a relatively simple existence, and nothing in space was superior to earth in a way that mattered to the Demigods.

The Demigods see the need to live exclusively in outer space, nor did not feel at home in heaven, and they did not feel as if there was a home for them anywhere in creation, except perhaps on earth.

Because the Demigods were a genetic variation of Demigoddess, they could not father children in heaven with any of the Demigoddesses. If the Demigods produced children they would have introduced genetic defects into the gene pool.

The facts concerning the Demigods emotional & spiritual condition in heaven were well known, but the magnitude of their unhappiness, was to them a form of suffering, was something only the Demigods experienced and understood.

The Demigoddesses governed heaven, and made an administrative decision to send Demigods to earth as SolarDark Mission Watchers. The decision failed to take into consideration the true emotional condition of the Demigods, and therefore the consequences were not foreseeable.

After thousands of years, the Demigods had returned to earth, to

live, even if only temporarily. In their ancestral birthplace, for the first timeThey found happiness for the first time, in their ancestral birthplace.

The Demigods were capable custodians of the technology, and

15

enjoyed the company of the humans also. The Demigods performed magic tricks which entertained & amazed the humans, and the Demigods enjoyed a position of great esteem. It was the company of the human women which truly made the Demigods feel as if they had returned to Paradise.

The problem with loving gods, is that they and human produced viable fertile offspring. The children of this union were exceptionally large, strong, and smart. Before the children could develop a moral compass, the children of the gods by virtue of their superior physical qualities became uncontrollable bullies.

The Demigods were happy with their children, and so they produced as many as they could, with as many human women as were available. The Demigods could see nothing wrong with their presence in the human communities on this earth.

The humans secretly held a community meeting concerning the suffering of human children at the hands of the redheaded children of the gods. The humans would not allow their children to continue to be harmed!

A move against the children of there gods is in fact a move against the gods, and it brought down upon the human men, the wrath of the Demigods.

The Pantheon believed that their migration to!outer space was a natural progression of the higher species. The Demigods over time begun to feel, not just think, but also feel deep within their being, that it was also natural to want to go home. Space was not a home for the Demigods.

They know that someday would return to earth, they would go home!

Humanity had been saved once against from extinction. Human beings had been moved to beautiful equatorial communities built for them by the gods. The Orbital Photosphere Network was in place for the next eight thousand years; and members of the Pantheon, the Demigods, had been returned to earth to insure that the plan would go well.

As the earth experienced another Ice Age, It grow quiet, and there was no longer a need to devote the Pantheon full attention to the affairs of humanity, for now the Demigods would watch over them.

It had been a few years since the last SolarDark on earth. The Demigoddesses had returned to their other pursuits, not knowing that the Creator Alpha Omega wanted them to be concerned about this little ball of ice populated by a actually ordinary biology.

Faraway somewhere in our Local Star Group. The Demigoddesses were busy studying unexplored worlds, as the unoffical search for a planet called Utopia Continued. Other Demigoddesses where searching for clues that might put them on the trail of the Ancient Ones who!left earth long long ago, but left behind great monolithic monuments.

The nights in space were always peaceful sleeping in zero gravity, until the night, in their dreams, the Demigoddesses heard the cries of women, billions and billions of miles away on earth.

The Demigoddesses could nor determine the facts based on what the Demigods were not telling them, and so it was decided that as soon as possible an earth reconnaissance mission would be organized. It would still be months before they could return to earth, till then the earth was in the safe hands of the Demigods.

After a interstellar crossing four months later, the Demigoddesses ships came out of the Sun, and moved into formation around the earth. The Reconnaissance ships landed on earth to a strange silence. There were still humans and Demigods on earth, but none to greet the Demigoddesses.

17

There were, no celebrations, only sadness drifting on the winds, and blowing through their long hair atop the mountain.

When the Demigoddesses came down from the mountain to the humans communities below, what they found broke their hearts. They had failed.

The humans communities were is complete disorder and near collapse. The natives told of how they had been plagued by monsters, shortly after the watchers made themselves at home in the human communities. (this was before the advant of the kingdom of the great god Lucifer, so there were no monsters on earth at this time, because Lucifer had not made them yet. ). The gods were no longer welcome on earth. They asked them to leave and take the monsters with them.

It was the cries of the earth women which summoned the Demigoddesses back to earth, and it was the tears of the earth women which told the story of how they had been loved by the gods. How the women had

> given birth to beautiful healthy children. How everything seem O.K. till they were about six or seven, and as big as twelve year olds. They were little monsters indeed.
>
> These little monsters besieged the human communities, and ruled them with force and intimidation. But they where still just children, not even teenagers yet. But they were Big & Strong, more then a human mother could handle. So where were their fathers the Demigods?
>
> The monsters were only children, but their feathers were adults who should have understood what they had done. Instead they defended their children, they loved their children, and they allowed them to terrorize the humans. And the humans were afraid to do anything about these children, because their Demigod fathers were worst then tyrants when it came to their children.

The Demigods would not allow the Demigoddesses to do anything to the children either. The disagreement was in how the children were perceived, based on the objectives of the observer. The Demigoddesses saw only the longterm consequences. The Demigods believed that this was simply a fact of nature, since the Demigoddesses & Demigods were actually native to earth themselves, and homo sapiens, in some crazy theories, is a subspecies of Demigoddess.

The Demigoddesses could feel sympathy for the Watchers. They immediately blamed the Demigods for everything, and moved to bring them before the council in heaven. It was the beginning of what would become;

A War Between The Gods &

A War In Heaven.

The Universe would get its first good glimpse of The Celestial-God who would become known as;

The Great God Lucifer,

The God Of Perfection, and

The God Of War.

The minor tragedy on earth, would produce an unimaginable crisis in heaven, and change the universe forever.

Somewhere in all this escalating war of ideas and truth on trial, the children of the gods would be forgotten, became insignificant, and they and their fathers & human mothers, would find peace on earth, and become the stuff of legends & myths. Even after all the pure bloods died out, their descendants continue to walk this earth today, and many of us have unknowingly within our bodies a portion of their flesh & blood. As the Demigoddesses feared.

History is always a story told by someone of a time that others have not known, and a interpretation colored by the ideas we hold dear. One can not argue with the gods about history they have seen, but amongst the gods, there was argument over the meaning of the history they were making, and could not undo once it was done. The gods realized their limitations.

# Sec. III: Fall of The Great God Lucifer

Note:

1) The Pantheon of Haven in our Local Star Group, consisted of six higher evolved species;( in order of the least powerful to mist powerful)

   a.  the Demigoddesses Minor,

   b.  the Demigoddesses intermediate,

   c.  the Demigoddesses Major,

   d.  the Terrestrial gods,

   e.  the Celestial gods, and,

   f.  the Universal gods.

1) The earth was the only source of higher evolved intelligent life in our Local Star Group. This was not unusual for the universe of trillions of planets, and millions of Local Star Groups.

2) The Celesial-God Lucifer was a mortal creature, but at the time a sole Celestial in heaven.

3) As the sacred vessels of the Creator Alpha Omega, the Demi-goddesses are the messengers & interpreter of the divine message. The Demigoddesses are not the Law-Givers, but rather the mortal creatures who receive the law from the Creator Alpha Omega, who is the sole Law-Giver in all the universe.

4) The opposition in heaven to the Demigoddesses spiritual & governmental role in the Pantheon & Matriarchate, was in fact a indirect opposition to Divine law, which is in fact a poorly disguised opposition to the Creator Alpha Omega. Lucifer sought to replace the Creator Alpha Omega with a creature (himself). There is much more to this then anyone in heaven understood at the time. The Creator Alpha Omega would reveal the full truth concerning Lucifer, after the war in heaven, and to the astonishment of all creation.

5) The events concerning Lucifer set the stage for the establishment of the Matriarchates on earth, which were modelled after the Matriarchates of heaven. The opposition to the Matriarchates was spiritual in nature. The religion CEBAGII of course emerged along with the Matriarchates, and was the target of relentless attacks which continue to this day. The narrative involving the Demigods and The Great God Lucifer explain the origin of the opposition to the true religions on earth.

Narrative:

The Demigoddesses had planned the future of humanity, and they were not plans for the conspicuous involvement of gods in human affairs. The gods would guide humanity quietly, and save humanity when necessary.

The higher evolved species and humanity had separated thousands of years ago, and there was no reason to go back to the way things once were. In fact the past could never be recreated.

In the Pantheon the Demigoddesses lead the government, and there was no disagreement as to the limited presence the gods would have on earth as humanity matured. It is easy to make plans, but sometimes impossible to make plans work.

The pantheon had drafted Civil law restricting the type of interaction between gods and humans, following their plans for humanity's future. Ultimately all Civil law, and all things in the universe, must agree with Divine law.

What had happened on earth was a moment in which a group of gods had defied Civil Law, Divine Law, and Natural Law in that they had altered human communities in a way that would change the course of humanity, and threaten the plans of the gods for humanity's future.

The Demigods believed that the separation of humanity and the higher evolved species after the migration and transformation, was the setting for the civil laws that now governed the heavens. The return to earth was a return to a different place & state where the civil laws of the Pantheon could not apply.

Unlike the opposition that would emerge in heaven, The SolarDark Mission Watchers were not fighting against Divine Law, nor did the wish to replace thee Creator Alpha Omega. The watchers simply wanted to be

happy again, to have family, and to live with their children on earth. The

Demigoddesses would not support their objectives and allow the situation on earth to continue.

The Demigoddesses opposition to the wishes of the Demigods, created great animosity in heaven towards the sacred vessels, amongst those sympathetic to the Demigods. Eventually one third (1/3) of the residents of heaven would leave heaven and return to their ancestral birthplaces throughout the universe.

The Demigoddesses were deeply concerned and insisted that something be done about the changes made on earth by the SolarDark Mission Watchers.

Before the council was The question of what could be done; But however the Demigoddesses had failed to perceive a much deeper question was involved here. The answer to that unspoken fundamental question would be determined by a war In heaven, and by the rise and the fall of a Celestial-god, The Great God Lucifer.

Earth had become the spark which lite a fire that would burn throughout the entire universe. Lucifer would kindle that fire as the gods watched and failed to comprehend what Lucifer was actually doing until it was all over and heaven was torn apart.

The day before council was to be simple procedure, the facts had aslreay been established, the accused admitted to the acts, and the request was to remove the children, the Demigods their Fathers, and their human mothers, too Mars Colony, and replace the watchers with cyborgnetic systems, or non biological lifeforms designed by the scientist of the Pantheon.

It bseemed that the father of those in violation was sealed, and then Lucifer made his appearance. Like a dark horse entry in a race where the outcome was all!but certain, Lucifer introduced himself as a third party whose voice in this democracy represented the silent majority who because they were males, were powerless in heaven.

Lucifer was the sole celestial in heaven at the time and very little was known about celestial- gods. Lucifer was known for never having lost a debate ever on any subject. The superior intellectual abilities of Lucifer

made him a serious adversary, even when Lucifer was wrong, he could not been shown to be wrong.

This Was War!

Narrative:

The war of words and idea begun in council in heaven before the entire Pantheon. Lucifer was extraordinarily convincing in his arguments that no laws had been broken except the laws which were erroneously construct-ed. It was the intent of these laws which was in question, and Lucifer reinterpreted it as a attempt to create a unnatural state of affairs on earth. What was a natural state of affairs became the question.

Lucifer argued that the facts had not been determined in their entirety and without distortion by those with vested interest in producing a partic-ular outcome. The Demigoddesses had long believed in a Utopian Theory, which had no historical basis in fact. The departure of the higher species from earth thousands of years ago allowed the pursuit of the Utopian Plan which as of yet had failed on earth.

The human condition is the result of the removal of an essential quality from the world, and the SolarDark Mission Watchers were correcting that error. It was not our ancestors who had made this critical error, but rather the Callipygian Aristocracy that emerged after the Great Transformation.

The Great Transformation gave us the Sacred Vessels who were the sole intermediaries between the creations and the Creator Alpha Omega. These creatures had demonstrated their propensity for error, and this had lead to the establishment of erroneous civil laws.

Lucifer ignored many details, and summarized the state of affairs in heaven from the perspective of one whose perspective has never be known to be contrary to reality. Lucifer did not seek to diminish the Sacred Vessels, but to destroy the illusion of their perfection, which blinded thee gods to the error that the Demigoddesses were committing.

Like any good advocate Lucifer defended the acts of the accused as a necessary act due to a great wrong that had endured too long uncorrected. The Demigods were not attempting to return to the past, but to allow nature to take its course, and then outcome was what nature dictated.

To act against the Demigods and their wives and children, was in itself an unnatural and unjust act. Those we home advocated such horrible acts were misguiding the Pantheon, and had been misguiding the Pantheon for ages. Those in authority based the validity on the past achievements of the founders and not on the facts which were unrevealed or distorted to make wrong appear right.

That was Lucifer's introduction, the argument was a powerful indictment of the stays quo in heaven, and in particular of the Callipygian Aristocracy. Beneath this attack on the sacred vessels was a hatred of everything womenly in creation. This misogyny went unspoken, but the Sacred Vessels could feel the hatred directed at them.

Lucifer had always been a mystery in heaven. Lucifer could assume any form, but preferred to go about in the physical manifestation of a human male. Lucifer lived in a Matriarchate, were authority was vested solely in compatent women. If Lucifer were to assume the female, and be known as Lucy, then power would be Lucy's. But Lucy would have share power with other women. As a man, Lucifer, if he could steal power, Lucifer would not have to share it with anyone. That was what Lucifer wanted.

Lucifer as a Celestial was at least three orders of magnitudes a greater intellectual then any other being in the Pantheon. Therefore even when Lucifer was wrong, his errors were not discernible by lesser intellects.

Lucifer defeated the Demigoddesses in council for three straight days and nights, until it was settled that the Demigods, their children, and their many wives, would remain on earth, and be given their own territories on earth.

Lucifer know that the SolarDark Mission Watchers were not necessary his allies, but he would use them for his purposes, and they allowed themselves to be used by Lucifer.

The true victory was that Lucifer destroyed the Pantheon's confidence in the sacred vessels. This allowed Lucifer to argue that the sacred vessels time had come and gone, that others more perfect then them, should take the helm. Who could be more perfect then the sacred vessels, only the one who had defeated them before the entire Pantheon.

Now the entire universe was taking notice of what was going on in this Local Star Group. Lucifer was destroying the concept of divinely appointed sacred vessels in the Matriarchates of the heavens. Now unappointed celestials could assume leadership roles, even MEN!

This development sent the Demigoddesses into crisis mode everywhere in the universe. Something had to be dfoned about Lucifer.

The Demigoddesses High Temple Priestesses could discern the progression of all beings, but Lucifer had no future progression & transition;

    A.  Lucifer was a none existent illusion.

    B.  Lucifer had no future because Lucifer was about to die very shortly, and would not spiritually progress because he was in perpetual digression.

This divination confused the High Priestesses because they could not imagine how either could be possible inside of heaven, it simply made no sense.

It was clear that the validity of divine revelation would be compromised if non divinely appointed celestials could assume the sacred vessels functions. False interpretations could be introduced into the religion.

Lucifer allowed his supporters to portray him as the God of perfection. Lucifer himself suggested that if one wishes to be perfect, then one should be like Lucifer. Lucifer was replacing the Creator Alpha Omega, as the standard of emulation in the pursuit of the purpose of human existence. The Demigoddesses could not test Lucifer's divinity, no test exist at that time for manifestations of the creator in the form of Celestial-gods. So they could not declare Lucifer to be a, " false idol ".

# Sec. IV: The War In Heaven / War Of The Gods.

Narrative :

Some of the Demigoddesses decided that a police action in heaven was appropriate and necessary. Lucifer would need to be forced into silence.

Why would sacred vessels contemplate an act of violence? They feared that Lucifer could destroy everything they cherished in heaven. But there was something more important then all the heavens, which Lucifer was tearing apart. He was destroying their obedience to divine law, he was silencing the voice of the Creator Alpha Omega within them. Lucifer valued something of more importance then all the stars in heaven.

The Demigoddesses would end this unholy war Lucifer was waging against the Creator Alpha Omega, by force if necessary.

The decision to compelled another heavenly being into obedience of divine law, and to do so by the use of physical force, was simply unimaginable, but so was Lucifer.

Lucifer wanted chaos in heaven because when the work of the Creator Alpha Omega stopped, the work of Lucifer could begin. Lucifer was building his kingdom in heaven and on earth, a new religion, culture, and way of life. Lucifer believed that he was perfection, and deserved to be worshipped and adored.

In order to subdue the moist powerful being in the Local Star Group, the Demigoddesses created a police force in heaven called the Amazons. '' Amazon '' referred to the function served, not the place, race, nationality, or religion, of the individual.

The Demigoddess-Special were asked to become the Amazons, and they agreed to allow the sacred vessels to transform them physically using secret rituals. The Amazons were tall, strong, had great stamina, long lived, healed quickly from injury, and were almost indestructible. They were also the most beautiful of women.

The army of Amazons arrived at the Mars temple complex of Lucifer's to take him into custody. There they encountered Lucifer's allies.

The struggle begin and slowly the Amazons made the way the Lucifer's front door.

Suddenly every object in the courtyard was flung through the air at the Amazons. The Amazons made an effort to defend themselves because they would never retreat. As one Amazon knocked an object out of the air with her staff, the object fell to the ground, shattered, and transformed back into Lucifer.

The entire universe was in shock, right before their eyes, a Celestial-god had been killed. everyone stopped and stood in silence looking at Lucifer's dead body.

It was at that moment that the Creator Alpha Omega stopped time.

Then the Creator reversed time and Lucifer was once again alive, the first resurrection had been done in heaven. The war was over!

The Creator Alpha Omega took Lucifer by the left hand not the right hand, and placed him on earth. The Amazons, and all Lucifer's followers also were exiled to earth.

This was a strange outcome to what was a strange condition in the heavens, which only the Creator alpha omega could help them understand.

Lucifer had always known that the Creator Alpha Omega would not allow him to die in heaven. Lucifer manipulated the Demigoddesses, the Council, and the Amazons, in order to get what he had wanted all a along.

The Creator Alpha Omega decreed the following;

I.     No one shall ever intentionally do harm to Lucifer, nor attempt to take his life, ever again.

II.    II. Lucifer would never die as long as his feet are planted in the soil of this earth.

III.   Lucifer and his followers have the right to return to their ancestral birthplaces.

IV.    That which is of the earth shall not come up to live in heaven except by means of the spiritual transition to higher forms.

V.     Never again shall a act of violence be performed anywhere in the creation, and never done in the name of the Creator Alpha Omega.

VI.    It is the spiritual obligation of all beings to work towards the spiritual progression of all beings not just themselves. Lucifer's

redemption is the objective which all the Pantheon shall pursue indefinitely until they succeed. The Pantheon shall never leave this Local Star Group until they have returned Lucifer to the Pantheon.

The Pantheon had been wrong in how they responded to Lucifer's actions. Lucifer was a Celestial-god, and his species is a extreme shape shifter. Theory are born and within minutes transform into fully developed adults physically. This is a mimic of the adults present at their birth. But However; Lucifer still must mentally & spiritually grow and mature. Lucifer was the most powerful being in the Pantheon, and he was still only a child!

Like most children, Lucifer pursued his desires with limited understanding, and reckless abandon, with no regard for anything or anyone else who is in his way.

Suddenly everyone understood Lucifer's behavior. What was important was that some people performed acts of violence, following this child. They had not developed spiritual discernment, and were not ready for heaven, and so they were returned to the many earths. This was not punishment, but rather putting things in order, where they can start over and move forward down the correct paths.

Punishment for wrongs done, even for blasphemy, was not a divine act, but a human concept. The Creator Alpha Omega preferred to give creatures the opportunity to improve themselves. Forgiveness was not the word to be used, because the Creator Alpha Omega never angered at, and never condemned, any creation, The Creator Alpha Omega simply understood what is beyond human capacity to comprehend about life.

The Amazons would be the thorns in Lucifer's crown. They would also give birth to the earth women we today know as the Legendary Amazons. There descendants would continue the fight against Lucifer till this day, and into eternity. The Demigoddesses would aide them always.

It would not be easy.

Narrative:

Lucifer taught the Amazons the meaning of death. These invincible women would face the monsters created by Lucifer. It was a hell on earth made by the kingdom of Lucifer, and an endless battle against what has become the greatest evil in the Local Star Group.

The heavenly Amazons came to earth at the same time as Lucifer. The Amazon is a title used to describe a superior woman who fights against the physical manifestation of spiritual evil in this world, and those human beings who have given themselves over to the service of that evil influence. They are warriors, in a war older then human civilization.

The daughters of the heavenly Amazons would continue the fight their mothers waged all over the earth. Lucifer's digression would intensify and he would resort to new acts of evil in his fight against the Amazons and there allies.

There were no monsters in the earth before the arrival of Lucifer. Lucifer is the Creator of monsters.

The ancestors of the sacred vessels once lived on earth amongst the hominoids. There are monuments recalling their civilization. There are also cemeteries full of the bodies of Demigoddesses.

Lucifer would hunt down the burial places of the ancient Demigoddesses. When the tomb was opened and the body removed, the women looked exactly as she looked when she was alive. This was an indicator that the body would be useful for the magic Lucifer was planning.

After Lucifer's priest would desecrate the body fully, the body would be burned to ash and the bones crushed to power and mixed into a blood potion. The blood would come from the children sacrificed to Lucifer by their mothers.

Lucifer would then select one of his fallen, who would drink the blood potion and die. The selected individual would have his chest cut open and the heart of a innocent child previously sacrificed to Lucifer, would be put in his chest and the chest sawn close.

The selected individual would then be buried in a mass grave, lie in the earth for three days and nights, then be exhumed.

The selected individual would then be bathed in the moonlight of a blood moon, in the river Euphrates, or the Jordan. Lucifer and his priest would perform ceremonies in the waters. The dance of death would be performed by drugged women, who would dance till the died.

Lucifer would then fallout the name of one of the Fallen from heaven calling him back from the spiritual realm, toma new vessel , and the body would rise from the waters, reborn as a monster.

If the monster is not feed within two moons it will die. The priest would not allow it to be feed yet. The army oif Lucifer would go into the countryside destroying and killing. The Amazons would arrive to protect the innocent.

The armies of Lucifer would retreat but nor without one captured Amazon. One was all they needed. They would bring their captive to a field, surrounded by the hungry monsters, and the monsters would feast on her flesh, drink her blood, and chew on her bones.

The ritual was now complete, from that day on, the monsters would have an insatiable hunger for the flesh of Amazon women.

# Sec. V: The Great Deluge.

Narrative: A Scientific Theory on SolarDarkAs Possible Real Explanation of Earth Climatic Variation Causing Global Glaciation.

The Russian scientist were the only people brave enough to go one the record with a hypothesis that ran contrary to the current line of reasoning in the scientific establishment. That is why we enjoy their company at the club.

The Russians suggested that our star ( The Sun ) was in fact a variable star. The energy output level of variable stars is not constant. So the star cycles through two opposite extremes, and the earth grows exceeding hot, and unbelievably cold. Between the extremes is our current Goldilocks conditions.

The Russians suggested that the photosphere of plasma which transmits our visible radiation, could cool temporarily and become absorbative of energy rather then transmissive. This was at the time, a radical idea quickly rejected.

Many years later a space probe passing the Moon and heading into deep space, turned it's expensive sensors towards the earth.

What the machine saw made the Russians cheer and celebrate. Earth is continually bombarded with large asteroids made of dirty ice, frozen water. These strange objects exist in infinite quantities in the vast Orrt Cloud. But clearly they don't remain there for ever. Just as they come crashing down on our earth, the Sun's gravitational energy field pulls many into collision courses with it.

There have been occasional spectral readings showing the existence of certain heavy metals at the Sun's surface, which is only possible if these metals originate outside the sun and arrive on dirty ice asteroids in collisions.

The Sun's fusion process in incredibly inefficient, but bits massive size hides this secret. The energy required to heat the surface to the plasma state is of a magnitude per square meter which would ionize the gases at a very slow rate. Once cooled, the Sun's surface remains non transmissive for an extended period of time. Water in asteroids provides ample electrons to deionized large regions of the Sun's surface.

Narrative: The Personal Account Of The Deluge:

The catastrophic natural events occur on this earth rarely, but often enough to remind us of human civilization mortality and it's finite duration.

The last great flood did not cover the entire earth with water, no flood has ever done that, since before the emergence of intelligent life on earth.

The minor deluge would claim the lives of 90% of humanity because of unpreparedness.

The members of hesects built arks as directed. They filled the arks with provisions, provided roomenough for their families, animals, tools, all the things needed to rebuild after the minor cataclysmic event.

The religious sects were not inhuman, they also made room for strangers. They built arks for their people, and in these arks they made room for people whom were not members of their spiritual communities.

Sections set aside for the refugees were simply whatever spaces could be made empty. Sometimes as many as many as six people stuffed into a room no bigger then a kitchen pantry.

Six men were placed in a small room with a window looking out over an endless stormy sea in the darkness. The coast was gone, and all the beautiful homes along the beach front properties washed away. There was nothing there but an endless angry sea.

These men were the lucky ones who had been pulled onboard as an act of mercy. They were cold, dirty, wet, and tired. Three small space heaters warmed the tiny space full of beds already occupied by sleeping strangers. It was clear that the deck would become beds for the latecomers.

When dinner was served, the room was still quiet, no one talked a out the humanity lost, or their own fears that they would not survive. But however they would survive, and live to tell their grandchildren about this Great Deluge, and it would become another myth, fiction, and unbelievable tale.

The rains did end, and there were only the stars in the skies to guide us to sanctuary. It was time once again, for humanity to begin over.

Narrative:

After the Sun returned to normal, the rains ended, and the waters

drained to the seas, dry land reappeared. The oceans were replenished,and the world was colder. At the higher latitudes glaciation would develop as it begin to snow constantly. Only a small strip of the earth at the equator was habitable.

But for the followers of the Demigoddesses, It was time once again to begin the rebuilding of community and civilization.

Because Humans needs are finite,

a.  food & water

b.  rest & sleep

c.  exercise & mental stimulation

d.  companionship & sexual relations

-the Arks were designed to carry everything needed, but it was not enough.

Some people who were not prepared, who did not heed the warnings, who survived by accident or be cause of the mercy of the people of the Arks, did not take up the hard work, but instead found another means of survival.

These men turned to violence to fulfill their human needs & desires.

Man became a wolf to men.

These men devoted their time not to rebuilding their communities & improving themselves, but rather to killing. Men killed other men in a battles over harems. Men killed women who would not submitted. Men killed children whom were inconvenient burdens. Men became a killer and in time killed the pacifist, the pious, the saints, and the good men of the communities.

These men then became a tyrants. Men beat women and forced them to produce all things needed by the community. Under the Brute-males, women were beast of burden all the long day, and sex slaves all the long nights. Men did not even spare their own daughters, and abused them freely. These men made earth into hell.

The old text say that when the gates of heaven are closed to the prayers of men, they always remain open to the tears of mothers, of Rachel crying for her children who are not!

It was not the gods on Mt. Olympus, nor those of the North, nor those of the South which heard the Cry's of women, and who came to earth to free them. It was a spiritual community of living beings, descendants of earthlings, and mortal imperfect and not the supernatural hero's of mythology, who came to set women free.

It was the species called the Demigoddesses who set aside their own affairs, who returned to earth, and who answered the prayers of women and their children living in human bondage.

Narrative:

We are human beings and we are earthlings. Earth is the place where our species, Homo Sapiens, has evolved under creation. We are tied to this earth instinctively, psychologically as if it is our mother and our home, physically dependant on for survival, spiritually we are part of this world.

Humanity is not ready to leave earth.

We stay and endure the ravages of nature. The rains which fall on the planes, then flow in rivers to the deep blue oceans. The beaches are covered with human foot prints, and we stand on the edge of the seas, performing rituals to the gods of the earth, space, universe, and energy time & space.

Water is the blood of all living things. The Creator Alpha Omega at the beginning of time gave earth all the water its life will ever need, and that water is stored in The Ice Asteroids, in the vast deep cold dark regions of planetary space.

Nature is not a cruel killer. Nature is without feeling. We have been given by nature the intellectual means to rise above the waves of water which drown the lesser living things. Extinction of humanity can only come by human action or human failure to act, both in a combination called suicide.

The higher evolved species will not humanity disappear from the face of this earth. In times of great pending cataclysm, the Demigoddesses have come to us in our dreams, told of the coming crisis, and instructed us on how to survive natures essential processes.

The intervention of higher evolved beings has save humanity time and again.

The last great cataclysm was a flood which our ancestors prepared for as instructed. The cities were lost, but humanity and life survived. It was civilization which did not survive.

A barbaric culture called Tribalism emerged, and civilization was re-placed by a New Stone Age. Humanity reminded in this condition for far to long.

From their observatories in the temples of Heaven, the demigoddess-es could see that humanity was holding itself back, and did not want to revive civilization.

The strongest members of humanity, violently resisted civilization. Those controlling Humanity did not want to go back to want they had before the great flood.

The question was why!

The Answer To That Question Is Relevant Today. We Must Find Ways To Live As Not To Repeat The Human Errors Of The Past. THAT IS A FUNCTION OF TRUE RATIONAL RELIGION.

Finding the answer requires that we look into history from a different prospective. We must open our eyes to a truth about ourselves and the world we build, and the societies we live in.

The Religious Interpretation of History & Mystery, seeks to answer to the question;

" why did human civilization fail ? "

Our current civilization emerged from the ashes of another long ago world, one unknown to historians, but one the gods remember well and relive in their dreams. It is a greatest mystery.

There was no reason to believe that the most temporally proximate SolarDark/Deluge event would lead to social chaos of an extended duration. It was even less imaginable that TribalecticCulture, or a New Stone Age would occur in the aftermath of the natural catastrophe. Finally the status of women would fall precipitously into that of a ordinary household slave or chattel property.

The destruction of humanity's cites was a expected outcome, but the total disappearance of culture, morality, religion, and civilized behavior, was simply unpredictable. Historians shall never know then what the true factors where, which enabled the Fall of Human Civilization after the great flood.

We view civilization as a commonly experienced psychological state. This mental state disappeared long before the building were washed away. People were living in a automated physical state facilitated by the multiple efficient institutions of society. Inside of the humans, they were in chaos already, living lives of " quiet desperation ". And then the rains came, and washed that all away.

Our human condition is a direct consequence of human actions. Our expectations of human behavior is based not on objective reality, but rather on social norms derived from obligations we have according to our Culture, Religion, Laws, and Interpersonal Relationships. Our social norms are inadequate at facilitating fulfillment of our subjectively perceived needs & desires, but however mandate certain behaviors even in light of these unfulfilled needs & desires.

The, '' quiet desperation '', is the experience conflicting motivations, based upon powerful diametrically opposing forces acting on our Psyche.

The mainstream religions emphasize our struggle with our human needs, but we see life as a struggle to live in a society under the control of a religion which is opposed to the fulfillment of human needs & desires, and calls these natural instincts sins.

They say the truth will set you free but how can that be when you are under the authority of men who actions result from a religion opposed to the acknowledgment of the truth. They have made truth, into, '' the forbidden fruit ''; and to live ones life in the light of truth is to them, '' the original sin ''.

This, civilization had already cease to be a act of free will, it became a prison in which men were already dying inside, a life they could not escape not even in their dreams. The end of civilization was awaited and silently prayed for every night, men fought tragic world wars one after another, and they couldn't kill the beast, so they succumbed to him, and died inside.

THIS WAS THE UNDERLYING HUMAN SPIRITUAL CONDITION AT THE TIME OF THE LAST GREAT FLOOD.

# Sec. VI: The Return Of The Demi-Goddesses.

Narrative:

Before the last Great flood, humanity built a most prosperous human civilization, but despite their wealth, humanity existed in a spiritual darkness, the vast majority of humanity unable to Perfect & Transition.

True Religion had been destroyed in the secret war against religion, and the survivors simply abandoned what was left of the true faith, and it was replaced by an imposter. This was a harbinger to;

a.   the fall of civilization,

b.   the New Stone Age, and

c.   the establishment of the brutal Tribalectic Culture.

d.   extremes of human suffering.

These became real and defined the human condition.

The human condition was not correctable by human means.

Humanity require the intervention of higher evolved beings who were guided by the Creator Alpha Omega.

Long long ago six higher evolved species separated from the hominoids of this earth, and migrated to three spiritual communities in outer space called '' Heaven ''. Our ancestors call the Higher Evolved Beings, '' gods ".

These gods are mortal creatures like ourselves. They blood. They have hearts which can be broken. They love. They hate. They struggle to survive and grow, as finite beings in a vast indifferent universe, which seems to be working on their destruction.

Of the six higher evolved species in heaven, the Demigoddesses are the most emotionally devoted to human salvation, and they have for 100,000 years been deeply quietly involved in the affairs of humanity.

They have been worshipped and called upon in times of need. They have been called the " Goddesses of Love ", because they induce a instinctual feeling of love when humans are in their presence.

Human beings have always been in awe of their beauty, intelligence, strength, moral integrity, and their devotion to the Creator Alpha Omega.

The Demigoddesses have given their followers, their religion, culture, and social organization. Above all they have saved humanity from extinction, but never enslaved us under their authority, we are free because they value Free Will.

A few years after the great flood was over, and the New Stone Age was well established. From high above us in their starships in the heavens, they watch over us, as, " The True Guardians of the Earth "; there the Demigoddesses could hear the Cry's of human women enslaved on this earth. The Demigoddesses could feel the extreme suffering.

Demigoddesses intervention in the affairs of humanity, had been the least intrusive necessary to prevent an extinction level event. It was now time for a intervention of the highest degree possible, in order to save humanity from going into perpetual digression.

A entire planet in Perpetual Digression could trigger the end of earth

43

& humanity. The Creator Alpha Omega, would not destroy humanity, but however, would leave them to self-destruction.

Self-destruction; followed by the wrath of Nemesis & Karma; and followed by the end of matter time & space. The end of this Local Star Group, followed by the beginning of a new one.

Only the six species of higher evolved beings living in the heavens would be allowed to depart the Local Star Group via the Sun, before the end. It would be the premature end of humanity in an orgy of self inflicted agony. Such is the inescapable destination which the blind are lead to in spiritual darkness.

Nemesis & Karma,

Saints & Archangels,

Thor & Hercules,

step aside,

Amazons & Valkyrie,

lay down your swords,Hatuibwari& Mawu,

rest!

For the coming of the Omega!

That is what gods & beast see in the darkness. They fear, not for themselves, but for the planet of the children who will never have but
one chance to grow old.

This Apocalyptic Vision is what drove the entire race of Demigoddesses to assemble in earth orbit on a mission to achieve the salvation of humanity which standing at the threshold to the higher state, and the edge of the abyss.

The leaders of the Pantheon, the three High Temple Priestesses themselves, in their flagship floating above the earth, gently reached into the dreams of the the living beings sleeping on earth below.

They say there is no rest for the wicked. The great god Lucifer dreaming in his castle keep, was awaken by a old familiar feeling in his being. This would be the last night Lucifer would sleep peacefully in what he called his kingdom on earth. There would be no peace for the wicked on earth after tonight.

Lucifer felt a sensation, a warmth, and a gentleness, he had not experienced since the day he fell from heaven. It was as if a hundred Venuses had visited him in his sleep. But it was not those familiar spirits which had reached out and touched him in his sleep, there was only one living species in creation, which could induce such a state of tranquility. He know it had to be the sacred vessels of the Creator Alpha Omega.

Lucifer ran out into the rain, sounding the alarm, this was war, looking into the dark skies for a sign, but there was none, only the thunder of the storm rageing all around the world. He know his most powerful weapon would be inadequate for the quality of immortal minds which were now reaching into this world from a greater kingdom above.

Lucifer smiled, his terrestrial immortality, his gift & curse from the Creator Alpha Omega, had allowed him to live long and to witness this moment, it had finally begun after a thousands of years of making it hell on earth, after he had killed more Amazons then there are hairs on his head, after killing religion and declaring god was dead, the dreadful moment had finally come.

The Demigoddesses Great GrandDaughters All Grownup Now Have Come to Earth In Vast Numbers Like The Stars in the Heavens To Finish What Their Great GrandMothers Had Started.

# SEC. VII: THE RISE OF THE TEMPLE PRIESTESSES:

Notes:

1) Temple Priestesses: A human girl or women specialist having extensive (a). knowledge, (2). experience, and (3). particular expertise in the;

The Religious Beliefs and Practices of

The religion CEBAGII.

Temples Priestesses are spiritually aware participants in the invisible forces creating and controlling reality as the ordinary people know it to be. Temple Priestesses are selected for their profession by the third means of acquiring knowledge, by spiritual experiences.

Temple Priestesses function as healers, counselors, teachers, doctors, farmers, pharmaceutical expert, scientist, architects, biologist, musicians, dancers, therapist, matchmakers, historians, prophets, community leaders, mothers, guru, spiritual guide, protectors, peace makers, and all other functions needed to build & maintain a vibrant spiritual community.

2) Human sexuality is presented herein as an important part of life, and as an important part of the religion CEBAGII, and

THE BOOK OF CEGBAGII

a important part of human history. The sexual ethics in CE-BAGII are unlike those of any mainstream religion or cult. Sexuality as we envision it to be is a matter which should be guided by religion. Herein the discussion of the historical role of sexuality in the transformation of the Tribalectic culture into a Modern civilization, is presented for the edification of the practitioners of CEBAGII. Sexual gratification is not the goal of this writing & presentation of the sexual history of CEBAGII.

3) The Temple Priestesses who performed sexual therapies, and provide guidance & education in sexuality, and preside over ceremonies & memorials having sexual elements in their rituals, all within their spiritual communities; are not Temple Prostitutes. The term Temple Prostitutes was placed on the Temple

Priestesses by the practitioners of other religions in which sex in a sin and not a blessing. It is precisely their religious beliefs concerning sexuality, which have given rise to various types of sexual perversions.

4) Temple Priestesses refers not to a actual manmade structure, but rather to the sacred vessels, whose created bodies are the place where humanity and the Creator meet, communicate, and transformative events occur in their presence. The Priestesses are the temple!

Narrative:

The entire world was engulfed in a great storm, in darkness, and in pain & suffering. The Demigoddesses high above the earth in their spaceships, contemplated their mission to save this world and humanity. The spiritual realm was in chaos as the two forces ( good& evil ) were colliding. The balance of power on the earth was in flux.

The Kingdom Of The Great God Lucifer on Earth, was about to go too battle against The Kingdom Of Love In The Pantheon of Heaven. Earth would become their battle ground.

This would not be the first or the last time the Demigoddesses opposed Lucifer. There was once a War In Heaven, which the Creator brought to a sudden end. The great spiritual wars seemed always to be wars between women & men.

All wars seem to be in Essene battles over beliefs and practices, over right and wrong, over life and death, all these have the same underlying direction, to plot the course of creation too it's ultimate destination which lies beyond the here and now, in infinity and eternity, neither our past nor our future. And yet all wars appear to be continuation of one endless war, which humanity has not the power to win.


The Earth Is Beautiful,

Warm, Soft, And Peaceful

From Space. An Island

In The Middle Of A Vast

Sea Of Nothingness!

Each Time They Return

They Return To A World

In Crisis, And They Have Become

    The Guardians Of The Earth !


The Demigoddesses Know that earth and humanity had no future if they did not intervene.

Humanity required periodic assistance. In their present condition humanity could not survive another catastrophic natural event. A remnant of Humanity was desperately holding on too the last artifacts of civility, faith. That would have to be enough to build human salvation upon.

There was much work too do before humanity awakened; and it begun with a prayer, a petition to the Creator Alpha Omega, for strength & guidance, wisdom & discernment, and the assistance of the higher power.

It would have to be the Temple Priestesses who would bring light back into this world. Like a opium addict, Humanity was now enslaved, by many forces both natural and supernatural, external and internal.

Above in space all the Demigoddesses had assembled and moved deeper into prayer, their immortal minds reaching out and becoming one with the immortal minds of every Temple Priestesses on earth below.

In that spiritual realm was light, and there stood the Temple Priestesses and the Demigoddesses. On earth the bodies of the Temple Priestesses awakened before sunrise, and disappeared Into the forest gardens to collect various ingredients. They collected the first water of the mountain springs. They milked the best cow before it eat the morning grass. They collected the poisonous fish of the sea, and the snakes while they slept before dawn. They ground minerals and precious stones into fine power. This was their profession before there were pharmaceutical companies and chemist.

The Temple Priestesses were busy making potions not made since the times when the gods walked amongst humans in the green gardens, in the hidden valley, east of eden, and prayer to the one Creator Alpha Omega. They Demigoddesses guided their hands as they did their work in secret. Only Lucifer know their true objective, but there was little he could do to stopped them. The Demigoddesses had come en masse, and together they were an unstoppable force.

The Temple Priestesses prepared the traps for the brute-males enslaving their communities.

NOTES: On The Key Event In History Which Saved Humanity And Allowed The Religion CEBAGII To Be Born, The Transformation Of The Brute-Males By Controlled Spiritual Experiences With Demigod-desses.

1) the Demigoddesses know that the brute-males were the obstacles to the advancement of the humans communities and the return of civilized way of life.

2) the use of sexual stimulation, drugs, hypnosis, to produce a elevated state of mind, was essential in facilitating a spirituasl union between thee brute-males and the Demigoddesses.

3) the outcome was an expansion of the minds of the men after the knowledge of life was passed on to them during their contact with Demigoddesses in the spiritual realm. This resulted in a new perspective on life, which lead to a pursuit of higher asperastions.

4) the temple priestesses use botanicals, animals, bacteria, minerals, in the much the same way which modern pharmaceutical chemist use organic chemistry. They create drugs which can enhance or modify biological processes within the body, as well as modify mental processes.

5) an environment conductive to the achievement of altered mental states is also produced with rhythmic sounds, music, human voice ,(hypnosis), incense, and certain periodic variations in the wavelength of light.

6) techniques of message, and methods of sexual intercourse also enable sensations which block the minds awareness of distrac-

tions in the environment, and focus the minds attention.

7) certain types of stimulation and excitation accumulate energies within the body, these cash be redirected at the performance of spiritual functions which enable thee mind to cross the threshold separating the physical and the spiritual realms.

8) the objective of producing elevated mental states is to enable the mind to cross the threshold separating the physical and the spiritual realms.

9) it is when the mind is in the spiritual realm, that the individual can have transformative spiritual experiences. These experiences are unlike anything which we can ever experience in the physical

realm. Things are possible which we wish we could produce in therapy but lack the technology to do so.

10) in fact no modern men have ever had sexual intercourse with a Demigoddesses. In the critical event in our history, it was the human Temple Priestesses whose bodies were used by multiple Demigoddesses who simultaneously inhabited them. This condition produces a psychological state in the minds of the men who are present, in which they see the Demigoddesses. But the Demigoddesses are not actually present. Today in certain special ceremonies the same process is performed by Today's Temple Priestesses & the Demigoddesses.

# Sec. VIII: The Establishment Of The Matriarchates.

Narrative: Kingdom Of Love.

Once again the little planet earth, with it's peculiar race of homo sapiens, and the small community of higher beings lead by the sacred vessels, was at the center of the universe.

The Pantheon of Heaven 's intervention, lead by the sacred vessels, was beyond impressive, it was to do the impossible, it was a miracle, and it was testimony of their true dedication to the highest ideas at all cost.

This was more then just Noblesse Oblige, it was an act of Love.

When the Demigoddesses were still a very young race on earth, and the sapiens were still wondering through the fields & valleys of earth, looking for a home of their own; the ancients had left earth in search of a world called Utopia we believe. They left the Demigoddesses their religion. Suddenly it seemed, the Demigoddesses became the dominant species on earth, possessing a higher quality which lead them too establish the most successful society.

The Demigoddesses are single gender Isogynic beings. There are no males born except for the special form, which has many disabilities. Rule by women was logical. Demigoddesses possessed more then the finer attributes of both human genders. They exhibited a far greater synergistic quality of internal mental & spiritual balance & harmony that was also present in their society.

In ancient times, before the Demigoddesses migrated to heaven and became the race of endogenous sacred vessels they now are; the Human species and Demigoddesses species living close together were deeply connected. They had interbreed and produced exceptional redheaded children ( today we call these Xenomorphs, they being unlike either parent, unique creatures ).

Those offspring of the union of the two species, became legends; Helen of Troy, Hercules, Ester queen of Persia were of that linage. The Viking kings & queens as well.

The Demigoddesses left earth to continue their spiritual pilgrimage to Utopia, following the path of the ancients. They cease to interbreed with the sapiens, but could not cease to be concerned about the sapiens welfare.

The universe would watch over and again, as every human tear that fell would bring the Demigoddesses flying back across the Star system, back to earth, to mend the wounds and ease the pains of the humans, to go to extreme measures for this peculiar semi barbarian species. Perhaps theirs was a natural symbiotic relationship. Perhaps the Demigoddesses needed the sapiens, just as much as the sapiens needed them.

It was no surprise when the Demigoddesses had become the Guardians of Earth & of Humanity.

This time, this incredible mission back to their ancestral birthplace, it appeared that the Demigoddesses finally got it right, this time they might have fixed the problem with the strange race of sapiens. ( that is, If there was actually a problem with the sapiens in the first place! )

Many in the universe wondered if the Celestial Being, Lucifer, was a powerful spiritual obstacle to the progression of creation, in this Local Star Group! This would be very consistent with Lucifer's character before being exiled from heaven after attempting to alter the meaning and purpose of creation ?

Dispute Lucifer great powers, and vastly superior intellect, many took note of his inability to control his rival the small race of Demigoddesses, or to even fully rule the childlike race of humans. We now assume that a greater gentle force is at play in the universe, compensating for Lucifer's evil acts, limiting his range and influence.

"An intervention is not an invasion.

An invasion is what the great god Lucifer
has done on earth.
The Demigoddesses are here
to correct that error!"
-( unprintable symbolic language)
see; names in the cropcircles entries

Those were the words of the High Temple Priestesses, and they were not just words, they were followed by the greatest assembly of Priestesses ever to occur in the universe. Demigoddesses Spiritual warfare was being

waged. But despite their heroic acts, the Problem with the great god Lucifer was not within the scope of the Demigoddesses power to correct. John the Baptist was still in the spirit realm waiting to be born. The

Final Revelation had not yet been given. The time of the coming of the armies of angelic beings, and the Last Great War to be fought in heaven, called the Apocalypse, was still to come. For now, Lucifer would remain free to damage whatever the Demigoddesses could build on earth, the place of his exile.

Lucifer could not stop the Demigoddesses. The Demigoddesses would rule the moment, and lead the Temple Priestess in building on earth what they had built in heaven;The first human Matriarchate ( what Lucifer would politely call, " The Little Callipygian Aristocracy " ).

The Demigoddesses taught government (and science, religion, arts, agriculture, etc) to the Temple Priestesses who taught it to the community. The women embraced it as a form of liberation and government logically superior to male rule which they outlawed by civil law, and the men agreed.

The Matriarchates were a advanced society based on religion, science, technology, and arts taught to humanity by the Demigoddesses. Their work was motivated in part by their religious duties.

The Matriarchates ended many evil practices;

a. infacide
b. harems
c. incest
d. mass-murder
e. slavery
f. brutality against women & children
g. e. totalitarian male rule
h. lack of education for the youth
i. lack of medical care & poor hygiene

j.  lack of efficient agriculture

k.  expulsion of males at puberty

l.  suppression of true religion

m.  human sacrifice

n.  rape & pillage

o.  violence against the weak neighbors

p.  beating children

q.  indiscriminate killing

Narrative: The End Of The Matriarchates.

The matriarchates were very successful because of their religious foundation, and their devotion to teaching their young, and caring for their old. Humans spiritually progress and then transition into Demigoddesses in their next life. Thus as humans neared perfection they would naturally become more like the Demigoddesses. The Matriarchates were best suited to humans who had grown & developed spiritually.

The matriarchates were extremely prosperous and this attracted the attention of evil men, and Lucifer begun his vacious war against the matriarchates the first day they were established.

The Demigoddesses had used sex as one of many tools in their repertoire of techniques to enable men to cross the threshold and produce in them a spiritual awakening. The transformation of the brute-males was essential to freeing the communities from enslavement to the dark side.

Lucifer would use sex in a purely base fashion to build a army of barbaric men living under a unholy philosophy which morphed into what was called The Cult Of The One. They sought not just to be like the god of perfection, who blinded them to what he really was, but they desired to unite with the perfect one, and become one with him.

This enhanced Lucifer's power in earth, and his armies became societies, these became nations, these became empires which would enslave all the known world, and destroy what they could not enslave.

Lucifer taught men the pleasure of extremes; of raping and pillaging, of fighting and killing, of enslaving the meek free people, and killing myrtrs. The Priestesses and the most beautiful women, became the spoils of war, which were given as rewards to the fiercest warriors. This became the basis of the warrior culture and way of life, the diametrical opposite of the Matriarchal societies.

Thus on this earth two spiritual communities came into existence. The first was modelled after the Matriarchates of heaven. The second was modelled after a society Lucifer created from his philosophy. The two were complete diametrical opposites, and they were at war.

One must oppose evil without becoming like them, this is a difficult task, because one must be willing to lose everything of the material world to that evil empire. One has only two options, either violence or love.

Love tames the savage. But humanity has never understood love, and

religion & philosophy have distorted it beyond recognition, and yet the simplest creatures exhibit it naturally & instinctively.

Love was a elusive mystery more enigmatic then the meaning of life. Because humanity has never fully understood love, it has never been able to fully express love, nor live amongst one another in love. Love is the true basis of civilization. War & aggression is the absence of love in men, the state of an unfulfilled need. Humans know how to fight, but few know how to love.

Because they failed to tame the barbarians, and bring them into their community, the matriarchates would all fall in time to the armies of barbarians.

One day it begin, the barbarians came out of the north and east like a plague and decimated the kingdom of love. Dispite the presence of the Amazons on this earth, the people of the matriarchates could not match the savagery & violence which the barbarians were capable of.

The age of tranquility was brief. It had been a sweat golden age of humanity, which lasted one summer in the Sun, and die with the lilies of the field, and the last honey.

The idea would never die, and someday when the human remnant assume the role of Guardians of the Earth, men will understand love, and the Matriarchates will return. As in heaven so on earth.

# SEC. IX: FINAL THOUGHTS ON THE RELIGIOUS INTERPRETATION OF HISTORY & MYSTERY.

The disagreements in religion are between the monotheist. When two monotheist talk about how their way of life which their god has given them, they can not agree that their god gave them the same way of life, one believes the other is lying. This is because the two are discussing two different gods, they simply don't realize this is the case.

All monotheist believe that the god they know is the only god that exist. Because of their belief, they can not comprehend the fact that two or more believers can each believe in a different god.

The problem with religion yes even more complicated when the various elements of their religious beliefs, are shown to be in consistent with logic & reality. Because these elements of belief are given them by a perfect god, they are unable to acknowledge the errors in those elements of belief.

Finally the matter of acquisition of knowledge by communication with their god is problematical. Not all believers have these spiritual experiences, their god does not want to talk to them, instead the receive their or religious beliefs for on other people. They know of no objective means of validating other peoples religious beliefs, and simply assume them to be valid, and adapt those beliefs as their own.

Those are some major problems with monotheism. The most important problem is that higher evolved beings misrepresent themselves as, " the God", to the monotheist. The monotheist fail to realize that there is a infinite quantity of higher being, who go by the title, "god", but however are not the Creator of the universe. but rather creatures like ourselves.

The polytheists recognize the existence of a infinity of living creatures who are called gods. The polytheists also recognize that every real thing has an Associated-Mind, and that these minds can exist independent of a physical manifestation, and interact with people, and are called gods.

Religion is a complicated system of theories which are contradictions of reality, and logically inconsistent, because they contain untruths which are fundamental elements of the system of belief. From these untruths are derived the strange beliefs & practices of false religions.

If all religions were open systems, subject to change, growth, development, they could identify and remove their internal errors. Almost all Religions are closed systems incapable of change, and they cause their current practitioners to relive the same errors as the generations of believers prior to them.

It is not possible to change all this with a simple book like this one.

This book serves to communicate ideas & knowledge to those in the world who already are seeking change, growth, development, and who have been lead to this religion, one of an infinite many.

As polytheists we do not believe in one god, nor in one religion, and we seek to live peacefully with these many other religions.

- Oba Kavii Lez Arah. the polytheists.

Notes:

Our religion denies the gods their traditional place of high esteem above all creation. Clearly we believe in many gods, but we do not credit any of the gods with the creation of; the universe, living things, and humanity. We perceive these gods as creatures like ourselves, imperfect, semi powerful, and mortal.

The gods like all created things have immortal minds, which a within the Creator alpha omega, and part of the Creator. We have no independent existence.

The immoral minds are the only real things. the universe is noth- ing more then a derived transitory state produced by the Creator alpha omega via the forces in the spiritual realm, where the immortal minds are active.

We envision that history and mystery are intentionally hidden and distorted by those wishing to maintain control over the lives of other human beings. Most of humanity is born slaves to false religions. False religions come !not from the Creator Alpha Omega, but rather from certain groups of immortal minds which are in diametrical opposition to the Creator Alpha Omega.

Life is a series of physical manifestations as transitory as the rest of the universe, and we are not the form we temporarily appear to be, and we will have many more lives in many different higher forms in an end-less succession.

We were once a particle, an atom, a molecule, a bacteria, a tree, a woman, a man, before our current form.

We seek to live at peace with the world, but we do not live in a peaceful world. We therefore refrain from acts of extremes, and at times accept that we must endure extremes of human suffering.

The religious interpretation of history and mystery reveals all this to us, and we are at peace.

# Volume 2

# Introduction To Volume Two

The Future Of Humanity On This Earth & Beyond

Humans can make works of art,

because they can envision Perfection.

Although we do not know how to achieve

perfection, we dream of it, and at some point

we pursue those dreams.

- Kavii

Synopsis: The future of this earth is a continuation of the past. Thus;

The Religious Interpretation Of History & Mystery is vital to our understanding of our future.

I.    Highest Probability:

This earth will experience a global warming, catastrophic global drought, food shortages, starvation driven conflict, social unrest, war, extremes of human suffering, and death.

I.    Second Highest Probability:

The burning of hydrocarbon fuels will increase the severity of the global climatic crisis.

I.    Third Highest Probability:

The increase in the occurance of deadly noval infectious diseases, will reduce the productive capacity of the workforce, render children without parents to provide for their needs, and undermine clan confidence in the institutions of government, resulting in large anarchistic & paramilitary groups controlled by cult-like leadership.

I.    Fourth Highest Probability:

Technological solutions will destroy the existing social structure by reshaping the way of life of billions of people around the world, and two hundred fifty million Americans. Government

support will become the daily lifeline of many
millions of Americans.

I.    Fifth Highest Probability:

People will increasingly turn to false religion and
in particular the UFO cults for salvation,
increasingly abandoning true religion.

The Unique Religious Perspective:

Due to humanity's inability to efficiently respond to these challenges. we see the natural environmental changes as being the greatest threat to the continuation of the species. It is not possible for a handful of individuals to create the necessary solutions to problems as large as those the human race will face. The solutions require the collective work of all of peoples of this world, if we can not do that then we are doomed!

The Fallen and their society will not suffer to any degree comparable to the human condition due to their technologically advanced society here on this earth, and their access to unlimited energy. But however they will use these assets to undermine the faith in the true religion and accelerate the fall of human government and human civilization.

The Future Of Our Society:

In our religious interpretation of history & mystery we reveal that the Demigoddesses from heaven, gave us their religion. The Matriarchate, culture, religion, and way of life, which they gave us, was done to elevate humanity. The Demigoddesses also intended to elevate some individuals to the level at which they would be ready for a life in outer space and the duties as the New Guardians Of This Earth. But not until after their's, the Fallen's, and Lucifer's departure.

The natural processes will bring about another SolarDark and Global Flood event, but that will not occur for quite some time. In the interim humanity will need to build no communities capable of protecting human life from the intensification of environmental extremes.

Our society will supply this earth with energy and water. The Sun will be the source of energy collected by Solar Energy Power Stations in outer space. The Orrt Cloud will be the source of vital water for life on this earth. We will not be able to supply energy in quantities necessary for water desalination and detoxification. Thus earth life will be dependant on Space based water sources.

The Supreme End:

From our positions in outer space, will will constantly provide communal prayer for the wellbeing of humanity and this earth, and the redemption of the Fallen gods and their children. This being vital to the maintenance of the spirit of hope in the world.

THE HUMAN CONDITION SHALL CHANGE:

(There Is Light, And We Shall Find It!)

THOUGHTS IN GENERAL:

we as mortal beings in this human civilization, are truly obsessed with two main aspects of existence, which have become the focus of religion, philosophy, and taboo;

A. Our obsession with sexual reproduction

B. Our obsession with death

When we can see ourselves as one immortal being, then death would no longer be death, but rather the continuation of life; and death would lose its power over our minds.

When we can see intercourse as a part of life, and much much more

65

then simply copulation, then we can accept it as natural, and we can be at peace with sex, and sex would lose its power over men.

what our obsessions reveal is our society's need for change & growth, which are natural & essential functions of creation and existence.

when we can see the perfect creator alpha omega as continually growing & changing, then we can recognize the need for change in all things in creation including ourselves.

this is a age old call for human realization of our purpose in creation, and yet it is something few humans comprehend.

the demonstrated potential of human intelligence is such that we as a species have the potential to eliminate all human physical suffering, and only our psychological suffering remains as a challenge to out understanding of our own existence.

we study the universe in the hope of understanding our place and purpose in it. What we seek has already been given too us, and we have rejected it, suppressed it, and waged war against the messengers & prophets. While the human condition has continued to deteriorate.

this has always been the pattern of human life!

the struggle for improvement, growth & change, has always been fought with resistance based on a collective human imagination & amnesia which erases our knowledge our our past errors, thus we find ourselves repeating the same errors in every generation.

this is not human nature, it is a stage in human development, and at this stage it is the domination of human civilization by human who have yet to develop higher moral & spiritual values, and therefore they can justify to themselves the suffering allowed to continue in our human condition.

CHANGE CAN NOT OCCUR UNTIL THE TRANSFORMATIVE

# VOLUME 3

\*       \*       \*

A

\*       \*       \*

## ABUNDANT PRODUCTIVE CAPACITY (APC)

APC is a major quantitative indicator of the prosperity of a society as a measurement of it's capacity to meet 95% of the needs of it's population, within a certain time frame.

APC is calculated using various factors including ( but not limited to ) their following variables;

M1. maximum industrial productive capacity

M2. maximum personal services prod. cap.

M3. maximum amenities prod. cap.

M4. maximum import/exchange capacity.

The Numerical value of the APC is indicative of;

a.  the gross level of happiness

b.  peaceful coexistence

c.  domestic tranquillity

The limits of our understanding of human needs, human biology, human psychology, and the limits to our productive techniques, all combine to establish a limit to the value of the APC. Thus as society advances it will require less time energy and resources to meet 95% of the needs of all it's population.

*       *       *

## ALPHA OMEGA THE CREATOR

The Alpha Omega is the name given to the Creator of all things which constitute creation and living creatures like ourselves. The qualities of the Alpha Omega define Divinity, and include but are not limited too the following;

I.    omnipotence

II.    omnipresence

III.    all knowing

IV.    immortal & eternal

V.    truthfulness

VI.    Creator of energy time and space

VII.    originator of the design & intent of creation

VIII.    originator of the purpose of creation

IX.    originator of the purpose of human existence

The Creator Alpha Omega's name represents two main functions of the Creator Alpha Omega;

a.  to create

b.  to uncreate

We can envision the Alpha as a supernova.

We can envision the Omega as a black hole.

All things are immortal minds created at the beginning of time. We exist as part of the Creator Alpha Omega.

The two realms of reality;

a.  the spiritual realm

b.  the physical realm

both exist within the immortal minds, within the Creator Alpha Omega.

All physical objects are states of the physical realm, which prior to being real were virtual States in a collection of all the possible states of the universe. The immortal minds made the states transition from virtual to actual.

The progression of immortal minds ends when they acquire the qualities of divinity, a point in the infinite future.

The condition of perpetual digression ends when the immortal mind is nullified and the physical manifestation absorbed in the Omega.

*     *     *


## AMAZONS

The Amazons are a group of human women who have been

given the task of containing the fight on earth against all those

who fight against the Creator Alpha Omega.

There were two types of Amazons;

A. THE HEAVENLY AMAZONS:

Created in heaven to police the Celestial-god Lucifer, who was establishing a religion diametrically opposite of that of the worship of the Creator Alpha Omega. These Amazons have all perfected & transitioned to higher stages and forms.

A. THE EARTH AMAZONS:

The daughters of the Heavenly Amazons, and their descendants, who continue the fight against those on earth who;

     a.  fight against the Creator Alpha Omega, and

     b.  oppose the achievement of the Supreme End, and

     c.  seek to elevate Lucifer above the Creator Alpha Omega.

The Heavenly Amazons were made by the Three High Temple Priestesses of the Pantheon in the spiritual community in outer space calls, " Heaven ". The high Temple Priestesses persuaded the special form of the Demigoddesses to volunteer to be permanently transformed. They were transformed into a special group called The Amazons to police heaven.

The qualities the Amazons have are the following;

     1.  instantaneous healing

     2.  physical regeneration

3. supernatural physical strength

4. supernatural stamina

5. longest lifespan of any living creature

6. extraordinary intelligence & memory

7. clairvoyance

8. extrasensory perception

9. spiritual gifts & gift of tongues

10. health

11. moral integrity & wisdom

12. extraordinary beauty

After the First War In Heaven, the great god Lucifer, the heavenly residents who worshipped him, and the demigods who worship Lucifer in his male form, and as Lucy in the female form, were all exiled to!the earth worlds of the billions of Local Star Groups throughout the universe.

The Amazons we're also sent to earth and become the thorns in Lucifer's crown. They served to limit the power of Lucifer and his followers here on earth amongst the homo sapiens.

The Heavenly Amazons also have the task of managing the Xenomorphs, or the redheaded children of the gods ( SolarDark Mission Watchers ), who live here on earth amongst the sapiens.

The Heavenly Amazons did have children by sapiens males. Their offspring became legendary, and we know them as the (female) Earth Amazons, and the (male) wizards ( like Marlin ).

The inbreeding of the two species did result in additional introduction of Demigoddess DNA into the Homo sapiens gene pool. But however the sexual reproduction of Amazons is a very managed affair, and not haphazard like the sexual practices of the modern day sapiens.

\*        \*        \*

## AMAZONS - POLICE

( See Also the entry on the Amazons)

After the War In Heaven was ended by the Creator Alpha Omega, the antagonist Lucifer and his followers were exiled. The Heavenly Amazons, the police of heaven, also went into exile.

After the establishment of the exiles on the earths, the Heavenly Amazons continued to police Lucifer on this earth. Some mistakenly see the Amazon Police as an instrument of violence. They are in fact a means to resist violence and prevent human suffering.

There are a few essential beliefs concerning the Heavenly Amazons use of force to Police the behaviors of others;

A.  Police are not a instrument of violence, but rathera force to restrain certain types of violence insociety between its

members.

B.  Freewill is not intrinsically good. There is the willto do good, and the will to do evil.

C.  Violence in itself is a extreme violation of anotherpersons exercise of freewill.

D.  The idea of a police force is based on the beliefthat there can be justice at times only if thefreewill to do evil is responded too with anopposing force sufficient too prevent the exerciseof that particular freewill. We call the resultantoder produced by police action Justice.

E. Even when justice fails we do not abandon thebelief in justice, only the assumption that thepresent means is adequate to create justice, andwe seek to create a more perfect means to achievethat true justice which we believe is possible.

F. In the minds of some, there is a conflict between natural and unnatural actions, such as " force of nature", and " force of a intelligent creature ".When the forces of nature destroy, we do not cease to believe that there can made a realorder in nature, and we seek a effective means to police nature and produce order. When nature goes to an extreme which threatens life, we do not hesitate to control that nature, be it wild-nature, or human-nature. If we fail to directly regulate nature when needed, then someday nature will destroy us due to our fault, our lack of action.

In conclusion one can not be an religious conscientious objector to the use of force in the pursuit of justice, unless one is willing to live in a world without justice, without order, a world of extremes of human suffering, a world of violence, and a world of untimely violent unnatural death. That is not the condition which the Creator Alpha Omega created the world to be. People ask why does the Creator Alpha Omega allow the world to be in such a condition, the true question is why do we allow the world to be in such a condition.

The presence of the Amazons, and their use of force to create justice, was not contrary to the design & intent of the Creator Alpha Omega.

\*        \*        \*

## AMNESIA IN REINCARNATION

KEY RELIGIOUS BELIEF:

BOTH NATURAL DEATH OF THE BODY, AND AMNESIA IN SUCCESSIVE LIFES, ARE ESSENTIAL ELEMENTS IN NATURAL REINCARNATION.

Narrative:

A succession of lifetimes, different circumstances, different bodies, different times & places; are all required to achieve the Supreme End. A single human lifetime is insufficient for two sets of reasons:

Firstly; In life the Personality of the physical manifestation creates limitations on range of experiences of the Associated Immortal Mind.

Secondly; A single human lifetime is insufficient to provide the immortal mind with the necessary range of experiences to facilitate the continuation of the fullest possible growth & development of the Associated Immortal Mind.

Natural Death is a stage in reincarnation, which facilitates the provisioning of the succession of humans lifetimes, which are required by the immortal mind for it's growth & development.

Amnesia is a tool that terminates the previous individual Personality when the immortal mind forms a association with a new physical manifestation, so that it can not restrict the previous personality in the successive physical manifestation.

NOTES:

Applicable Terms & Concepts To This Subject:

I. REINCARNATION;

1. The process in which; (a) a Immortal Mind permanently ceases to associate with one physical manifestation ( or form ) resulting in the cessation of life signs in that form; and then ( b ) that same Immortal Mind gives life to another physical manifestation (

   form ) by establishment of a longterm association with that form at it's conception.

2. The process were by an Immortal Mind transitions from one physical manifestation to another physical manifestation, and thereby continues the Immortal Mind's growth & development, which consist of it's continuing to acquire additional divine qualities.

3. The death of one individual form followed by the birth of another individual form of the same kind, in which both individual forms share the same associated Immortal Mind.

Reincarnation creates a new living soul consisting of two parts;

1. The Physical Manifestation of the TemporalSpacial Energy Material Realm, whose transitory qualities are related to its physical existence, and

75

2.  The Associated Immortal Mind whose eternal qual-
    ities are of The Creator Alpha Omega, which it is a
    infinitesimal portion of, and which creates;

    a.  the physical realm ( three dimensional space
        ) and

    b.  all Physical Manifestations ( the physical
        qualities of things in three dimensional space
        ) in creation.

I.   AMNESIA IN REINCARNATION;

The natural condition in which the individual physical manifestation can not recall the previous life of the physical manifestation
which preceded it; despite the fact that both share the same associated Immortal Mind.

II.   PERSONALITY;

1.  . the distinctive individual qualities of a person, con-
    sidered collectively. ( Websters New World Dict.)

III.   SELF;

1.  . the identity, character, or essential qualities of any
    person or thing. ( Websters New World Dict.)

2.  .the unique set of innate and acquired physical,

mental, moral & spiritual qualities possessed by an
individual being which come to define that person in
the thoughts of her/himself and others, in this realm
of existence.

The qualities which define our self are the consequences of a hierarchy of forces within us;

A. Our innate biological instincts which are the basis of our predatory nature.

B. Our mental faculties which enable us to modify both our environment and ourselves to fulfill our perceived needs.

C. Our moral/spiritual qualities which allow us to emulate the higher qualities of a Immortal Mind, having greater aspirations then the fulfilment of ones own needs and desires related to physical existence.

The immortal mind has only it's divine qualities which define it, these, and not the previous personality, determine the fundamental qualities of the next physical manifestation. If a living being could remember the previous life of it's Immortal Mind, then this memory would resurrect the previous personality. That personality would then become a controlling factor in the Physical Manifestations actions.

IV.   DEATH OF A BODY:

the permanent termination of the connection between that physical manifestation and that particular Immortal Mind, which renders the physical manifestation incapable of exhibiting the qualities of living beings (lifeless).

*       *       *

<u>ANARCHY:</u>

An antisocial & anti communal way of life, based on the fundamental belief that ones subjective perspective is always superior

to that of others, and this frees one from any obligations to obey
any restrictions placed on one by society. Either one disobey
openly or secretly.

An anarchist seeks and demands that others join him in the
destruction of the vital functions required to sustain a viable progressive society, and thereby threatens the well being and future
of human civilization.

One significant factor in the failure of government to achieve
it's objectives, is the anarchist activities of government workers,
who serve their own objectives, which are destructive to the objectives of democratic government.

\*        \*        \*

<u>ANCESTRAL BIRTHPLACE:</u>

Creation consist of the universe and all things in the universe.
There are trillions of Stars, and even more planets. Most mature
stars are arranged in Local Star Groups. Each Local Star Group
has living things on at least one of its planets, in at least one it's
solar systems.

It is natural pattern of life to progress, develop technologies,
migrate to the regions of space in it's Local Star Group, and establish colonies. This pattern is repeated throughout the universe.

The planet on which the higher evolved creatures originated is their Descendants, " Ancestral Birthplace ".

This earth has been the birthplace of many many species. A very few species develop technologies enabling them to live in outer space. Some a benevolent some are hostile. Morality is not a innate quality of all living things regardless of the level of evolution & development.

This earth is the Ancestral birthplace of six higher evolve species of the Pantheon in the spiritual communities in outer space called heavens. These are the descendants on seven species which prior to 100,000 years ago live on earth. The six species are limited to the following;

MAJOR GODS:

A. Universal Gods

B. Celestial Gods

C. Terrestrial Gods

MINOR GODS:

D. Demigoddess: (A Isogynic Race by choice)

    1. Upper D.

    2. Middle D.

    3. Lower D.

These creatures have the right of return, but however that right has been suspended during the period of the Lucifurian Exile.

This planet is called, " Earth ", because it is currently the temporary place of exile of the Fallen. The earth actual name is unknown to humans.

There were many earths established after the War in Heaven. Our earth is the home to the leader of the rebellion, the great god Lucifer. Because this of the earths, is Lucifer's Ancestral Birth-place, he was permitted to exile here, under Divine, Natural, and Civil Laws.

*       *       *


## ANCIENTS

Historical Background:

The Ancients were a technologically advanced higher evolved species native too this planet 300,000 years ago; which preced-ed both; (a) the Hominoid species on this earth and, (b) the six higher evolved species currently living in this Local Star Group.

The Known Intelligent Life Of This Local Star Group:

I.    The Highest of The Higher Evolved Beings.

II.   The Extinct Ancients.

III.  The Major Gods:

IV.   Universal-gods

V.    Celestial-gods

VI.   Terrestrial-gods

VII.   The Minor Gods:

VIII.  Upper Demigoddesses

IX.   Middle Demigoddesses

X.    Lower Demigoddesses

XI.   The Hominids:

XII.    Homo Sapiens

100,000 years ago the Ancients gave the three species of Demigoddesses their Religion, Culture, Social Organization & Governmental Structure, Arts & Sciences. This transformed the Demigoddesses and give birth to their distinctive qualities which over the next 100 millennium were greatly enhanced.

After transforming the Demigoddesses, the Ancients left this earth, leaving behind their monumental stone structures & mysteries. The Demigoddesses then transformed spiritually into the Sacred Vessels of the Creator Alpha Omega.

The Guardians Of Earth:

The six higher evolved species, especially the Demigoddesses, have accepted their necessary role as The Guardians Of This World. 25,000 years after the Ancients departed, the six higher species migrated into outer space of this Local Star Group.

Since that time the Demigoddesses have unsuccessfully searched this collection of heavenly bodies for physicasl evidence which would put them on the path of the Ancients. It is said that the Ancients know of a place we called utopia.

The Demigoddesses once believed that if they find that place they would find the Ancients; and if they found the Ancients they would find that place. They searched the stars of this LSG, and finding nothing they have returned to our world, the only world they haven't searched!

The Ancients Transformation:

The process of transition into a being of a higher evolved species, require that multiple Immortal Minds unite into one greater

Immoral Mind. Even the Ancients reincarnate, progress, perfect, and transition. The Ancients were just a stage in the progression of the Immortal Minds; as all things in the universe/creation are.

It is now accepted that the Ancients never left this Local Star Group. The Ancients underwent a spiritual transition too a unique

higher species, which is of a form which is no form!

The Immortal Minds of the Ancients who were in perpetual digression became lower species; (a) The three species of Demigoddesses, and (b) the many species of hominids.

Thus after 75,000 years of searching, the Demigoddesses concluded that the Ancients are still here in this Local Star Group, as much higher evolved beings then themselves.

THE ANCIENTS HAVE BECOME

THE GODS OF THE GODS !

*      *      *


APOCALYPSE

KEY BELIEF:

THE END OF THE PRESENT IS THE BEGINNING OF THE FUTURE

In this age a rational belief and wildly popular idea, which sounds true, is that the end of civilization is also the end of the world, the end of life, and the end of humanity; It is a compelling misconception.

The facts is civilizations in the distant past were more technically advanced then the current moon landing civilization. Abandoned Stone cities are evidence that those civilizations existed and disappeared. Hominids coexisted peacefully with those civilizations. We are the proof, that humanity did not perish with those ancient civilizations..

Human beings existed before there was human civilization, and humanity existed without civilization, and humanity will survive without the end of this current civilization! That is a Fact of Life. The only question is How Will We Survive! No human has the answer unless they derived it from a higher authority.

Humanity continues to migrate into every corner of this earth. They search the world for a better society. The next civilization can not be the better society they seek, if they build it like this one, with human strength and human ingenuity. The better world must be built on higher principles, designs and plans. A higher

authority must guide humanity.

The End Is A New Beginning,

That is A Law of the Creator Alpha Omega.

*     *     *

## ASSOCIATED-MIND

The Creator Alpha Omega. By reducing the qualities of a portion of it's being, a lesser portion is established. The lesser portion is not equivalent to the whole or the greater part, and it is relatively imperfect. Each of these lesser portions in the Creator Alpha Omega is capable of thought, and perceive itself as an distinction called an individual, and is an, " Immortal Mind ".

All Immortal Minds were created before The Physical Realm was created;

    A.  Before Time & Space were created.

    B.  Before Energy was created.

The universe was created in the Immortal Minds. Every Physical Manifestation In The Universe Which Is A Whole Thing Is A Manifestation Of The Thoughts In The Immortal Minds, And Has An Associated-Mind, which is an Immortal Mind. The Immortal Minds must continually increase in the level of perfection, obtaining higher qualities.

Our perfection is not measured in the level of technological, artist, philosophical, or even religious development we achieve.

Our perfection is in the accumulative changes which occur within us, and which gradually reduce & eliminate the differences between our conscious thoughts & desires, and that internal moral conscious, which is the voice of the Creator Alpha Omega, in all creation, in all creatures, in all ages, eons, and eras.

*      *      *

## ASTEROIDS OF ICE:

This planet was created to be inhabited by living things and in

this Local Star Group is all the water this planet will ever need to maintain the surface in. condition which can support life.

The surface water on this planet is continually replenished by the arrival of water from!outside this planet. On the edge of this solar system exist a vast region of outer space known as the Orrt Cloud. The Orrt Cloud consist of billions of asteroids made of frozen water.

Natural processes enable the asteroids to leave their orbits in the Orrt Cloud, and travel into the inner solar system. Some of these asteroids will collide with the planet, turn to vapor, and make it down to the surface as precipitation or snow. In fact most of the ice in deep glaciation is directly from outer space.

At times the ice asteroids can arrive in swarms so large that they cause torrential rains which cause widespread flooding on the planets surface. These natural catastrophic event are called Deluges.

\*     \*     \*

B

\*     \*     \*

## BALANCED ISOGYNIC BEING

In the three higher evolved species call Demigoddesses, each species has three possible physical forms.

A.  THE FEMALE-MALE FORM. (normal form)

This form has all the reproductive functions of the female and the male, as well as the external secondary sexual characteristics of both human genders.

B.  THE FEMALE FORM. (special form)

This form is a biological anomaly caused by the incomplete

formation of a Demigoddess form, due to the absence of one of

the male soulmates in the transitional process of unification of soulmates, which produces a Demigoddess. We call this a special form.

### C.  THE MALE FORM. (special form)

This form is a biological anomaly caused by the incomplete formation of a Demigoddess form, due to the absence of one of the female soulmates in the transitional process of unification of soulmates, which produces a Demigoddess. We call this a special form.

The Female-Male Form of Demigoddesses is called a balenced ISOGYNIC being. All the Female-Male Forms in the three species of Demigoddesses have the ability to transition between three physical forms which take on the appearance of each of the forms above.

The three species of demigoddesses migrated from earth to their spiritual communities in outer space 100,000 years ago. After leaving earth their species became Endogenous ( breeding only with other Female-Males Forms ). They scientifically managed all their sexual reproduction and were able to eliminate all naturally occuring adverse effects of their third-gender physiology. After 25,000 years the Demigoddesses became a pure race of physiologically perfect Isogynic beings.

*        *        *

The Future Of Humanity On This Earth & Beyond.

Creation Of Body:

The power of the immortal mind creates the physical manifestation by selecting a future state from the virtual set of all possible states. The degree to which the immortal mind can comprehend the set of all possible states, determines the limits the immortal minds creative powers, and the degree to which the laws of nature dictate conditions.

The Body Beautiful:

It is said that the value humans place on physical beauty in a reflection of our vanity. But this saying was from a time before we understood genetics. Our genes control our qualities, abilities, health, and lifespan. It would benefit the species if the best genes were passed on to our offspring, and the worst genes were prevented from passing on to our children.

The body is an expression of the genetic information it carries, and physical beauty is too some extinct an indicator of the quality of our genes. Nature by tying asexual attraction to physical beauty, encourages sexual relations with the beautiful ones and thus improves the quality of future generations.

A Important Key Belief:

Once We Understand The Natural Biological Rational For These Natural Impulses, We No Longer Have To Be A Slave To Those Impulses. Understanding Is Power.

The genetic utility of degrees of sexual attraction, does not diminish the human value of unattractive indiviuals people who are not endowed with superior genes. These people can make good parents to children who whose genetics come from superior doners. Such a arrangement would scientifically improve the human species, and possibly eliminate many genetically inherited disease and disabilities.

The Plan For Future Generations Today:

The Demigoddesses used science to plan artificial reproductive programs which did not change the lives of those living, but improved the next generation significantly. This practice was repeated in every generation, and over time the demigoddesses became species of exceptional qualities; physically, intellectually, and spiritually/morally.

The same will be possible for homo sapiens if we make invetro fertilization the standard practice for all prenatal planning. We can select from seven billion people the best gene pool, and design the optimal combinations of ova and sperm.

Sex will still happen, but sexual intercourse will no longer lead to pregnancies. A governmental agency will be responsible for planning and creating all new children. Once parents are approved, then they can select which fertilized ova will be implanted

in the women's womb. It many cases it can be a family of one parent, or eleven samesex couples. People can receive better children then they would have produced naturally. All at state expense!

We can then allow everyone who wants children, and is suitable to be parents to receive the healthiest children possible. Not all people should have children, but biology allows anyone to become a parent, and this has resulted untold suffering of young children at the hands of psychologically unstable parents.

Clearly many more factors will be taken into consideration when a scientific assessment is made of an individuals genet- ic makeup, and suitability of their genes for state ran selective reproduction programs which will provide fertilized ova to qualified recipients along with prenatal/postnatal care, free of charge. ( The French have a saying that today's children are the future France. That is a quite true )

There are many people who object to science taking over human reproduction, and they will not want to participate in this, that's O.K. This is not a plan for the American society at large, but for our select sub society & religious community. This is incredibly humane and rational and doable.

Future Body:

We can all be made beautiful on the outside! As we move into outer space we will take science to the next level, replacing the human body with a machine body. The Brain Would Be Retained along with the internal organs. The bone marrow would be in a new manmade organ so there would be no bones. This is the Ghost In The Shell Technology. This also is something many people would not see the benefits of.

The Isogynic machine body would also be an option some people would select in our spiritual community, in imitation of the Demigoddesses. That would be a most beautiful thing too do!

*      *      *

## BODY

The body is also called the physical manifestation because the body originally is a a member of a set of infinite possible states in the universe, and the Associated-Mind determines which of those will be real for a fraction of time. The body like all real things is created via the Immortal Minds, and its condition is influenced by the Associated-Mind.

*       *       *

## BODY THIEVERY

Body Thievery is an ancient process for the exchange of Associated-Minds between two bodies. It is used to steal bodies.  A Associated-Mind in a dying body can steal a healthy body, by causing the mind in!the healthy body to return to the wrong body, while it assumes the healthy body, and then killing the unhealthy body before the Associated-Mind realizes its be tricked into the wrong body. Once the body is dead the Associated-Mind with enter the cycle of reincarnation, and be born into!a newly conceived body.

In the old country ( Eastern Europe & Eurasia) this has been going on for thousands of years. When children recall their last life, sometimes it's because their last body is still alive somewhere being occupied by another Associated-Mind. If the investigators were to obtain permit to exhume the body of the person the child knows he/she is, they would find the wrong person buried in that grave. They would never find the stolen body. Lastly the body must be stolen while both bodies are still alive.

In the West this occurs also today, and has been practiced since the 1860's in large urban metropolitan areas, where no one will report the disappearance of a homeless teenager or young adult.

*  *  *

## BILOXI, Queen of Sheba

Another Demigoddess of this sect.

*  *  *

## BREAST AS SYMBOLS IN THE MATRIARCHATE

Every unique society of human beings has their particular set of beliefs & practices, ways of life, means of survival, place the call their own, and symbols which are related to all the above. Their art tells us how the envision the world, creation, life, death, and the meaning of all these.

CEBAGII is a religion in which woman are the authority, leadership, spiritual gurus, mother, sister, wife, and friend. The essence of CEBAGII is it's undeniable matriarchal nature.

Breast are a major symbol of CEBAGII. The artistic representation of Breast conveys a large body of meanings. We are an intelligent people, and It is not necessary for me to list every possible meaning in this brief dictionary entry. I would like the artist &

91

members of this religion to express their own impressions of what breast mean to them.

The Demigoddesses who returned to earth to give us their Religion, Culture, Art, Science, Government, and a unique way of life, were tripartite beings, and they were women. They are remembered as women of great intelligence, strength, beauty, and as living beings much like ourselves, only better!

35,000 years ago artist created icons which survive to this day, they are the oldest surviving art on this of the earths. These figurines have enormous breast & hips, and the are clearly human women. These works of art were important enough to the people of that age, to be protected so that the would survive into perpetuity.

In a matriarchal world, the most important symbolism reflects the physical attributes of women, and holds these attributes to

be cherished and deeply respected. That was the case 100,000 years ago, 40,000 years ago, 24,000 years ago, and it is still true today and tomorrow!

Note:

1.  Nudity in religious art, icons, and symbols, is not for the purpose of sexual gratification, but because the gods were relative physical perfection, and art must represent that perfection;

2.  Nudity exist also because the gods did not see the need for clothing in the climate of North & Central Africa, they were not embarrassed by the bodies.

C

*       *       *

## CANNON OF THE CREATOR ALPHA OMEGA

The Order the cannon is listed in is arbitrary, and all cannon is of equal importance.

1. Each individual has a obligation to work towards the growth & development not only of oneself but also that of other human beings, as a fulfillment of the Supreme End.

2. Each individual has a obligation to work towards the redemption & salvation of other human beings who are in perpetual digression, as a fulfillment of the Supreme End.

3. No created thing can be elevated to a status equal too, or above that of the Creator Alpha Omega.

4. The practices of slavery, harems, forced marriage, incest, arranged marriages of children, involuntary prostitution, are taboo.

5. No person shall allow the abuse use of children, the deprivation of the needs of children, the denial of education of children, the isolation of children from their peers, the participation of children in soldiery, the forced labor of children, nor the alienation of affection of parents.

6. No person shall seek to injure, harm, or kill another living creature without extreme necessity.

## CATASTROPHISM

The Creator Alpha Omega has provided the material and the energy reserves, and the natural processes & conditions, needed to ensure that life on the inhabited worlds does not disappear from the universe.

The natural processes ensure that this earth can continually sustain life on its surface and in it's oceans, lakes, and rivers. These natural processes are sometimes very dynamic and destructive. The can erase civilization, and bring about mass extinctions , or Extinction Level Events.

Catastrophism is an old theory that the natural processes which ensure life, also threaten life, and that our earth endures endless cycles of building up and tearing down, since the first day of creation.

Here in I gave two (2) relevant examples of dynamic essential natural processes;

A. SOLARDARK ; is the natural variation in the energy output of our nearest star ( The Sun), which displays extremes, including the total cessation of light & heat. SolarDark is necessary in order to cool the earth enough to prevent it from becoming another planet Venus.

B. Bombardment of this Earth by swarms of Orrt Cloud ICE ASTEROIDS; is another of the vital natural processes. The Orrt Cloud contains all the water this earth will ever need. Ice Asteroids provide water & oxygen, by leaving their stable orbits, tracing into the inner solar system, and colliding with the earth and the Sun's plasma corona.

When large swarms of ice asteroids enter the inner solar system, then occurs the extremes which endanger life on earth, giving earth its periodic great global floods, and providing the material for precipitation accumulating as large scale glaciation. These conditions have long term impact on earths climate & environment.

The Creator Alpha Omega, has infinite wisdom, and has provided a means by which the progression of creation is not destroyed by natural processes. One important means is the distribution of life in all its variety throughout the universe. The other is the natural instincts which drive higher evolved beings to care for the lesser creatures of their worlds, or Natural Compassionate Noblesse Oblige.

After each natural catastrophe human rebuilds, but this would not always be the case if not for the intervention of certain higher evolved species, who come the humanity's aide in times of extreme crisis.

It is also true that there are higher evolved beings who care nothing for other lifeforms. The valence in the universe between good and evil, always tips in the favor of good, because of that factor Catastrophes are not the end of creation as we know it to be.

*     *     *

## THE CEBAGIlian

We are not the atoms in our body. Those atoms are replaced constantly, and yet we are not diminished, we remain. We are not the air in our lungs, the air enters and leaves the body, and yet we are not diminished, we remain. We are not our hands, feet, lungs, those things can be removed and replaced, and yet we are not diminished, we remain.

When our body dies, because we leave it and do not return, and yet we are not diminished, we remain. We do not die when the body dies. What then are we?

We are Human Being for only a Moment in time and place.

Had we been born on another world we would have been some other creature, and yet we are not diminished, we remain. We are not the creature!

All things in creation/universe are transitory and they all pass away, and yet we are not diminished, we remain. We are not those things, we are not of this world.

We are all within and indivisible portions of The Creator Alpha Omega. That Is All That There Is. We are All That There Is.

\*        \*        \*

## CELESTIAL-GODS

The Celestial-gods are one species belonging to a group of six ( the Pantheon ) higher evolved species, who originated on this

96

earth, spiritually, culturally, and technologically progressed, and now living is spiritual communities ( Matriarchates ) in regions of outer space we call heaven.

God is a relative term not referring to the Creator Alpha Omega, but rather to any living creature constantly displaying qualities & abilities of a level of perfection beyond what homo sapiens are naturally capable of, and also having other natural qualities of a nature which is totally incomprehensible to homo sapiens. By virtue of their natural and developed attributes, they create the means to alter the material world in a manner & degree which our ancestors called magic.

The most well known of the Celestial-god species is the great god Lucifer, who is in exile to this of the earths after fighting the War In Heaven.

Lucifer was referred to as the, " god of perfection " be his followers, and he taught them that if the wish to be perfect be like him, then he lead them into a religious war in heaven. He then became known as, " the god of war ".

Lucifer is in perpetual digression, but however the Unitarian Universalistic beliefs of this religion indicate that the Pantheon is obligated to continue to work towards Lucifer's redemption & salvation. The progression of all creation in this Local Star Group requires Lucifer's return to the Pantheon. The Celestial-gods such as Lucifer being a essential part of this creation, but not in his present state.

The Celestial-gods do not experience a biological childhood stage. But however they do go through a process of psychological growth, which has a child stage. This can result in them being a most powerful being relative to other beings, while they still in the psychological condition of a child.

The ability of shape shifting means that no one is ever sure of what a particular Celestial-god actually looks like. But however they have a tendency to develop a consistent personal appearance, when in the presence of a select society they interact with regularly.

Finally the intellectual capacities of the Celestial-god species gives them creative & cognitive abilities beyond human comprehension. Because of these qualities, Celestial-gods are mistaken for the Creator Alpha Omega by more primitive societies.

The Celestial-god species is only one stage and lifeforms, which all immortal minds will go through in the progression in our Local Star Group. So we too will someday be Celestials, but hopefully we will not behave like the great god Lucifer.

*       *       *


## CEBAGII, Part I

CEBAGII is the name for sect practiced by myself, of the religion given to humanity by the higher evolved species called, The Demigoddesses. CEBAGII is an acronym for;

The Creed Of Eclectic/Esoteric Beliefs

Ad-infintum and General and Ideosycratic

Ideologies.

CEBAGII is the name I have given to the set of personal beliefs and practices concerning;

    A. the divine origin of the universe,

    B. the divine design, intent, and purpose of creation,

    C. the true spiritual nature of human beings,

      D. the purpose for human creation & existence

      E. the Supreme End of the divine way of life.

The origins of the particular beliefs and practices in CEBAGII are;

    A. the subjective interpretation of my subjectivespiritual experiences which have come throughdreams and inspiration,

    B. the history of humanity,

    C. the laws of nature,

    D. science and

    E. inspired art, and

    F. the divine revelations given to other human beingsin other times and religions which have becomepart of our human collective learning.

The Primary text in CEBAGII is the volume called;The Religious Interpretation ofHistory and Mystery.

This volume explains the forgotten divine interventions in the history of humanity, in the past interventions of higher evolved benevolent mortal beings, in human affairs.

These interventions did save human life on this world from natural extinction, and to guide the spiritual/moral development of human society through the transmission of a unique religion, culture, government, social structure, and way of life. These are the based on CEBAGII.

The singular true living entity in CEBAGII is the Creator Alpha Omega, who is both the beginning and the end of everything. Alll true understanding and All real things originate in the Creator Alpha Omega, including;

    A.  the spiritual realm of immortal minds

    B.  the physical realm of

        1.  Time

        2.  Space

        3.  Energy & Matter

    A.  The laws ( Science) governing nature

    B.  The Divine laws ( Cannon ) governing intelligentlife

    C.  The Design, Form, Functions of all real things

The secondary text in CEBAGII concerns the future of the practitioners of this religion, referred to as the remnant, and includes the following predictions;

    A.  their inevitable migration to and establishment ofspiritual communities beyond this world;

    B.  their spiritual obligation to the well being of

        1.  this world,

        2.  living things, and

        3.  humanity;

    C.  their continual struggle with natural imperfectionhuman & spiritual digression.

D.  and their relationship with other intelligent life in the universe

The Cannon Of The Create Alpha Omega, is the fundamental basis of the bodies of;

I.    Divine,

II.   Civil, and

III.  Natural Laws.

From these all ideas & concepts governing life are drawn, and other ideas & concepts compared to.

CEBAGII and the Laws, are not fixed, but evolve as the spiritual community of practitioners grow and develop. Aanology is in the progressive stages of a students learning;

FIRSTLY; addition, subtraction, multiplication, and division;

SECONDLY; followed by algebra, trigonometry, geometry;

THIRDLY; followed by calculus, complex logic, analytics;

FOURTHLY; followed by even higher forms of precise quantitative understandings of the reality.

Like all growing developing things in creation so are our beliefs & practices. CEBAGII is a infinite series of evolving progressively more comprehensive and precise teachings/revelations of the nature of reality in all its dimensions, passed to humanity through our spiritual experiences.

In the final stages CEBAGII will lead humanity to the realization of the beginning of everything, and a complete understanding of the only true existing being, our Creator Alpha Omega, which we recognize ourselves as being within and a inseparable part of.via the,

\*        \*        \*

## CEREMONIAL DANCES

All members of the spiritual community participate in dances. The Spiritual Community performs dances which have meaning and purpose, and each member of the community is fought their meaning. These are often Rhythmic Pantomimes.

Pan' to' mine: a drama played out without words, usingonly actions and gestures.

Cere' mo' ny: a set of formal acts proper to aspecial occasion, as a religious rite.

- Webster's New World Dictionary

Dance consist of the actions of humans in coordinated organized motion, and it serves more then one function;

A.  Dance is a dynamic physical representation of conditions and events which are not actual at the time & place of the performance.

B.  Dance is expression of the spiritual, and emotional personal union of two or more people, through specialized reciprocal synchronized motions

Ritual Dances in CEBAGII involve as many people as can be accommodated, and who have the necessary familiarity with the rituals being performed. The arrangement of the participants relative to one another, the center alter or temple priestess, and the energy structure of the surrounding architecture, is dictated by the type of ritual also.

The various degrees of elevated spiritual states are created by the environment, music, motion, and ambient energies both living being energies, and the stored and earth energies upon Transfer

( the release and then absorption ) into the bodies present.

Each type of dance has a central form of event represented by the actions (dance) of the participants, each playing a part in the whole. Each ring of dancers representing a stage or evolution in the event. The center being completion or perfection. The high temple priestess being the gateway to the spiritual realm through which comes and goes the immortal minds, while their bodies are still in motion here on earth.

There is no random motion, no irrational energy, and no individuality. Together as they become closer to one, they come closer to the representation of essence of the Creator Alpha Omega. Achievement of the purpose of creation, The Supreme End.

All This In A Dance!

\*　　　\*　　　\*


## COMMON ANCESTOR

100,000 years ago the Demigoddesses lived on earth, and there communities were proximity of the human habitats. The two species;

A.　Homo Sapiens

B.  Demigoddess

are known to be genetically compatible and produce viable fertile healthy offspring called Xenomorphs.

One theory is that the two species both derive from the same
common ancestor.

Another (but least likely ) theory is that the two species may be
the one species, but two distinct expressions of the same gene
pool, which have become fixed over time and the separation of
habitats eliminating interbreeding.

*      *      *

## COMMUNICATION WITH DEMIGODDESSES

There are three means by which human beings come to

possess knowledge;

A.  Human Experience, and the sharing of humanexperienc-
es through collective learning.
B.  Innate & instinctual
C.  Spiritual Revelations & Divinations.

The careful and logical interpretation of the above knowledge
can lead to a rational theology, and way of life based upon it.

The higher evolved beings are living creatures and subject to
the same processes in the acquisition of knowledge. They also
have the ability to share their knowledge via spiritual processes.
Human beings can acquire knowledge through spiritual process-

es where the transmitter of that knowledge is a higher evolved being or Demigoddess.

The ability to share & receive knowledge via spiritual experiences requires that we are in a Physical, Mental/Emotional, and Spiritual state conductive to spiritual processes.

Various methods of producing Elevated Spiritual States in the human being, do aide in the creation of a state conductive to spiritual experiences. ( See the entry on Elevated Spiritual States ).

CEBAGII is a religious based social order, culture, art & science, and a way of life, which is acquired from the spiritual experiences in which the human being is in communication with one or more Demigoddesses. The particular interpretation of these spiritual experiences leads to the unique body of beliefs & practices which distinguish one sect from another. CEBAGII being actually the name of our sect.

One of the most important types of religious practices are those which facilitate the obtainment of hestate necessary to have spiritual experiences of a controlled beneficial form.

Communications with Demigoddesses once established, obligates us to cease the spiritual communication with other beings who are diametrically opposed to the religion of the Demigoddesses.

Within the religious system, the Temple Priestesses are the authority on all matters, the leadership of he religion, civil government, the cadre of teachers, artist, doctors, and other professionals required for the viable progressive advanced society.

Although today the Temple Priestesses are no longer direct

descendants of the children of the gods, the possess unique innate qualities which with training & practice, make them particularly capable at communication with demigoddesses.

All human beings have spiritual experiences, because we all can hear the voice of the Creator Alpha Omega within us, in the form of our moral conscious. The spiritual experiences with living creatures is not a innate quality all human beings possess, but one which all human beings can learn.

Finally each sect has it's own set of one or more Demigoddesses they worship as spiritual guides; and their own sets of demigoddesses in waiting.

Those nor of this religion and who deny the existence of higher evolved beings, are most often people who have not developed the abilities required for spiritual experiences & communications with the Demigoddesses.

*      *      *

## COMMUNITIES, SPIRITUAL

Human beings, are imperfect beings, and they are incomplete Immortal Minds. This is true for all things in creation, atoms, rocks, trees, animals, peoples, demigoddesses, etc,etc.

The Supreme End is achieved daily by a existence in which the immoral minds are becoming more complete, moving towards poerfection, and the human being in each successive reincarnation, is perfecting the qualities of the human being. Once perfected one moves on the the next higher form and state.

A misconception is that people are spiritual united by the shared beliefs & practices. Sharing a religion is not enough to form a spiritual community. The immortal minds were united at the time of their creation, and they were the first creations.

In our physical manifestations we are united by qualities we can not readily perceive. We are made soulmates by what we are, not what we think, believe, and do in this world. What we are is not subject to our freewill, we were created before the universe was.

We do not fully know what we are, we only see this shell we inhabit for a brief moment in time & place; and then the succession of shells ( physical manifestations ) we will inhabit as the immortal minds progress.

Slowly, as we move though the succession of lifeforms, we grow and come to realize what sort of thing we actually are ( and it is something incomprehensible, The human beings life is a series of autonomous functions, until we must decide it is time for change.)

And in this change, we assume those qualities which now are incomplete. It is those qualities which develop which are the basis of our union and formation of a spiritual community.

The spiritual communities require the Temple Priestesses to help us unlearn our way of living so that we can live together regardless of our personal distinctions, and become the spiritual community which our true nature & qualities allows us to be apart of. But first the Temple Priestesses must teach us what we do not know before we can live together, because it is what we believe which prevents what we are from being expressed in our life.

We are made soulmates of particular beings at the time before the universe was created. The perception and space separating us is an illusion. The immortal minds may exist in physical manifestations anywhere on the planet and universe.

Those unknown processes in the universe will bring soulmates together, but the culture we are born into will keep soulmates apart. Soulmates can not form unions & spiritual community until they overcome the involuntary culture they are born into and did not chose. Only then can they become free to be what they truly are.

The spiritual community consist of free people, and people becoming free, and people who have been drawn to the community but are still held mentally by the culture they are trying to escape. Even in the heavens, this is true, even amongst the gods.

The purpose of creation require that all things in creation progress. In a spiritual community, if any soulmate is not progressing, then the spiritual community is not progressing.

Despite all outward appearance, despite material prosperity, despite the advanced arts & sciences, despite all the good deeds the spiritual community does in the world, it can only progress when everyone in the spiritual community is progressing.

The relationship between the Pantheon and the great god Lucifer is a perfect example. Lucifer and all of the fallen are still a member of the spiritual community of heaven, despite his exile to this of the earths. Lucifer started a war in heaven; attempted to replace the Creator Alpha Omega; lead his fellow creatures to rebellion & exile; attempted to mislead humanity, and he lives in perpetual digression till this very day.

And Yet; the Creator Alpha Omega has decreed that never again will any creature hurt a hair on Lucifer's head, that Lucifer shall not die at the hands of a creature ever again, and that the Pantheon shall every day engage Lucifer and work towards his redemption & salvation, and his eventual return to the Pantheon someday. The spiritual community of Lucifer's, which is still in heaven, can not progress without him!

The purpose for which each spiritual community is established, must be consistent with the Supreme End; the progression of all creation, of all members, and of all strangers within their territories. The earth and all it's inhabitants are also in need of assistance and the material resources of the spiritual community must be applied to facilitating that purpose by eliminating human property, suffering, and deprivation of needs.

The necessity to constantly work towards ones survival, denying one the time and energy to work towards ones own improvement and the improvement of others, is a adverse human condition which the spiritual community must work to eliminate through the use of unique sciences & technologies

The Spiritual Community must teach the religious practices to the members to assist them in their growth & development, and an educastion which can assist them in practicing a way of life which leads to their improvement, perfection, and transition after this lifetime.

The spiritual community has many communal celebrations.

The first being Birth of a new human being. Thee last celebration being the death of that human being. Both celebrations are
reflections of the beliefs that our lives are part of a much bigger
process in the universe in which each human birth, existence, and
death, are essential to the universes future states. We envi- sion
all of creation as A participatory universe as they say, in both large
and small frames of reference. The infinitesimal particle we begin
as, and the infinite we are becoming

*        *        *

## COPELAND, MISTY

Each of The sects of CEBAGII has their own demigoddesses
(" Goddess" being a relative term applied to a higher evolved
being exhibiting qualities vastly superior to those of the homo
sapiens ).

The cycle of life requires repeated reincarnations, until the perfection in the qualities of the current form & species is achieved,
then transition can occur. Transition is the process whereby immortal minds move from one species to the next highest species.
Demigoddess is a species of higher evolved beings. Each demigoddess is created from the union of multiple immortal minds of
human " soulmates ", to form a single Associated-Mind & individual being.

The Temple Priestess is able to foresee the transition of a individual while they are still in the human form. Pending Transitional
State, is a refection of human qualities perfected over many stag-

es of human reincarnation.

Misty Copeland was born on the 10th of September in the year 1982, in Kansas City, Missouri. She became world famous when in the year 2015 she became the first Afroamerican Principal Dancer at The American Ballet Theatre Group, after many years as a ballerina.

One might even say that she has the qualities of a goddess. In the higher spiritual sense, she is nearly perfected in the human qualities.

Because of many perfected qualities sensed in her being, it has been determined that Misty Copeland Will Transition After Her Current Physical Manifestation. Thus Misty is a Demigoddess in waiting. We recognize her a one of our future Demigoddesses.

*        *        *


## CREATION

In the beginning let there exist only one real being, thing, entity, and reality. LET us refer to this as The Creator Alpha Omega. LET us use the symbol (A) to represent the Creator Alpha Omega in diagrams.

THE FIRST CREATION:

(LET all created forces, elements of the set; {B,...,W.}, be individuals.)

1.  a single great force (A) exist.
2.  great force (A) creates a second force (B)

3.  now two (2) forces exist.

4.  the union (A,B) creates a third force (C)

5.  now three (3) forces exist.

6.  the union (A,C) creates a fourth force (D).

7.  the union (B,C) creates a fifth force (E).

8.  the union (A,D) creates a sixth force (F).

9.  the union (B,D) creates a seventh force (G).

10. the union (C,D) creates a eighth force (H).

11. the union (A,E) creates a ninth force (I)etc.

Table One:

THE FIRST CREATION

AS TWO DIMENSIONAL INTERACTIONS

OF REAL BEINGS

| X | A | B | C | D | E | F | G |
|---|---|---|---|---|---|---|---|
| A | * | C | D | F | I | M | R |
| B | C | * | E | G | J | N | S |
| C | D | E | * | H | K | O | T |
| D | F | G | H | * | L | P | U |

| E | I | J | K | L | * | Q | V |
|---|---|---|---|---|---|---|---|
| F | M | N | O | P | Q | * | W |
| G | R | S | T | U | V | W | * |

THE SECOND CREATION:

LET us now image a third dimension to creation,and the real things of the first creation now intersecting to create the second creation. For example we will now have,

112

the union (A,B,C) creates a (x) force (a)

the union (A,B,D) creates a (x+1) force (b)

the union (A,B,E) creates a (x+2) force (c)

LET there exist an infinite quantity of dimensions of creation, and an infinite quantity of created things.

LET the set of all things in all dimensions of creation be called, '' Creation & Universe ''.

LET the number of each dimensions in creation be a stage in a hierarchy of stages of beings in creation, with the lowest number being closest to Divinity, and the highest number being the elementary fundamental particles.

*       *       *


## CREATION

THE CREATOR ALPHA OMEGA:

Creation is a process and a condition, it is an action and the thing being acted upon. We are creation, not as the human being, but rather as the immortal minds which are within and part of the Creator Alpha Omega. Our role in creation is to create this body we inhabit and this world this body occupies. And yet they are both the same thing. We are the Creator and yet we are not yet fully the Creator of the universe.

THE ALPHA:

We envision our beginning as an one of an infinite collection of immortal minds, having no qualities at all, and we then create an infinitesimal particle and call it self. As we realise the qualities asleep within us, we become more complete, and we are drawn together by a force which unites us into a new greater immortal

mind, and we then create a new physical manifestation an atom, and call it our next self.

THE OMEGA:

Before the beginning of time, We begin as an infinite collection of infinitesimal immortal minds, and when time ends, We become a singular infinite immortal mind. The history of our creation, of our existence, says nothing of the brief moment in time when We were human beings, long long ago before We reached the Supreme End of creation.

THE CREATOR ALPHA OMEGA:

We are Creation & Creator, but only when We are completely One! We Can Never Be One Until We Are All Complete. Thus one must conclude that we are the immortal minds who existed before the beginning of time, and who shall know no end, if if time were to cease.

Notes:

( See: entry on The War In Heaven, in which the Creator Alpha Omega caused time throughout the universe too stop, in order to end the fighting after Lucifer was killed by an Amazon; But However; our ancestors recalled that they continued to existence, even while the universe stood still in the absence of time. They continued to exist while their bodies were frozen in time. They realized that they existed separate from their shells! A clue as to our true nature not overlooked by the ancients, who left the children of earth many secrets written in stone. )

(( I kind of got entries out of order during the rewrite ))

## COHABITATION

The physical manifestation is a temporary vessel which can be occupied by any number of immortal minds. It is in fact not real, but a spiritual state of (...) sustained by the power of the Creator Alpha Omega channeled through the immortal minds.

Other entries will show that this state can be captured by hostile immortal minds, and shared by higher evolve beings.

The Demigoddesses can easily occupy human bodies because they share many human qualities. The Temple Priestesses in particular are easily occupied by the Demigoddesses because they are in a natural harmony with these creatures. We call the occupation of Temple Priestesses by Demigoddesses, " Cohabitation ".

During cohabitation the body here on earth takes on the qualities of the Demigoddesses inhabiting it. The Temple Priestesses is no longer present, and the Demigoddesses are controlling in her body. During that time period the Temple Priestesses can perform many rituals unknown to humanity. They may also heal the sick sometimes.

The degree to which the human body & mind are permanently altered by many repeated cohabitations is directly proportional to the quantity of cohabitations which have occurred by the same Demigoddesses, and each cohabitation makes the next one even easier to achieve and maintain.

The evil practice of stealing bodies by tricking an individual into consenting to the exchanging immortal minds, then killing one of the bodies to make the cohabitation permanent, is an old secret practice of the cults of eastern Europe and the Mideast.

Immortal minds of significantly developed power a can achieve the cohabitation of machines. This practice is also abused by the European cults.

Because of the long history of abuse of this practice the techniques have become closely guarded secrets. Even in CEBAGII cohabitation is no longer practiced, except during special ceremonies, in special assemblies under controlled conditions, and under very close supervision.

*       *       *


## CULT

The worship of creatures is not contrary to Divine Law. There are many forms & degrees of worship. The worship of any creature in a manner which exults the creature to equality with the

Creator Alpha Omega, or elevates the creature above the Creator Alpha Omega, or creates the belief that the creature is the Creator Alpha Omega, and denies the truths taught through the sacred vessels of the Creator Alpha Omega; is Digression. These are the primary characteristics of a cult. There are other qualities, but these are the fundamental & essential attributes of all cults on this of the earths.

Thus any religion started by any creature which has the above qualifiers is not a true religion, but rather, it is a cult.

The Kingdom Of The Great God Lucifer is the primary cult on this of the earths.

\*     \*     \*

D

\*     \*     \*

## DEATH & REBIRTH

In The CEBAGII We Shall Always Celebrate Every One Of The Natural Stages In The Cycle Of Life:

Stage I. BIRTH,

Stage II. MATURATION,

Stage III. DEATH, and

Stage IV. REBIRTH.

BIRTH & MATURATION: The Supreme End requires that the immortal minds grow & develop all those qualities of the divine. The growth & development only occurs through living. Therefore all things must exist in order that they can grow & develop.

MATURATION; The revelations & collective learning of people of CEBAGII, form the basis of our vade mecum in living to achieve the purpose of creation. Living is the means to perfection and the evolution of more perfect forms and States in creation. Without the past & present there would be no future. Without growth & development there would be new evolution.

UNNATURAL DEATH; The untimely & unnatural death of any

real thing is a disruption of its grow & development, and does not serve to achiever the Supreme End.

NATURAL DEATH; The termination of the life functions of the physical manifestations occurs in order that the Associated-Mind may progress either after full perfection followed by transition, or progression towards perfection followed by reincarnation. Therefore natural death is a part of the natural process that serves to achieve the Supreme End.

REBIRTH; IN THE BEGINNING; We existenced as the most fundamental elementary particle having only one quality, our existence! We die as a fundamental & elementary particle to be reborn as a higher particle. Each rebirth moving us to a higher form & stage. This is Reincarnation. Therefore rebirth is a part of the cycle of creation, and we will be all real things, and yet we are not those things we have been, are currently, and shall be in the future.

Therefore, in the true religion, there is no intrinsic evil in life, and in the the stages of life: BIRTH, MATURATION, DEATH, and REBIRTH; and we celebrate each and everyone!

NOTES:

1.  The science of genetics informs us that the mutations occurring during reproduction are not necessarily improvements to the creatures. But we know that in the participatory universe, the intelligence guiding of evolution of new forms of greater complexity & perfection, is a product of the energies of the existing forms in their perfection; and that this evolution occurs within the infinite set of possible

future states of of everything of the universe, designed by the Creator Alpoha Omega.

\*        \*        \*

## DEATH OF THE BODY

When a Immortal Mind establishes a physical manifestation in the TemporalSpacial Material Realm, it creates a real thing and becomes the Associated-Mind of that real thing.

The Associated-Mind can permanently cease to be associated with the real thing, and the physical manifestation sustain its form in a state called Death. The disassociation of Associated-Mind and Physical Manifestation can occur for either of two reasons;

A. The Physical Manifestation can no longer perform the essential higher functions of it's kind, and therefore the Associated-Mind's progression can no longer continue if it remains associated with the physical manifestation. The Associated-Mind must create a new physical mani-festation of the same kind, and then form a association with the new physical manifestation of the same kind.

B. The Associated-Mind has fully developed those higher spiritual qualites of that kind of physical manifestation, and the Associated-Mind's progression can no longer continue if it remains associated with the physical mani-festation. The Associated-Mind must create a new phys-ical manifestation of the same kind, and then must form a new association with the physical manifestation of the next higher form and state.

The Essential Spiritual Qualities Of The Physical Manifestation are not known to the real thing until that real thing is enlightened. But such knowledge is not necessary prerequisite in order to fully develop those qualities.

Death of the physical manifestation then is necessary for rein- carnation/transition of the immortal mind from one physical man- ifestation to another successive physical manifestation; which is necessary if the immortal mind is to continue to progress; which is necessary if the immortal mind is to fulfill the Supreme End.

Once a physical manifestation is created, it can continue to exist ( sustain its state in the TemporalSpacial Material Realm ) even after the Associated-Mind permanently separates from it; But However it will be unable to display the higher spiritual qual- ities, because these are qualities belonging to the immortal mind and not belonging to the physical manifestation.

*     *     *


## DEIFICATION

Deification is the formal recognition by a sect of the estab- lishment of a spiritual association between members of that sect and a higher evolved creature/being. Deification establishes the worship of that higher evolved creature/being by members of that sect, but this type worship does not elevate that higher evolved creature/being to the status equal too or greater then, The Creator Alpha Omega.

The higher evolved creature/being is determined to possess certain qualities which are compatible with & complementary to the set of higher spiritual qualities of he collection of higher evolved creature/being which are worshipped by that sect; And these are the same qualities which the members of the sect embrace and seek to grow and develop within themselves.

The sect has a unique way of life which is derived from the guidance of theses higher evolved creature/beings, and remains consistent with the universe beliefs & practices of the primary religion which the sect is a subgroup/denomination of.

Prior to official deification, while the demigoddess to be remains in the form of multiple homo sapiens soulmates here on earth, she is considered a Demigoddess In Waiting.

None of the higher evolved creature/beings here on earth are worshipped in CEBAGII, as they are members of the fallen. After the war in heaven, the Creator Alpha Omega allowed those in PERPETUAL DIGRESSION to return to their ancestral birthplaces.

This present age is the time period in which the select planets are called," earth(s) ",which means," exile of the gods fallen from heaven ".

The earths were established by Divine decree, which stated in part, that no being from the heavens will come to earths in physical form during the period of exile. No creature in while in perpetual digression can go to the heavens, nor can she ever be worshipped ( deified ) in CEBAGII. All the higher evolved creatures of the earths are in perpetual digression.

*     *     *

## DELUSIONS

Delusions are complex misconceptions of reality, present in the human mind, conscious or subconscious. These are important because of their influence on human behavior.

Delusions can be produced by either; natural illusion which is produced by the biology of humans, or by intentional deception. Both can give rise to false beliefs. The weak minded who have no resistance, and absorb all varieties of harmful ideas.

The most powerful delusions are not recognized as Delusions. Powerful delusions psychologically deny humans the use of their freewill, which is psychologically restrained by unrecognized false beliefs.

Delusions often cause human to pursue what they can never ever have, by means which can never obtain their objective, in a reckless manner, which has no end because it can never be satisfied because it knows no success.

The qualities of the cults are in their entirety are clearly very clever delusional systems based on human weaknesses, which Psychologically rob human of their strength and freewill. One personality, with one set of desirable but flawed ideas can rule over millions and lead them to their own end.

Delusion as publicly dissimilated systems of beliefs & practices, are another of the tools employed by the Fallen to destroy

122

human civilization on this earth, and ultimately bring about hu-manity's self destruction.

\*        \*        \*

## DEMIGODS

The universe is full of Local Star Groups, each having many worlds, and of those worlds one of those will always has higher evolved living creatures. The separation of Interstellar space is a

illusion, which they can not overcome until they develop certain higher spiritual qualities. Till then it keeps the lifeforms separated as they evolve, grow, and develop.

For the last 100,000 years this Local Star Group has been the home to six (6) higher evolved species. They live in regions of outer space, in spiritual communities called, the " Heavens ".

Three species of higher evolve species are known as the, " Demigoddesses ". The Demigoddess species(s) has a special form, which has diminished qualities, known as the, " Demigods ".

The demigods have the physical appearance of homo sapiens males (men). They are divided into two groups;

A. The Fallen in perpetual digression here onthis of the earths.

1. Those of the former SolarDark MissionWatchers. Who harmed the lesser specieshomo sapiens reck-lessly, by giving themchildren & sciences, and be-

come the firstcults of this of the earth.

2.  Those who joined the great god Lucifer, inthe rebel-
    lion which lead to the war inheaven, and their exile
    to their ancestralbirthplaces.

B.  Those who continue in the progression, still livingin the
    Pantheon in spiritual communities ofheavens.

The situation is similar to this throughout the universe, because the Celestial-god ( a higher evolved mortal nondivine species of creatures ) Lucifer started a rebellion in all of creation.

The Demigods never adjusted to life in the stars, and did not lead a life in heaven that was progressive. Their unhappiness was their weaknesses exploited by Lucifer to lead them astray.

When the Demigods were sent to this planet for a extended duration to work, they were dynamically emotionally affected by the natural world. They returned to a way of life which has been outlawed for the six higher species, and fathered children with the women of this planet.

This lead to the introduction of sciences to the earth commu-nities which forever altered the course of human development.

The religion exile have Transitory Immortality because they can not follow the natural reincarnation cycle, because it would result in their rebirth in heaven, which is impossible because the Creator Alpha Omega has set the strong angels to keep us in exile. And so they die, and yet they do not die, because they can not until they be released!

\*          \*          \*

## DEMIGODDESSES

There have been many many higher evolved species which originated on this earth since its beginning. Most species native to this earth have become extinct.

In this current earth age, there are six (6) species of higher evolved creatures, which are called, " gods ", living in regions of outer space. Three (3) of those species which are known to humanity as the, " DEMIGODDESSES ", lived on this earth 100,000 years ago. They were preceded by the ancients, who left this earth 100,000 years ago for the stars.

Approximately 75,000 years ago the Demigoddesses built their spiritual communities in beyond this earth in outer space. They called their new homes, " The Heavens ", and their Matriarchate society became known as the, " Pantheon ". The Demigoddesses's society is over 100,000 years old.

The Demigoddesses are mortal beings, and they are the divinely appointed Sacred Vessels of the Creator Alpha Omega ( who is not a god ). In heaven they are the government of the Pantheon. The society in heaven is called a Matriarchate, because authority is held by women, and men are excluded from positions of authority.

The Demigoddesses are naturally divisible into three (3) species of Demigoddesses based on the significant distinctions in the magnitudes of their relative observed general qualities. The three (3) species consist of the following;

THE MINOR GODS:

A.  THE UPPER DEMIGODDESSES

3rd. level of scientifically guided evolutionexhibiting the highest levels of; intellectual,physical, and spiritual development

B.  THE MIDDLE DEMIGODDESSES

2nd. level of scientifically guided evolutionexhibiting the intermediate levels of; intellectual,physical, and spiritual development

C.  THE LOWER DEMIGODDESSES

1st. level of scientifically guided evolutionexhibiting the first levels of intellectual, physical,and spiritual development

The General Qualities Of Demigoddesses;

1.  Sacred Vessels of the Creator Alpha Omega.
2.  Isogynic Tripartite Sexuality
3.  Highest level of intelligence of any earth creature
4.  Strength of five men ( Sexual dimorphism )
5.  Incredible stamina
6.  Shapeshifting ability.
7.  Outward appearance of a human women
8.  Extrasensory Perception
9.  Wisdom, patience, calm nature
10. Longevity

THE THREE SUBSPECIES OF THE DEMIGODDESS SPECIES:

1.  THE ISOGYNIC TRIPARTITE BEINGS we callDemigoddesses. The are 98% of theDemigoddesses, and are the

majority of theresidents of the heavens

2. THE MALE SPECIAL FORM called, '' Demigods '. As-ingle gender, with human male secondarysexual characteristics. Are not sacred vessels,and whose qualities are an order of magnitudeless then the ordinary Demigoddesses. Theymake up approximately 1% of Demigoddessesspecies.

3. THE FEMALE SPECIAL FORM called, ''Demigod- dess-Special ''. They are female inappearance, are not sacred vessels, havequalities of Demigoddesses to a

lesser degree.They make up approximately 1% of the-Demigoddesses.

OTHER PHYSICAL QUALITIES:

The Upper Demigoddesses have highly elongated heads, and exhibit perfect Proportional Gigantism ( 7 - 9 feet in height ), with the human female model as the reference standard.

The Middle Demigoddesses display cranial elongation less- er magnitudes then the Upper Demigoddesses, and also exhibit Proportional Gigantism ( 6- 7.5 feet in height ).

The Lower Demigoddesses do not display cranial elongation, and are equivalent to tall human women ( 5 - 6 feet in height ).

The Demigoddesses lack the complex birthing process of human beings, due to anatomical difference in the birth canal, hips, and a smaller birth size of the offspring after gestation. The offspring have a longer period of neonatal growth & dependence on their mothers, then the homo sapiens.

Due to the successful scientific genetic management of their species sexual reproduction, and the designed physical transformation of their species, these Isogynic beings do not suffer the biological abnormalities seen in human Isogynic individuals.

The Demigoddesses are famous for their legendary physical beauty. Their bodies became the standard by which human women were measured.

QUALITIES OF THE DEMIGODDESSES:

In the spiritual communities of outer space the Demigoddesses no longer needed to perform labors to sustain their life. They had all the time they required to devote themselves to their spiritual pursuits. They worked on the physical improvement of their species, the intellectual development of their society, their arts, and their development of a religious based society lead by sacred vessels.

After 75,000 years in the spiritual communities of heaven, their society developed all the unique qualities of the Matriarchate & Pantheon.

Spiritual Qualities:

The sacred vessels enhanced their capacity to commune with the Creator Alpha Omega, and with the human Temple Priestess-

es of earths spiritual communities. They became the connection between creation and Creator. They receive and interpret the divine messages to this Local Star Group. They are the keepers of the secret knowledge given by the Creator Alpha Omega.

The Demigoddesses became the religious leaders of the Pantheon; the High Temple Priestesses became the civil leaders of the Matriarchate; The Lower Demigoddesses became the civil servants in heaven; The Middle Demigoddesses became the heads of institutions of the society in heaven, the teachers, the doctors, the counselors, the artist & scientist, and professionals in every area of activity.

HISTORY OF THE DEMIGODDESSES:

The Goddess Of Love:

The Demigoddesses became known as the original Goddess Of Love, due to three main events;

1) Unification of Immortal Minds
2) Transformative Spiritual Experiences
3) Repeated Interventions in human afairs

   A. The unification of multiple immortal minds of soulmates, creates a single Demigoddesses immortal mind. The soulmates must truly love one another or the transition & unification into one will not occur. Thus Demigoddesses are born as a result of true love.

   B. After the last Major Solar Event, in the wake of the great flood, people became barbaric. Human beings simply killed one another, and many times ate human flesh. Their were less then 100,000 human beings left on this earth. This doesn't count the Fallen and their hybrid children.

After the last natural catastrophe Human civilization fell, and could not rebuild itself, we entered a barbaric period know as the

New Stone Age, of a Tribalectic Culture, and of domination of human communites by the Brute-Males. The New Stone Age lasted 250 years.

When The Demigoddesses cause Brute-Males to have Transformative Spiritual Experiences, they used a entire repertoire rituals & techniques, the must important was true Love. This ended the New Stone Age.

(3). The repeated interventions in human affairs by the Demigoddesses demonstrated how strongly they cared for human beings. They felt a strong paternalistic love for the human species.

The Kingdom Of Love:

The Matriarchate on this of the earths was modelled after the Society in heaven. Both the Earth & Heavenly Matriarchates were known as the Kingdoms Of Love.

The Spiritual Advancement Of The Demigoddesses:

Humanity has always formed a unstable society. The human condition has always been precarious due to the human way of life. We have never reached the technological level sufficient to!enable us to survive the Natural Extinction Level Events in our Local Star Group. The Demigoddesses have given so much of their time & energies to ensuring the well being of humanity.

The purpose of humanity in this Local Star Group seems to help the higher evolved species develop empathic qualities, freely sacrifice without gain, and exhibit patience & compassion for other beings. No matter how far the Demigoddesses develop technologically, they must also continue their moral and spiritual lives. Humanity helps the development of the spiritual & moral

130

Demigoddesses.

The Human Temple Priestesses:

The Demigoddesses once lived on this earth, and at times breed with homo sapiens. Children born to demigoddesses and fathered by homo sapiens, were the Xenomorphs. Them first xenomorphs were sent to live amongst the humans, and they became the first Temple Priestesses to the human communities.

The Temple Priestesses have always had the ability to spiritually interact with the Demigoddesses. They Demigoddesses have also occupied the bodies of Temple Priestesses during ceremonies, performance of rituals, and teaching the human communities important skills, and during certain types of divinations. This is called Cohabitation.

Much of what the Demigoddesses taught the Temple Priest-

esses are secrets because of the tendency of humans to misuse and abuse the unique sciences & arts they acquired from higher evolved beings, to the detriment of human communities.

The Future:

The Demigoddesses are the Guardians of Earth & Humanity, but that shall not always be the case. Someday like the ancients the Demigoddesses will leave this Local Star Group and never return. Their hope is that a spiritual community will grow an develop on earn to the point were they are able to take over the duties of Guardians of the Earth & Humanity. The Demigoddesses work towards this objective with the humans, but the humans do not seem to be ready for the heavens yet.

After the birth of John The Baptist, we here on earth received the Apocalyptic Revelation. This is an warning that the period of exile is coming to an end in the lifetime of this physical manifestation. Humanity may need to assume their higher obligations without a introduction or warning and much sooner then they think.

That day will mark the end of Demigoddesses intervention on this earth, and the beginning of a new human species which will become the New Guardians Of This Planet called by it's old name Reincarnation/Transition/Progression

Demigoddesses are the next higher stage after human, in the progression of the immortal minds. The immortal minds begin Associated-Mind is a fundamental elementary particle, and end as a fully developed portion of the Creator Alpha Omega.

The Succession Of Forms:
Particle
Atom
Molecule
Aggregate Matter
Rock
Virus
Bacteria
Fungi
Plant
Insect

Bird
Animal
Human

THE BOOK OF CEGBAGII

Demigoddesses

Terrestrial-god

Celestial-god

Universal-god

Creator Alpha Omega

Note;

we the immortal minds are a part of the CreatorAlpha Omega, thus once we fully grow anddevelop all our qualities, we become fully like theCreator Alpha Omega, and we always remain apart of the Creator Alpha Omega, not someseparate being. The Creator Alpha Omega is theonly true real being.

Demigoddesses In Waiting:

As we the immortal minds in human physical manifestation perfect the qualities of human form ( physical, intellectual, and spiritual ) through successive cycles of reincarnation, we become ready to transition to the next higher evolved lifeform.

Those about to transition are called, Demigoddesses In Waiting, while theory are still in their last human lifetime.

The Temple High Priestesses can see the future transition, and notify us who is about to transition to the next higher form.

We can then declare that Pierson to be one of our future Demigoddesses of our sect.

Demigoddesses Of The Sect:

Amila Earhart

Misy Copeland

Harriet Tubman

Helen of Troy

Joan D Arc

Susan B Anthony

Many sects can share the same Demigoddesses.

The sects look towards the Demigoddesses for guidance because they are closer to the spiritual realm the humans and can

see the past, present, future without distortion and in its entirety.
They

also have access to the knowledge of the universe.


Names Of The Demigoddesses:

Each Demigoddesses has as name, which we of the sect must
learn the pronunciation and the symbolic spelling.

The names of demigoddesses are written in the earth as cropcircles on the day of their celebration as as message to their sects
all over the world. This has been a practice for tens of thousands
of years, after the Demigoddesses migrated into outer space.


Religion/Culture/Government:

The Demigoddesses gave humanity their true Religion which
was given to them by the ancients. The religion became the basis
of a matriarchal culture, government, and society. The Matriarchates are a form of women lead society modelled after the society
in the heavens where the Demigoddesses reside.

The religion/culture/government which the Demigoddesses
gave human created the human spiritual communities and end-

ed the New Stone Age Tribalectic Culture, and transformed the Brute-Males into gentlemen. This was the beginning of pres- ent-day civilization.

Humans Living With Demigoddesses:

It has always been a wish of the Demigoddesses that humanity could join them in the stars where humanity could filly grow and develop. But mankind has never been ready for the stars, someday the human will leave.

On occasion individuals have been taken into the heavens to live with the Demigoddesses, and those individuals do well in outer space. But no entire human community has ever successfully adopted to life off world.

Enoch is one example of an individual taken to heaven to alive amongst the Demigoddesses. There were many others who the Demigoddesses found to their liking.

Today humans are taken by the Fallen who are exiled here on earth as part of the Fallens activities here on earth. The modern descendants of the Heavenly Amazons still fight against the fallen to!recover the humans the fallen take. No human has been taken to heaven since the arrival of the Fallen to earth in their exile.

Demigoddesses & Amazons:

The Demigoddesses created the Amazons through spiritual practices which transformed the subspecies Demigoddess- es-Special Form. Just as the Demigoddesses transformed the Brute-Males to a much lesser degree into civilized humans.

Qualities Of The Amazons:

A. Incredible Beauty

B. Super human strength

C. Wisdom

D. Instantaneous Healing

E. Stamina

F. Speed

G. Clairvoyance

H. Extrasensory Perception

I. Ability To Commune With The Demigoddesses

J. Priestesses Of The True Religion

K. Longevity

The Amazons conducted the War in Heaven, which was never intended to be a war. The Heavenly Amazons were intended to be a Police In Heaven. Lucifer who made the rebellion & war occur, was the individual god who was to be regulated by the Demigoddesses's Amazons.

After the war in heaven, the Heavenly Amazons came to earth to continue to police Lucifer, and these Amazons became the mother's to the legendary Amazons of this earth, who continue the fight against the fallen gods in exile on this earth, and protect humanity.

*     *     *

## DEMIGODDESSES - REPRODUCTION &/ SEXUALITY

The topic of reproduction & sexuality of the Demigoddesses

changes as the demigoddesses home changes, and as the demigoddesses mature as a species.

I.    In The Beginning:

Demigoddesses were three species which originated here on this earth at about the same time as the species homo sapiens emerged. The three species of demigoddesses were preceded by other intelligent species oh higher evolved beings. Therefore earth has seen many species evolve and either migrate to outer space, or become extinct. We humans are no the highest evolved beings to have lived on this earth.

The ancients gave young species their religion/culture, then the ancients migrated to the stars, approximately 100,000 years ago. At that point the Demigoddesses Civilization truly begun.

The Demigoddesses lived amongst human being in the beginning, and homo sapiens and Demigoddesses are biologically compatible species. At one time homo sapiens and Demigoddesses breed together and produced viable fertile offspring.

The offspring of Demigoddesses and Homos sapiens were called, Xenomorphs. Xenomorph is a term indicating that the offspring are unique, unlike either parent, and seem to be their own subspecies.

The Xenomorphs became great men and women in the human communities which they helped grow advance. One set of Xenomorphs became the first Human Temple Priestesses.

I.    The Establishment Of The Heavenly Communities:

Even while living on this of the earths, the Demigoddesses did not regularly breed with humans, or with the other species   of higher evolved beings on earth. It was after their migration to the heavens, approximately 75,000 years ago, that the Demigoddesses became fully Indigenous, that is they breed only with other Demigoddesses ( their own species ).

In the heavens the Demigoddesses utilized science & reproductive technologies to selectively breed their species. This enabled them to perfect their unique Isogynic condition and it became the norm for the three species of Demigoddesses. Using science they were able to eliminate most biological abnormalities, and reduce the rate of occurrence of others. Thus after 75,000 years the Demigoddesses produced a complete transformation of the three Demigoddesses species.

I.   After The Fallen Of Gods:

Two events occurred in our lifetime which enormously impacted the relationship between Demigoddesses and Homo Sapiens.

A.  The First Event:

During the last SolarDark Mission, the subspecies, Demigods, were assigned to the, SolarDark Mission Watch Post on this earth. The Demigods breed with many human women, and produced a race known as the, Redheaded Children Of The Gods. They were notorious, but it is the long-term effects of the introduction of Demigod DNA into the human Gene Pool which has been detrimental.

B.  The Second Event:

After the war in heaven the antagonistic and their leader were exiled to their ancestral birthplaces. The Beat God Lucifer unfortunately had right of return to this of the earths. As soon as The Fallen arrived they begin the interbreeding of human and Demigod species.

These two events lead to many spiritual wars in the human communities, and other tragic consequences followed.

Many Violent Battles between the offspring, the Xenomorphs ( Demigoddesses children ) and the Nephilim ( Demigods children ), have also occurred throughout earth's history, and have been recorded in the sacred writings of many religions, and can be seen in some great works of art.

Humanity has been caught in the middle of this war between the children of the gods, even though these offspring are half human they lack sympathy for the human condition, and have as their ultimate objective a human genocidal world war. Some groups of human beings ( secret societies, holy orders, cult of the one, death religions, Suicide cults, UFO cults, etc. the same groups under many different names & in many different places) have throughout history, cooperated with them in their attempts to bring about the end of humanity.

I.    After The Apocalypse:

The Demigoddesses have been forbidden to physically come to this earth during the period of the Luciferian Exile, as a result their new DNA has never entered the human gene pool. It seems that the exile will not end before the great angelic war in the uni-

139

verse. Thus present day humans and Demigoddesses will never meet.

People ask what will became of the Fallen gods, without realizing that they are creatures like ourselves whose fates will be decided by their own actions like any other creature.

The Demigoddesses will also be present at the Apocalypse because they are also creatures. After it ends, when the Demigoddesses are allowed to migrate to the stars beyond out Local Star Group, leaving this earth forever, Human & Demigoddesses intercourse while be a matter of history.

*   *   *

## DESIGN & INTENT

Design & Intent directs the forms and functions things shall take in the universe/creation.

The universe/creation and all things in it have forms and functions which were predetermined before the TemporalSpacial Energy Material Realm was created by the Creator Alpha Omega.

*   *   *

## DIGRESSION

1. a state of the Immortal Mind, in which the immortal mind no longer pursues the Physical, Intellectual, Moral/Spiritual growth & development of the physical manifestation. As a consequence the immortal mind can no longer ac-

quire additional divine qualities ,each Immortal Mind has the potential to achieve; which are necessary for the progression of the immortal minds.

2. in addition, It is a state in which the Immortal Mind stands in opposition to one or more of the following;

   a. Divine Law,

   b. The creator's design & intent,

   c. The meaning of human exist, and

   d. The purpose of creation The Supreme End.

3. Rather then fulling the creator's design & intent, the Immortal Mind seeks it's own ordering of creation.

How Digression Occurs:

Digression is a state in which the Immortal Mind lacks the range of comprehension to become fully self aware of all its flaws &errors, and is compelled by it's erroneous beliefs to live in a manner based on those erroneous subjective conceptions & interpretations.

Digression is a state in which the Immortal Mind desires something which can not ever be, and desires it strongly, that it conceives of a way of obtaining the forbidden or the impossible by changing the circumstances of nature, violating natural law, and forsaking its on salvation.

Consequences Of Digression:

Digression must end at any time in the lifetime of the physical manifestation, but if the physical manifestation should die while in digression, then the Immortal Mind will be rendered inna state of Perpetual Digression.

Perpetual Digression results in the Immortal Mind's rebirth/re-incarnation in a lesser form of physical manifestation.

Perpetual Digression & The Fallen In Exile:

The Fallen Currently in Exile to the Earths, are in perpetual digression, but they also have terrestrial immortality and can not reincarnate because it would enable them to escape exile. They simply continually resurrect.

The perpetual digression of those in exile, if they are not redeemed, ends in death of the Immortal Mind. This is the only way for any immortal mind to die, at the hands of the Creator's Omega. They simply return to what they came from, as if they never were! Not even the memory of them survives.

*       *       *

## DIGRESSION BY DECEPTION:

( The Six Stages Of Deception & Conversion )

KEY BELIEF:

THE DETERIORATION OF THE HUMAN CONDITION IS A PRODUCT OF HUMAN BEHAVIOR. THE HOMO SAPIENS HAVE BEEN MISLEAD BY THE HUMAN LEADERS WHO FOLLOW THE FALLEN GODS, AND HAVE INTRODUCED HUMANITY TO A GREAT DECEPTION WHICH NOW INFECTS THEIR SOCIETIES.

KEY HISTORICAL RELIGIOUS TRUTH:

The Fallen Gods Are Transitory Immortals Exiled To This Earth. They Have Continued Their Rebellion Against The Creator Alpha

Omega While Exiled On This Earth. They Have Given Rise To Endless Wars And The Deteriorating The Human Condition. This Is Precisely What The Demigoddesses Envisioned Tens of Thousands of Years Ago, And Tried To Prevent By Petitioning The Pantheon To Forcibly Remove Their Fellows The Solardark Mission Watchers And Their Nephilim Children From This To Planet. They Failed To Do So. That Was The Beginning Of The Catastrophe, The Fall Of Mankind!

The current human condition has persisted for approximately 5,000 years out of the last 75,000 years. This is 6.67% of our Current Eon, which beginning with the latest migration of the higher evolved species to the heavens.

Narrative:

The Fallen Gods in Exile not only introduced their own Religion & Creator, they also introduced a Philosophy which modified secular culture. Their philosophy became a fundamental element to the human culture, and thereby it modified all other religions practiced under that culture, in such a way as to install in those religions the errors fundamental to the religion of the Fallen Gods.

Through their Philosophy The Fallen Gods established a basic pattern of thought which infected all human activities both secular & religious. This distortion of thought has plagued the human race every since the arrival of the Fallen Gods in Exiled to this earth.

The way of life of the believers taught by the Demigoddesses is considered by some too be an extreme. The way of life established by the Fallen Gods deception has become the insidious normal. Change is difficult, because Humans find it extremely dif-

143

ficult to leave the normal and embrace the extreme, even when the extreme is truth and the normal erroneous.

The spiritual community is; a select religious society worshipping The Creator Alpha Omega, a Matriarchate modelled after the society of the Demigoddesses, and a community under the leadership of Human Temple Priestesses.

The Human Temple Priestesses help novice members to identify and correct errors in their thought processes, so that they may embrace the truths, and thereby become capable of working on their self improvement as members of the spiritual community.

There is a tremendous psychological resistance in men due to how they have been raised to believe certain untruths, and follow certain patterns of thoughts & behaviors. This psychological resistance leads to hostile actions called religious discrimination/ oppression in the society at large by those in positions of power over others.

The spiritually weak secular & religious leaders of the human societies were spiritually entrapped by the Fallen Gods ( who understand human needs, wants, and desires and how they can be made to generate moral weaknesses ) to manipulate their followers in the following manner;

I.    Human Beings Have Always Sought The Natural Pleasures Denied By Their Societies.

II.   Their Societies Manipulate Them By Using The Pleasures They Are Denied, Which Are Presented To Them Symbolically As Pleasures Wrapped In Sins. By This Mechanism The Human Come To Associate Pleasure

With Sin.

III.    The Confused Human Being Of Immature Intellect Are

Unable To Distinguish Sin From Pleasure, And Are Lead To Believe That Pleasure Is Sin.

IV.    Once The Human Has Accepted The Misconception That To Sin Is Natural, They Comes To Believe That It Is Acceptable To Commit Any Sins He Desires. A Dangerous Psychological Dichotomy Develops Which Leads To Hypocrite Behavior. The Individual Truly Wants To Be Good, But Becomes Convinced That He Must Do Evil In Order To Find Happiness In Life. He Seeks To Hide His Sins From The World.

V.    The Dichotomy Generates Extreme Mental Stress Which Leads To A Breakdown In The Ability To Consistently Make Rational Decissions And Display Rational Behavior. Emotions Rule The Man. Unleashed Desires Lead To Wild Extremes Of Behavior Which They Incorrectly Assume To Be Human Nature.

It Is Because They Have Attributed Moral Restraints Placed On Them As Denying Them Their Needs, That They Abandon All Restraints And Exhibit The Extreme Behaviors In The Human Condition.

VI.    Thereby The Human Is Converted Into A Being Who Is Diametrically Opposed To The Divine Cannon. By This Means The Fallen Gods In Exile On This Earth Have Sought To Convert The Homo Sapiens Into Their Willing

Slaves, Their Army On This Earth In Their War With The
Earth Amazons, And Insignificant Casualties In Their Rebellion Against The Heavens.

Most human beings today rely upon others to do their thinking
for them. Regardless of who those others are, and without consideration of their intentions and objectives. The Honor System
seems to be part of what people raised in society are taught too
depend upon. This allowed the establishment a basic pattern of
erroneous thinking which infected the activities of entire societies, and has plagued the human race every since the arrival of
the Fallen Gods in Exiled to this earth.

*     *     *

## DIVINATION

Divination is the process of entering an elevated spiritual state
which then facilitates spiritual experiences, for the purpose of acquiring knowledge from sources other then ordinary human experiences and innate/instinctual attributes.

The type of knowledge pursued is relevant to the determination of effective solutions to problems faced by individuals, the
spiritual community, human beings in this world, and the earth
itself.

The other processes;

A. communication with Demigoddesses
B. cohabitation

C.  ceremonial dances

All require us to become receptive to the influences & guidance of other immortal minds belonging to higher evolved species.

One common from of divination requires that psychological and/or physiological stimulation of natural attributes be used to accumulate energies which are redirected at the achievement of higher spiritual objectives (such as divination ).

Through divination one can see into the past, present , and future. One can come to know things one has never been taught

*     *     *

## DIVINE ( THE CREATOR ALPHA OMEGA )

The term Infinity is used to indicate a quantity not only beyond the ability to numerate, but also beyond the ability to visualize.

Universe:

The universe around us seems so enormous that there seems to be no end to it. The stars and other heavenly bodies number into the many trillions. The life throughout this universe has never been measured, even though spiritually humans have contacted

other living beings on other worlds. There is no factual evidence that any lifeforms has navigated this vast universe.

All this as the work of one real being, the Creator Alpha Omega. The universe is vast, but The Creator Alpha Omega is Infinite!

Life:

On this earth the incomprehensible nature surrounding us is

also beyond imagination. The varieties of life have never been fully catalogued. The planet itself is in many ways a mystery.

The Creator Alpha Omega has been known to many religious peoples throughout history. Care must be taken not to use the names of the gods, when thinking of and speaking of the Creator Alpha Omega.

We can only imagine a small subset of the qualities of the Creator Alpha Omega, who has unique higher qualites we can not even imagine. we have not seen any living creature exhibiting some of these unknown traits; nor will there ever be a creature like the Creator Alpha Omega.

The Known Qualities Of The Creator Alpha Omega include the following in human terms:

A.   Knowledge & Understanding of all things
B.   Present in all places at all times
C.   Eternal, existing before the beginning of time
D.   Immortal, existing after the end of time
E.   Infinite Wisdom
F.   Infinite Strength
G.   Infinite Power
H.   Infinite Goodness, Love, and Compassion
I.    Infinite Patience, Forgiveness, and Sympathy

Creation & The Immortal Minds:

We are the Immortal Minds which are all part of the Creator Alpha Omega. We each are a portion of the divine which begins as the small possible element of the divine, having all the Divine qualities to the infinitesimal degree. Thus we are real but infinitesimal parts of one infinite being, and an infinite collection of infinitesimal beings who are one.

The Created Realms:

There are two created realms;

A. The Spiritual Realm
B. The TemporalSpacial Energy Material Realm

Because the realms are creations, the Immortal Minds develop a power over the realms as the Immortal Minds grow & develop their Divine Qualities. Thus all things in them, are the products of the Immortal Minds.

Creation, Divine Design & Intent:

The Creator Alpha Omega set the forms for all created things before there was creation, and these are the limits the Immortal Minds operate within. The Divine gives Immortal Minds the power to create for themselves physical manifestations. We then associate with those physical manifestations and are called Associated-Minds.

We go through reincarnation cycles until our form perfects certain qualities of that kind of physical manifestation. By doing so we Immortal Minds slowly acquire higher Divine qualities of our kind. Then we transition to the next higher form of physical manifestation. Thus we are association of many lesser developed Immortal Minds in the form of particles, atoms, bacteria, working together, sometimes not.

We are not our physical manifestations! They are our transitory creations. We are part of the Creator Alpha Omega and we are Immortal, and we can die in Perpetual Digression ( see entry ), or we return to the Creator Alpha Omega after an infinity of time.

Guidance Of The Creator Alpha Omega:

The Creator Alpha Omega gives creation the Laws Of Nature to regulate the behaviors of The Immortal Minds not having developed the necessary intelligence to determine how to live. Particles, Atoms, Aggregate Matter, basically non biological creations.

We Immortal Minds even once we develop the higher qualities, are still incomplete & ignorant. We would have no idea what the purpose of creation is and how we the Immortal Minds are to achieve that purpose if not for Divine Guidance, which comes in the following three (3) forms;

A. The MORAL CONSCIOUS All Creature HearWithin

themselves.

B. The CANNON OF THE CREATOR ALPHA OMEGA. Which is an essential part of religious beliefs &practices.

C. Personal Transformative SPIRITUAL EXPERENCES. Communion with the Divine.

RULE II:

RELIGION NOT ONLY GUIDES US IN LIVING, BUT ALSO GIVES US AN UNDERSTANDING OF REALITY, WHICH CAN NOT BE ACQUIRED BY ANY OTHER MEANS, AND WHICH ENABLES US TO DO THINGS WE COULD NOT DO WITHOUT THAT KNOWLEDGE.

*        *        *

## DIVINATION BY BOOKS

DIVINATION; is the acquisition of unique useful knowledge, which is imparted in one's memory during a personal spiritual experience.

Divination, as a means of extrasensory perception, and requires that the Mind/Body are in condition in which they are no longer interfering with the Associated-Mind's perception of other immortal minds, primarily those higher evolved beings which the sect worships. The Associated-Mind can then establish a communication with those immortal minds.

When human beings intentionally seek to establish communication, it is done for two purposes;

A. Communication is sometimes done for thepurpose of worship.

B. Communication with higher evolved beings is alsodone in the pursuit of several types of assistancewhich can not be obtained by ordinary means,such as the following;

1. Guidance
2. Healing
3. Protection
4. Knowledge

5. Intermediary To The Divine
6. Manipulation Of Future Events/Conditions

The use of printed books is one of the oldest and most common of the techniques of divination. Each year over 70,000 new titles of printed books emerge from the U.S. printing industry. These books fall into several categories for powerful divination purposes;

A. All books
B. Books written specifically with hidden messages
C. Books written in unknown languages
D. Books containing works of inspired art
E. Books of science & mathematics

In Bibliographical Divination, first the select Book(s) are read either in part or whole. The practitioner will not comprehend the contents of the material he/she read of views prior to the divination, this is normal.

After reading passages from the printed book, the reader then has a spiritual experience, during one of two states;

A. ELEVATED SPIRITUAL STATE ( ESS ). Used inthose Techniques initiated by the practitioner.
B. DEEP REM SLEEP. Used in those techniques notinitiated by the practitioner, but initiated by thehigher evolved beings. Often preceded by impulseto obtain a particular book and read a particularpassage.

Certain Passages in books will be rearranged during a spiritual experience, and the resultant arrangement constitutes a useful message from higher evolved beings.

Notes:

Key Terms:

I.   Bibliographical Divination; the technique.

II.   II. Reader; the practitioner of this technique.

III.   Elevated Spiritual State; mind/body condition.

Authors:

This is a very old system which predated the printing press. Temple Priestesses secretly communicated knowledge in hidden form, through the distribution of written works which were highly valued, carefully copied by scribes, and safeguarded by librarians.

Many of the most popular books contain hidden knowledge, which can only be revealed by divination. Often the writers are unaware that portions of their works have been influenced by higher evolved beings, until much later after the book has gone out of print.

We collect books, and establish vast libraries of old dusty books for this purpose. We buy books which no one has as use for. We retain books which contain obsolete information. Yes, This is a very old system!

*     *     *

## DIVINE INTERVENTION

The Creator Alpha Omega did not simply create the universe, and then abandon it to the natural processes. We are the immortal minds of one mind, that of the Creator Alpha Omega. Our existence is only real because we are part of the Creator Alpha Omega. Everything else are transitory creations.

153

We are less then the Creator Alpha Omega in the number of qualities and magnitudes of qualities we possess. We are made incomplete, or imperfect. Our Creator Alpha Omega is that voice of moral conscious we all share, and most of us ignore. Even the Fallen are creatures, immortal minds, and they hear the voice of the Creator Alpha Omega in their minds as moral conscious., which they ignore.

The direct intervention in human affairs by the divine has occurred rarely. The stopping of time in the universe, and the Resurrection of the great god Lucifer, was a example of direct divine intervention.

Divine intervention has come most often thorough the acts of higher evolved creatures, such as the Demigoddesses in this age of human civilization. Higher creatures hear the voice of the Creator Alpha Omega as their moral conscious, and in their personal spiritual experiences, and those compelled them to become involved in human affairs.

Our own personal spiritual experiences also guide us, when they are true communions with the Creator Alpha Omega.

It has always been a question amongst the humans, how do they determine the real voice of the Creator Alpha Omega, when false voices of some of the more powerful but evil immortal minds are also seeking to commune with the humans and lead them astray.

\*       \*       \*

D

\*       \*       \*

## DRUGS

The Demigoddesses taught the human Temple Priestesses the precise techniques for making complex drugs using only the materials found in nature all around them. These drugs were then administered by the Temple Priestesses for four major purposes;

A. Treatment of illness
B. Creating Elevated Spiritual States
C. Rituals in ceremonies
D. Divination
E. Temporary Enhancement of human qualities

The Temple Priestesses making drugs was no different from what modern pharmaceutical technicians do everyday. In time the Temple Priestesses developed a entire body of secret knowledge on the subject of Drugs, Diagnosis & Treatment of illness, Treatment of psychological conditions, Medicine & Chemistry. This knowledge was applied to both human beings and their farm animals.

Historical Background:

During the New Stone Age Tribalectic Culture it was the Brute-Males who had reduced the human population to less then 100,000 human beings on the entire planet.

The Demigoddesses realized that the human communities were on the verge of extinction, and that the factor preventing the advancement of humanity, was the Brute-Male's impact on human communities at that time. The Brute-Males were killing

155

anyone who had the motivation to change the human condition for the better.

The key was not to kill the Brute-Males, but rather to bring about the transformation of the Brute-Males. This was consistent with the religious beliefs & practices of the Demigoddesses And what they had learned from the War In Heaven.

This religion begin with the Demigoddesses Intervention which transformed the human communities on this earth. The immediate major impact was enormous;

A. the end of the New Stone Age Tribalectic Culture,

B. the reintroduction of true religion,

C. the creation of human spiritual communities,

D. the establishment of the Matriarchate.

E. The end of Harems, slavery, killing of infants

F. reduction unwanted pregnancies

G. improved the health of women & children.

H. reduce domestic violence & murder

I. civilized the Brute-Males

J. introduced agriculture & husbandry

This was the beginning once again of human civilization, some 250 years after civilization fell in the last SolarDark event, and Global Flood.

Humanity returned to a way of life in which the human form begin to pursue perfection of it's physical, intellectual, and Moral/ Spiritual qualities. This also facilitated the growth and development of their Immortal Minds in higher divine qualities.

This would have been impossible if not for the brave, intelli-gent, strong, women called the Temple Priestesses.

Transformative Spiritual Experiences:

To produce transformative spiritual experiences in the Brute-Males, two things were necessary;

1. The Brute-Males had to obtain the ElevatedSpiritual State.

2. The Brute-Males needed to commune with thedemigoddesses and have spiritual experienceswhich resulted in enlightenment and theadaptation of higher aspirations life consistentwith the purpose for human creation andexistence.

The Night The World Changed:

The entire race of Demigoddesses occupied The entire population of temple priestesses here on earth While the Demigoddesses controlled their bodies, the Demigoddesses created the conditions need to achieve their objectives with the Brute-Males. These preparations included the following;

1. Making of psychologically powerful drugs
2. Special Music
3. Special Incense
4. A comfortable room with soft furs
5. Special Foods & Drink
6. Special candles ( lighting ).

The Demigoddesses used this combination of factors to produce the Elevated Spiritual State Brute-Males, in the huts of the Temple Priestesses.

The Brute-Males were taken into the spiritual realm. They were given history, knowledge, revelations, and taught the truth. In the end the Brute-Males acquired enlightenment and were no longer the Brute-Males, they were Gentleman!

That night the New Stone Age Tribalectic Culture came too an end, and civilization returned to this earth. It was something even the Great God Lucifer could not have imagined possible, and it diminished his stature and following in the universe, because all the universe was watching this glorious intervention in human

affairs to save the human race.

It would not have been possible without the Temple Priestess-es and their Drugs.

Epilogue:

The physical communities the Demigoddesses had built would not endure, but the true religion had come to this earth, and given birth to a idea and a dream which would never die, even after this earth and all things in it pass away.

Notes:

1.  During the New Stone Age the human population dropped to less then 100,000. This number does not take into account;

    a.  The Fallen now in exile

    b.  The Watchers were stayed on earth

    c.  The Redheaded Children Of The Gods

d.  The wives of the above.

The society of the Fallen did not attempt to save the homo sapiens, and their influence was always detrimental to the well being of the human communities. They were a kingdom all too themselves on this of the earths.

1.  Lucifer didn't call this an intervention, but rather an interference with the natural course of life in the universe. Lucifer's argument was that Humanity was weak and it should be left to die! Lucifer's people were the true strong Men of this earth! Lucifer revealed his desire to rule all the physical earth and all its new inhabitants, ignoring the transitory nature of the material realm.

*          *          *

E

*          *          *

## EARTH RESONANCE

The Heavenly Bodies Move Through

A Sea of Energy:

It is one of our beliefs that the earth is internally resonating to energy waves passing through the solar system. The atmosphere also resonates to a lesser degree. This resonance is undetectable. This internal planet wide resonance increases the climatic and geological instability. This natural phenomena adds energy to the earth. Certain temples are constructed of special natural materials, and these in precise arrangements, allow the temple to become a resonator and battery for storing the earth from the rest of the universe. Once this energy accumulates in the temple structure, the temple is energized, and may be used for ceremonies including directed energy rituals.

The Ancients determined the natural frequencies and geometrics too be used in the temple materials & constructions; and in the rituals for the extractions & conversion of accumulated natural universal energies.

The stages in the conversion of natural universal energies by natural processes;

1. Universe. ( Origin )
2. Local Star Group
3. Solar System
4. Earth
5. Temple
6. Temple Priestesses
7. Practitioners ( Recipients )

*       *       *

## EARHART, AMELIA

Amelia Earhart is a Demigoddess of our sect. In her last human life she was born on July 24, 1897. She was a aviation pioneer, author, and adventurer. She disappeared July 2, 1937. Amelia Earhart was a competent talented woman in fields reserved for men.

She was a inquisitive child, teenage dreamer, who benefited from the support of her mother & grandmother which was important in her growth & development into a woman who exceeded all expectations and limitations placed on her by both her family and society.

The Immortal Mind which is Amelia Earhart the Demigoddess achieved perfection in it's lifetimes and reincarnations, as a human being, and became a hero, role model, and idol for millions of people living around the world.

Deification:

Deification is the identification of a Associated-Mind in a human being as a Demigoddess In Waiting, who upon delegation from the material being, transitions to Demigoddess, and is worshipped by our sect and others.

Demigoddesses are creatures much like ourselves, they are mortal, imperfect, and a stage in the long progression of the Immortal Minds to Divinity.

In the secession of lifeforms, the Demigoddess is the next higher stage after the human form. Immortal Minds which perfect in human form, shall become Demigoddesses after the end of their last human physical manifestation.

RULE I:

EVERY HUMAN BEING WHO PERFECTS WILL BECOME A DEMIGODDESS.

Some of the Other Demigoddesses Of This Sect:

Jeanne D' Arc, (?)

Helen of Troy, 7th century BC.

Naked Benzaitan (?)

Hedy Lamerr, 1914 - 2000.

Josephine Baker, (?)

Misty Copeland, September 10, 1982

Herriot Tubman, (?)

Tracy Edwards, September 5, 1962.

Florence Nightingale, (?)

*  *  *

## EARTH

The true name of this world is not know to the present human civilization. -Kavii

Earth;

1. any of the inhabited worlds in our universe, which are today the homes to exiled Fallen, their children, and their wives.

2. term meaning '' Place of exile of the Fallen gods. '' were the Fallen gods are held by the Angels in exile, such as this planet.

To this very day this planet is the temporary home to many Fallen gods, their children & wives. There are six species of higher evolved beings in the heavens of our local Star Group. The right of return brought them back down here after they lost the War Of The Gods. We have not known peace & tranquility, since after the Fall. The eight higher evolved species fight a hidden battle over this transitory world which none can ever truly own.

At a time when the gods still walked this world and lived amongst humanity. They were not yet known as the gods. They had not yet acquired the power of technology, and the intoxication of perfection. The ancient forefathers of both men and gods, left this planet's name on the walls of their temples, and the monolithic monuments they left behind. These things were built before the higher species migrated to the stars, and fought The War In Heaven.

This earth has been the birthplace, and the burial place for

many higher evolved species. The present six higher evolved species call this world their ancestral birthplace, and some believe that they have a stronger claim to this world then the homo sapiens. The sapiens being the last intelligent native species to survive the war waged against the indigenous life on is world.

One by one, Australopithecus, Homo habilis, Homo erectus, Homo Neanderthalensis, Homo floresiensis, and even Cro-Magnon Man was finally driven to extinction, only the Sapiens remain refusing to die quietly vowing to take the world with them in Mutually Assured Destruction which ironically has bought humanity time to grow stronger & wiser.

This Earth is still our home, though we fight battles over whose home it actually is.

\*       \*       \*

# ECONOMIC MODEL

## &

## ECONOMIC SYSTEM

Human societies must create the means whereby their members may acquire the means to fulfill their personal & humans needs. In advanced societies, The society must have diverse abundant productive capacity, based on the organized labours of humans, animals, or machines.

The Economic System given by the Demigoddesses too the human spiritual community was designed to optimize the;

    a.  material resources,
    b.  the quantity of time,
    c.  guidance & education, and
    d.  professional assistance;

in such a way as to maske available to each member all that is required for their unobstructed pursuit of the growth & development! of their;

    (1) physical- qualities,
    (2) intellectual- qualities, and

    (3) moral/spiritual - qualities.

The achievement of such, enables their Associated-Mind, which is an Immortal Mind, to acquire additional divine qualities which they have the innate potential to realize.

The General & Universal Human Needs addressed by a civilized progressive society include the following;

A. Physical/Material;Air, Warmth, Exercise, and Food & Water.

B. Exercise, Mental;Intellectual activity

C. Neurological & Cerebral;Amusement or the relief of stress, and Pleasure.

D. Social & Spiritual;Parental Affection,Peer Companionship, and Sexual Relations,Opportunity for forms of self expression,A Meaningful Comprehension of life.

To produce a number of essential items, the society developed the key elements of a system;

A. Production Sites; Factory, Farm, Services.

B. Storerooms & distribution system.

C. Medium of exchange, money & Banks

D. Body of productive artisans, skill workers &service providers.

E. Institution Production Planning, LabourCoordination, and Management.

The Demigoddesses taught the temple priestesses all forms and techniques of human productive labour. The temple priestesses then taught these skills to members of the human communities, thereby organizing the productive institutions and human labour within the spiritual communities. This also lead to an educational system, trade schools and libraries. this required that basic reading, writing, and arithmetic, become a universal ability.

The society established by the Demigoddesses was the most advanced for it's time.

Free Enterprise:

Even if the productive institutions of the society can meet all

the needs of all the members of a society, their is an independent individual creative impulse. Society must accommodate this individual creative drive if there is to be a highest possible level of gross quiotent of happiness in that society.

The human creative impulses require room for expression, thus society must allow private productive hobbies & free enterprise, to coexist with communally owned and operated means of production.

The Demigoddesses provided the human spiritual community with a Basic Capitalistic Economic Model.

Economic Taboos:

It was not enough to have the technology, and the able bodied work force, there were moral obligations, restrictions, which Demigoddesses applied to human productive economic activities. All people at all levels of society, in all professions observed these economic taboos, and there was no inventive ways to violate them, economic taboos became Civil Laws.

The economic system given to humanity by the Demigoddesses came with certain moral caveats.

1. There was no Slavery, Involuntary Servitude.
2. There was no For Profit Lending or Debt
3. There was no Prostitution
4. There was no Production, Distribution, or Sell ofDrugs for recreational habitual use.

5.  The Medical Professional, Police, and CivilServants performed their duties according to astrict moral code.

6.  The private ownership of property was nottransferable as a form of debt payment, but wasallowed as voluntary exchange of property ofequal value.Economic activity was not the prime objective of society or human existence, the Supreme End was. Economics was not elevated above the Divine purpose for creation & human existence. Economics was only a tool of humanity, and not the master of, life.

*    *    *

## EDEN

This Planet has been the home of many higher evolved species. The surviving higher evolved creatures in outer space, whose ancestral birthplace is this world, have always regarded Eden as THEIR Most Sacred Place On This World, and they have long denied the hominids access to that place on this earth.

Humanity has known of the Demigoddesses for more then 100,000 years. For a long time the hominids and Demigoddesses lived together on this earth. Every place where humanity and demigoddesses lived together on this earth,was to humanity an Paradise. The higher evolved species wanted more thena earthly paradise, they sought out a spiritual paradise in the heavens. Well, most of them did at least.

Approximately 75,000 years ago the Demigoddesses migrated

to their spiritual communities in outer space called " The Heavens ". That permanent separation of humanity and the Demigoddesses marked the End Of Paradise on earth. At that time, The location of Eden was forgotten in human memory, and lost in history. Only the higher evolved species still return to Eden to perform memorial ceremonies and rituals to the Ancients. Yes even the Goddesses worship their Goddesses. A mystery they do not think it necessary to share with us, and a subject which this book can not speak on ever. ( Even the gods have their gods! ).

After the Pantheon allowed The Watchers to return too earth and live here with their Nephilim children; The Watcher Post was taken over by machines. When the secular peoples speak of angels guarding Eden, they are speaking of those machines. The Higher evolved species put machines to watch over Eden and keep the hominids out of Eden.

The Angels guarding earth with flaming swords, were placed here by the Creator Alpha Omega to keep the Fallen Gods in Exile on the earths. They do not guard that place called Eden. The Demigoddesses Machines do.

*     *     *


## EINSTEIN, ALBERT

The theoretical physicist Albert Einstein, helped to advance the scientific understanding of the laws of nature in the areas of;

A.  The TemporalSpacial Energy Material Realm

B. The Interaction of Matter Energy and Time.

C. The Instantaneous Connection between particles

D. of matter which are separated by vast distances.

E. The novel states of matter in which the propertiesof matter are synergistically enhanced.

The above were the major areas of concentration of his life's work. Albert Einstein was the beneficiary of divination by subconscious means, like Adolf Hitler and may other persons having enormous impact on the course of human civilization.

Albert Einstein like many of his contemporaries in the sciences in his day were under the influence of hostile higher evolved beings, who provided humanity with lethal sciences & technologies, which humanity was not mature enough to use properly.

There are higher evolved beings which use scientist and world leaders to pursue their objective of global human genocide by any means possible.

The development of thermonuclear weapons of mass destruction, was guided by hostile higher evolved beings on this of the earths.

Dispute the interference of hostile beings, humanity has not been exterminated from the face of hisof the earths. This is not the case on many of the other exile worlds.

Human Survival Against All Odds:

Humanity has survived in earth due to the quantity of nuclear weapons which exist, which have the capacity to render the entire earth inhabitable for centuries. Thus the plan of encouraging human self destruction by global thermonuclear warfare has had the opposite effect. Mankind will take the entire earth with him in his self destruction, leaving nothing for the higher evolved beings to takeover.

Other Leaders Used By Hostile Entities:

Einstein, Hitler, Pol Pot, Stalin, and so many others were completely unaware of their spiritual connection to hostile evolved beings, and that they were being used as part of a evil genocidal plan. The war against the other evil species on this world will never end until the entire world is made aware of their existence and their true nature.

*        *        *

## ELEVATED SPIRITUAL STATE

The Immoral Minds are connected to physical manifestations, and are temporary Associated-Minds. As Associated-Minds our perception of reality comes via the body senses, and as a result is limited by their biological capacities. Human intelligence can help use to comprehend reality beyond our sensory range, but the human mind is also limited by biology.

To more fully comprehend reality the sects turn to the higher evolved beings, who are creatures much like ourselves. In order to have spiritual experiences ( non physical interpersonal communication occurring in the spiritual realm ) humans must obtain a Elevated Spiritual State. ( that's what the condition is called in the English language. )

The Elevated Spiral State is a condition of the Mind/Body.

The body has a habitual learned condition in which it is the source of a type of interference which blocks our awareness of the spiritual realm, and prevents essential personal spiritual experiences.

There are many techniques which reduce the interference and free the Associated-Mind to perceive the spiritual realm. These techniques rise the Associated-Mind's awareness, or elevates it to the level of Extrasensory Perception ( ESP ).

The human being has three states ( PMS );

The Three States:

1. Physical;

2. Mental; and,

3. Spiritual/Moral.

The three states of the human being are Interconnected, Interactive, and Interdependent. Each state is aligned with the other two states.

The human being goes through three stages/changes which can produce the conditions ( ESS ) for human initiated interactive spiritual experiences;

The Three Transitions:

A. Physical Transitionperformed in conjunction with the mind,generates energies, reduces body's interference

B. Mental Transitioncalms the mind, directs it at the single objective

C. Spiritual Transition.the Immortal Mind is temporary freed to sensethe other minds in the spiritual realm.

Techniques:

The way of life consist of daily religious practices, which we taken in their entirety are like instruments in a Symphony, each part being essential to the whole.

Every religious practice influences the level of energy within the being. When done correctly certain practices can elevate the level of Free-Energies. These energies affect the range of activity within the Associated-Mind.

Peak Energy; is the elevated state created and maintained by regular religious practices.

Threshold Energy; is the highest elevated state possible in humans. Threshold Energy rises the Associated-Mind above the energies generated by the body/mind normal functions, and the Associated-Mind can perceive and interact in the spiritual realm. THE BEING IS NOW HAVING A SPIRITUAL EXPERIENCE!

The Temple Priestesses were taught these techniques by the Demigoddesses, and they taught some of these techniques to humans in the true religion. Each sect specializes in unique techniques which are optimized for particular objectives.

The simplest natural techniques are the most common. Basically natural biological & psychological process are activated in

order to generate human internal energies. These energies are accumulated then intentionally directed at the enhancement of the Associated-Mind's ability to penetrate the perceptional threshold.

There are advanced techniques which are also called the

MindBody Disciplines. There are techniques using lights, music, and drugs, and physical exercise. It is a large area of specialization in modern spirituality.

*      *      *

## END, HOW WORLDS -

No created thing is immortal. The Immortal Minds are immortal only because they are part of the Creator Alpha Omega. All Creation and created things may end in either of these three possible ways;

1. Return to the Creator Alpha Omega
2. reduced to nothing in perpetual digression
3. material universe reduced to nothing.

All Immortal Minds will return to the Creator Alpha Omega, either as perfected divinity, or as Perpetual Digression reduced to nothing.

A. The End of Creatures:
1. The Supreme End.

The perfection of the physical, mental, and moral/spiritual qualities of its kind, after successive reincarnations of that kind, allows the Associated-Mind to acquire another Divine Quality, leads to the transition to the next higher form, which first requires the unification of multiple soulmate Immortal Minds which go forward as one Immortal Mind. The ultimate is to arrive at the Divine.

The last stage in the progression.

    2.  Perpetual Digression.

The physical manifestation permanently separates from the Immortal Mind, while it is in digression, and in exile, and that Immortal Mind is then absorbed by the Omega of the Creator Alpha Omega.

    B.  The End of the Physical Manifestations:

        3.  The Local Star Group Lacking Immortal Minds.

The physical manifestation has permanently separates from the Immortal Mind, and retains it's physical material nature according to the laws of nature. That Local Star Group consisting of physical manifestations Not being associated with any Immortal Minds, will be absorbed by the Omega of the Creator Alpha Omega.

Other Religions See The End As We Do:

The BenBen Stones of Egyptian Temples tell us of two Creators who are One;

1. The Alpha, 2. The Omega; are

The Creator Alpha Omega.

The BenBen Stones depict one, The Alpha, as older, and the other, The Omega, as younger, and yet they are the same Creator Alpha Omega.

Note: The Immortal Minds at the beginning of creation are infinite in quantity, greater then the number of elementary fundamental particles in the entire universe. Thus the Ultimate Unification into a single greater Divine Mind occurs in a infinite quantity of time.

Note: Not every physical object in the universe has an Associated-Mind. When the Immortal Mind permanently separates from a physical manifestation, it becomes A unchanging still life condition of reality; which is sustained for an extended duration without the continual influence of the Immortal Minds, and until the Omega of the Creator absorbs that local portion of the universe/ creation.

Note: An anology would be to compare The Alpha to a Astronomical Supernova; and compare The Omega to a Astronomical Blackhole.

*     *     *

## ENERGY FIELDS

Condition Of The Universe:

There are two realms, The Spiritual Realm, the TemporalSpacial Energy Material Realm. Both realms are created by the Creator Alpha Omega. The things in the TemporalSpacial Energy Material Realm are produced by the Immortal Minds.

All real things exist for only a fragment of time, if they he an Associated-Mind. If they lack a Associated-Mind then they are sustained still life. The fragmentary reality is selected from a place in the Divine Mind in which all possible future states of the two realms axis virtually. The Immortal Mind selects the future state and it becomes real or actual in the TemporalSpacial Energy Material Realm.

The energy field around any real thing having an Immortal Mind is the sum of the multiple states occurring in that space which vary from one another. So the future state is not exactly like the present state or the antecedent states.

Active Energy Fields:

Directed Energy Practices require Synergy Energy Fields, because one human has insufficient power. Therefore a significant assembly of synchronized practitioners perform a routine of participatory rituals, such as the ceremonial dances.

When multiple beings combine the power of their Immortal Minds, they generate a Synergistic Point Energy Field. The center of this type field can alter reality in the present or remotely if the center contains an independent Immortal Minds which redirects the Synergistic Point Energy Field.

The Three Common Settings:

A. Assemblies of The spiritual community
B. The unions of soulmates
C. Ceremonial Participatory Rituals in the presenceof two or more temple priestesses.

The energy fields of two or more proximate real things having

Associated-Minds, can interact in either Constructive or Destructive fashion. The resultant magnitude is quantified as follows;

$FMag. = ( Pm \times Em )^{Qp}$

were:

FMag. Energy Field Magnitude

Pm. Permeability of TemporalSpacial realm

Em. Mean Human Energy Constant

QP. Quantity of participants

For Elevated Spiritual State ( ESS ):

Let the lower limit equal the Peak Energy state.

Let the upper limit equal Threshold Energy Level

Real things lacking Associated-Mind do not have active energy fields, they are sustained still lifes.

The non living environmental can enhance the Energy Field Effect if for example the temple structure contain monolithic natural stone, there are underground deposits of quartzite, and/or underground & surface water flowing in a polar orientation. These conditions store earth energy, and be induced to release the stored energy if stimulated by the proper humanmade patterns of energy frequencies.

*     *     *

## END TO GLOBAL WARMING

Today we can see the effects of climate change on this planet. The average temperature of this planet continues to increase every year, and scientist have measured these increases and determined that global warming is accelerating. Given this fact, within our lifetime, this planet will become unsuitable for supporting seven billion humans.

The sceptics points out that global warming is not a new development in nature. This has happened before on this planet, that is a fact. The planet did not die, that is a fact.

A. The truly important question to ask ourselves is what natural events took place on this planet to stop global warming?

The Religious Interpretation Of History & Mystery, reveals that the natural events which in the past have a stopped global warming have been catastrophic and extinction level events. The natural processes are unchanged, and these calamities will occur again too stop global warming.

B. The next question is what should humanity do in order to survive these inevitable natural processes?

Once again the Religious Interpretation Of History & Mystery, provides us with the answers.

In the past humans have built arks large enough to survive the storm, and with enough internal space to hold all the essential tools & supplies needed to begin again after the natural catastrophe.

We do not control the natural processes on a universal scale which determine the course of events on this planet, therefore we must deal wisely with what nature is doing and about to do to this planet.

The demigoddesses have spoken, and they have told us all that we need to know, everyone who hears them must decide what they will do. Is there a plan? Yes many societies, nations, groups, religions, corporations, wealthy people, have made proper and wise plans. They account for the 1,000,000 who are prepared to survive. What about the rest of the humans, the other seven billion ? If they don't pay attention they'll never see it coming! The natural events to come are as unbelievable as the global warming we are now experiencing!

The Inevitable Sequence Of Events InThe Future Of Humanity On Earth:

CURRENT EVENTS

1. Global Warming
2. Droughts
3. No Rains
4. Wildfires
5. Massive Crop Failure On A Global Scale
6. Water & Food Shortages
7. Social Unrest

8. Starvation

NEXT STAGE:

9. Civil Wars
10. Planet Wide Death Of Farm Animals
11. Large Scale Human Deaths
12. Years Of Human Civilization In Decline

NATURAL CORRECTIVE PROCESSES BEGIN:

13. Ice Asteroids Bombard The Earth
14. Torrential Rains
15. SolarDark
16. Great Deluge
17. Months In Darkness

18. Glaciation Begins

A CHANGED EARTH:

19. New Ice Age

20. Homo Sapiens Population Falls To Less Then1,000,000.

21. Civilization Ends, and Next Stone Age BeginsIn Equatorial Communities.

So, As you can see the Religious Interpretation Of History & Mystery, Natural calamity repeats itself over and over again, and humanity can't stopped the universe & laws of nature by not believing in them while we are still on this earth.

The Religious Interpretation Of History & Mystery, is not given to us simply to teach us about our past lives; but to prepare us for our future lives should we survive the storm.

For those of us who have a plan, Not surviving the storm, is not one of the options.

SECRET PROPHETS:

We can see visions of the future in our mass entertainment, or movies. Each movie containing a small pieces of things to come. These ideas are generated by that part of our minds which is free from the social obligation to think like everyone else around us. If we look closely we can see solutions to the problem of surviving the seeming impossible.

The pulp fiction authors are our prophets!

*        *        *

ENERGY & SEXUAL JOY

## SEX IN GENERAL:

Sex is a human need. Some people have psychologically suppressed their natural sex drive because they are unable to conceive of a appropriate sexual behavior which fulfills their particular sexual needs.

Religion must give people a set of religious practices, which constitute a way of life, which fulfills their natural needs. Religion must address the ways & means of sex because it is a human natural need.

The CEBAGII gives directions concerning how to practice sex in a manner consistent with human well being and the achievement of the purpose for creation and the purpose for human existence. Theses are CEBAGII religious practices.

Energy:

Worship at times involves elevated spiritual states, elevated levels of internal energies, and the expression of;

A. gratitude,

B. happiness, and

C. joy.

These are all things which our Creator Alpha Omega is pleased with. Sex is one method of expressing these, there are other ways, the ways are based on the inclinations of individuals expressing gratitude, happiness, and joy.

Thus sex has a place in human life, and a place in worship, and is a part of religious practices in the CEBAGII.

\*     \*     \*

## ESTER, Queen of Persia

Another Demigoddess of this sect.

*        *        *


## ETHICS & HUMANITY

The Essence Of Human Behavior:

Human behavior has its causation in the condition of the Mind/ Brain primarily, behavior is shaped by belief, and behavior is the practice of, and expression of belief. Religious, Philosophical, Political, Moral, and Scientific beliefs are a significant factor in determining the outcome of decision making and chose of actions.

Just as memory does not lie in the Brain/Body, our system of beliefs exist outside the TemporalSpacial Energy Material Realm, in the Immortal Mind.

Religious, Philosophical, Political, Moral, and Scientific beliefs form our conception of the universe, but however we do not truly know the universe until we leave the TemporalSpacial Energy Material Realm, via our personal spiritual experiences.

As we come to understand our personal spiritual experiences, we develop our religious beliefs & practices; these become the primary factor in our ability to follow the guidance of The Creator Alpha Omega, which is present in all Immortal Minds, in the form of our internal independent moral conscious; our impulse to do what is right!

The complexity of life does not escape the!awareness of our

Creator alpha omega. In our spiritual practices we have the means to obtain valid spiritual guidance in all areas of human affairs. Thus our religion provides us a complete basis for ethical/moral decision making & behavior.

Our Religious Beliefs Are Dominant:

Within the Creator Alpha Omega are we the Immortal Minds, each a lesser portion of the infinite & eternal, not yet what we

are to be someday, seeking to be like our Creator Alpha Omega someday, not knowing truly what that is! Only knowing that it is good! And that is what we seek to be!

The Immortal Minds grow & develop and this material body and universe reflect the Immortal Minds condition, their imperfection, and their Divinity.

We are guided by the Creator alpha Omega to behave like higher beings and the pursue higher aspirations.

The sources of spiritual ethical/moral guidance include the following;

A. Cannon of the Creator Alpha Omega

B. Taboos in the Economic System

C. Nublesse Oblige

D. The Professional Code Of Doctors

E. The Supreme End

F. Moral Conscious, voice of Creator Alpha Omega

G. Personal Spiritual Experiences.

H. Taboos in the religious & social system

\*      \*      \*

## EVIL, THE NATURE OF -

Evil consist of any;

A. physical action

B. thought or desire

C. spiritual energy directed as a forcewhich by it's intent and effect odstructs;

    a. the progression of Immortal Minds

    b. the pursuit of the Supreme End

    c. the observance of divine law

    d. the purpose of creation and human existencewhere it is done knowingly and of ones own freewill.

Becoming Evil:

Firstly:

All things have the potential to error, it is not evil until we ac-

cept the error, refuse to correct it, and refuse to refrain from repeating it in the future.

Secondly:

The coveting of things not our own, and the obsession over things we can not have, leads to evil thoughts, desires, and actions.

When The Good Do Evil!

There is a common misconception that when an act of evil has occurred, and it has impacted us, that our doing an act of evil in response to that evil will remedy the harm done.

That misconception is the causation of so much evil and human suffering in this world.

The evil that others do, impacts us only if it leads to us doing evil; Otherwise this evil is not done to us, but rather it is done to the evil doer by their acts. When we do evil to the evil doer in response, we are not just doing evil to them but also to ourselves.

\*　　　\*　　　\*

## EVIL CONSCIOUS

There are three sources of knowledge;

A. Biology. (instinctual)
B. Physical Experience. (mental)
C. Spiritual Experience. (spiritual)

Our Creator Alpha Omega is heard as our moral conscious regardless of who we are and what faith we belong too or do not belong too.

The history of humanity is full of powerful men who were lead by voices to destroy what good men had built. Adolf Hitler being a primary example. The voices which some people hear can be more powerful then the voice of moral conscious.

Quantum Physics, a Modern science, has known for half a century that there is instantaneous action at a distance in the TemporalSpacial Energy Material Realm between real things. As science increases it's understanding of these counterintuitive natural phenomenon, it will become clear that the mind is subject to external influences.

Some highly experienced human beings while in meditative practices, can influence the thoughts and/or disposition of others proximate to them, if those others are particularly susceptible. Higher evolved beings on this of the earths can do the same.

I would be incomplete if I did not acknowledge that the other two sources of knowledge;

A. Biology. ( instinctual)

B. Physical Experience. (mental)

also provide the basis for human error, and human desire, and human evil, in thought and action.

*       *       *

## EVOLUTION

The Creator Alpha Omega created the Immortal Minds before anything else, before even time, space, energy, and matter. The Immortal Minds existed before the stars were born.

The immortal minds progress by slowly acquiring the divine qualities over a period of association with a succession of physical manifestations. The succession appears like the following;

elementary particle

atom

molecule

aggregate matter

bacteria

plant

insect

bird

fish

animal

human

The Creator Alpha Omega by Design & Intent has determined the forms which all real things will take in creation, in the uni-

verse. Thus evolution proceeds according to a predetermined sequence.

Mutations do occur but they too are of a form that is within the possible states of the universe of real!things which the Creator alpha omega has predetermined.

*     *     *

## EXPERIENCES, TRANSFORMATIVE SPIRITUAL -

In the religious interpretation of history & mystery, we see how the Demigoddesses have historically sought to elevate humanity, and help humans to live better lives & pursue higher aspirations.

In all cases the Demigoddesses attempt to give human beings transformative spiritual experiences ( TSE ). TSE allow the human Associated-Mind to experience things which the human can never experience by any other means. TSE occur exclusively in the Spiritual Realm beyond the limitations of time & space. TSE have a much greater range then ordinary experiences confined to the TemporalSpacial Energy Material Realm.

The key transformative spiritual experiences were thus of Brute-Males which bought the New Stone Age Tribalectic Culture to an end.

The Religious Interpretation Of History & Mystery, contains this narrative of the essential transformative spiritual experiences:

'' A New Day Dawns:

'' After hundreds of years, in which the heavens had been silent, the Demigoddesses had returned to this of the earths. In the dark hut lit only by candle light, incense filling the air, laying on soft furs, the Brute-Male found himself in the presence of the goddesses of his ancestors, and the goddesses spoke of many things they had seen, and they gave the Brute visions of forgotten places and times, he perceived things which once were, are now, and will be some day long after he is forgotten.

'' Taking the Brute-Male by the hand the Demigoddesses travelled to the end of he universe and he a simple creature looked into the mirror, and saw the timeless smiling face of the Creator Alpha Omega, he touched the hands that had put him in his mother's womb, the hands that birthed him, and held him to a warm breast, and he cried as if born again. He saw the beginning of creation and the end of the universe, and the birth of the next universe.

'' There beyond this world he found the reason for life, the purpose for human existence, immortality and death and rebirth. His eyes were open for the first time, and he had compassion & enlightenment, and he understood many things.

'' The light of the ancient sun welcomed him to a new day as he stepped out of the hut of the temple priestesses, and the man was no longer the Brute-Male. ''

My favorite passage from, The Book Of CEBAGII !

- Kavii

*       *       *

F

*       *       *

## FALLEN GOVERNMENT SERVES MEN:

KEY IDEA:

A SELF-SERVING GOVERNMENT IS NOT A GOVERNMENT SERVING THE PEOPLE, AND IS NO LONGER RECOGNIZING THE PURPOSE FOR WHICH IT WAS ESTABLISHED, AND IS NO LONGER REGULATED BY THE FUNDAMENTAL LAWS OF THAT SOCIETY.

Divine Law means that the government SERVES The Creator Alpha Omega, by serving to help the people achieve the Supreme End, and not obstructing their religious practices & religious way of life.

The religious society has Divine Law which regulates government just as it regulates people. The war in heaven begun be-

cause Lucifer and his followers sought to nullify Divine Law, by placing persons in charge of interpretation of divine messages who were not servants of the Creator Alpha Omega.

Because Divine Law is the basis of government and of religion,

189

then members who no longer believe in the validity of Divine Law as the guide of government, no longer believe in Divine Law as valid, and no longer are believers in this religion.

The Light Does Not Shine

In The Hearts Of All People.

The Voice of The Creator Alpha Omega

Humanity's Moral Conscious

Is Not Heard By All People

The Evil Lead &

The Weak Follow

The Government Of The Fallen.

STAGES IN THE FALL OF GOVERNMENT:

A. Society forms because people find it easier tofulfill their needs when they work together withother people who have the same needs.

B. Society grows so large, that it becomesdisorganized and finds difficulty workingeffectively.

C. Government formed to organize society for;

1. to control the resources of the society in ordertoo apply those resources more efficiently inmeeting the needs of all members of the society

2. to provide for the defense of individuals

3. to provide for the common defense

D. Government fails to effectively meet the needsof the people.

E. People seek to form new government which willfulfill the purpose for which their government isformed.

F. Current Government's employees perceive theirneed to continue the existence of the current

G. government.

H. Current government applies resources ofsociety to perpetuate the existence of thecurrent government, regardless of the failure tofulfill the purpose for which government wasestablished.

I. Government is not longer the servant of thepeople. The goals of government are now

J. opposed to the needs of the people.

K. Government works to prevent the people ofsociety who formed the government fromreplacing that government with a new & bettergovernment.

L. Because government is the tool for enforcing theconstitution, when government ignores the intentof the constitution, then the true constitution isno longer enforceable in that society. We have afake constitution in effect

A Fundamental Truth:

Societies Fail When Their Government Places It's Needs Above The Needs Of The People; Works To Preserve Itself While It Fails At The Purpose For Which It Was Established; Turns Against The People In Order To Keep The People From Replacing Their Ineffective Government. Such Government Is Not A Real Thing But It Thinks That It Is A Real Thing. If It Were A Real Thing It Would Be Called A Evil Thing.

\*        \*        \*

## FALSE RESURRECTION

I.  REINCARNATION;

the natural process which allows the immortalmind to associate with a succession of physicalmanifestations, and experience
multiple lifetimes,a type of immortality.

II.  RESURRECTION;

the reinstatement of the association between anImmortal Mind
and a physical manifestation, afterthe association has been permanently terminatedin the death of the body. This process al-
sorequires the repair of the physical manifestation.The physical
manifestation and theAssociated-Mind go on too continue living.

False Resurrection:

False Resurrection is a reincarnation which is mistaken for a
Resurrection because the Immortal Mind involved in the event is
highly progressed so that it reincarnates in a physical manifestation which has no child stage, it is reborn as a adult.

There are ways of distinguishing Resurrection from Reincarnation. One is that in Reincarnation the body is of a different individual, and this is visible. In Resurrection the body is the same,
because its the same individual. Higher evolved beings can recall
their previous lives, so they can pretend to have been Resurrected.

The First Resurrection:

In our present age the first creature to be resurrected was the great god Lucifer, when the Creator alpha omega resurrected him during the War In Heaven, the sent him into exile. This event marked the end of at war.

\* \* \*

## FOOD & DRINK

The Future:

The human use of natural biological organism for nutritional purposes is a unnecessary cultural habit. Synthetic foods & beverage have all of the benefits of natural substance, and none of the disadvantages. The engineering of synthetic foods will improve over time and someday reach a level of sophistication which will make synthetic foods superior to natural foods and very desirable.

\* \* \*

## FREEDOM OF RELIGION

KEY BELIEF:

ONE CAN NOT BE FREE IN ANY SOCIETY, IF ONE IS NOT FREE TO EXPRESS AND PRACTICE THE RELIGIOUS BE-LIEFS ONE SINCERELY BELIEVE IN.

One's Religion is the expression of one's sincerely held personal beliefs about the nature of reality, creation, existence, life, purpose of life, death, and the afterlife.

One can not be free while one is being compelled to believe what one does not believe. One can be compelled to practice what one does not believe, but not compelled to believe. A free society may compelled observance of civil laws for the well being of the society at large, but however it can not compelled the observance of religious laws.

When one has been forced to follow the practices of a religion which is inconsistent with ones beliefs, one is not actually practicing a religion, one is actually carrying out the forced labours of religious enslavement.

Religions in which the practitioner forcibly compel others to convert and practice their religion, are not religion of free peo- ple, but rather they are religions of people forbidden to practice their own religion, and people held in slavery to a human master through that master's use of a religion.

Religious Freedom is not dictated or established by majority vote, but by society's understanding of life, which leads it to value human beings & human rights.

Freedom To Believe In Your Own Religious Beliefs, even if you are the sole believer, is the most fundamental right every human being who is a believer in anything, seeks and cherishes.

*     *     *

## FREEWILL

Freewill:

the power of the being to think and act in a manner consistent with it'sown;

A. Beliefs & Practices

B. Wants & Desires

C. Inclinations

D. Conception of Reality

E. Perceived needs, and perceived means offulfilling those needs.

The mind can perceive of the need for a certain condition and the means of producing that condition, then the individual may be compelled by his/her believe in the value of improving & perfecting, to pursue the realization of that better means. Freewill is the freedom in society to do just that!

*    *    *

G

*    *    *

## GHOST IN THE SHELL

I.    Cybernetics:

The use of artificial systems to maintain the human brain in a living state after the biological failure of the body.

II.    ( machine symbiosis )

The instillation of a human brain within a machine for the control of the machine, and the maintenance of the human brain as a living organism within the machine.

195

The Near Future:

The ability to survive in the low gravity high radiation environment of outer space, will require that the first workers at the far point station asteroid survey & mining fields in the main asteroid belt by Cyborgs. The spacesuit will be a machine-body their mind is encased within.

Some ask if a human being can be a human being without a human body. We know that there are certain qualities which make humans human. These essential qualities will not be eliminated by cybernetics. The human being will still be a human being, inside the machine.

There are some who suggest that because our human qualities are also weaknesses in the environment of outer space, that these qualities should be eliminated. But Human is a set of qualities that are determined by Divine Design & Intent, we do not correct the work of the Creator Alpha Omega, we respect it!

Human Being is an essential stage in the progression of the immortal minds. The machine-body will give human beings a greater opportunity to perfect their human qualities. Humans of this religion do not seek to escape their humanness, but to reach its greatest potentials.

*        *        *

## God

The term God refers to any creature, or any non-biological intelligent entity, which displays qualities of two or more orders of magnitude greater then human capacities and qualities, and whose use of their natural abilities is beyond the comprehension of human beings.

Gods are mortal, even the machine gods can die.

Gods are not divine.

Gods are not perfect.

Gods are not the Creator Alpha Omega.

*     *     *

## GODDESSES OF LOVE

The Demigoddesses were called, " The Goddesses Of Love ", not because of their beauty which caused all men love them, but because they taught Humanity what true love is!

The First Evidence That Demigoddesses Love Human Beings Is In Their Continually Intervening In Human Affairs To Aide Humanity In Every Crisis.

Humanity exist in the shadowsof a love made in heaven, andcast down upon our worldcompensating for the tragic cyclesof nature in our livesseeking humanity's wellbeing,transformation,and elevation ofform and mind.

The Second Evidence That Demigoddesses Love Humanity Is That Every Demigoddess Immortal Mind Was Born From The

Union Of Multiple Human Immortal Minds Who Were Soulmates In Love. Demigoddesses Are Born Of Human Love.

The Third Evidence That Demigoddesses Love Humanity Is

197

That Historically The Demigoddesses Took The Form Of Temple Priestesses To Transform The Brute-Males Through Spiritual Practices Which Included Loving Them.

'' if you try to create community firstthen, you shall fail. But if you loveone another, then you will createcommunity.''

- Eric Bonhoeffer

priest executed during WWII by Nazi's.

The Demigoddesses said it first, and proved it, by living it.

*       *       *

## GOVERNMENT OF THE MATRIARCHATES

Before migrating to spiritual communites in outer space, the Demigoddesses established their communities on earth governed by women, because all Demigoddesses are the same gender, all the Demigoddesses are women. ( Later called the Matriarchate )

The three species of Demigoddesses joined the other three species of higher evolved beings, and the six species left this earth, and established the Pantheon in heaven. In the Pantheon Demigoddesses became the leaders of the religion, and were recognized as the Sacred Vessels of the Creator Alpha Omega.

The Pantheon adopted the system of government of the Demigoddesses because it was the most effective & efficient of those known at the time, 100,000 years later and it is still the preferred government in the heavens.

When the last major intervention by Demigoddesses with the objective to save humanity occurred, the Demigoddesses established Matriarchates on this earth.

Matriarchates On This Earth:

The religious based society in which women are the religious leaders, has created a culture in which all authority in the society is vested in women. Men are forbidden from holding any positions of authority over others.

Because there is not a valid objective history available by which we may determine the qualities of women lead scientifically & industrially advanced societies, it is only our religious beliefs by which we can say that this system of social management is superior to any other forms.

*     *     *

## GREAT FLOOD

The Current State Of Knowledge:

There is evidence that this earth has experienced great floods multiple times. Modern science has not given this phenomenon careful investigation, and therefore the implications for humanity's future survival have not been considered outside of the religious community.

U.S. Space probes have confirmed the Russian theory that for millions of years, water has come to earth by ice asteroids colliding with our atmosphere.

The Science of Astronomy has established the existence of a vast region of space surrounding this earth, and that billions of asteroids occupy that region of outer space.

Astrophysics has determined that the asteroids of our solar system are the remains of materials from which the planets were formed when the solar system first was created.

There is an entire body of facts which must be determined, models built, analysis performed, before secular experts can make scientific predictions. It is our opinion that mainstream religion is obstructing this investigation.

The Religious Perspective:

The solar system contains all the water which this earth will ever require to remain fit for life in all it's varieties. The edge of this solar system is a vast region of outer space called the Orrt Cloud. It is called a cloud because it consist of an innumerable quantity of asteroids made entirely of frozen water.

The natural processes cause some of these ice asteroids to leave the Orrt Cloud and journey through the planetary space until they collide with this earth's atmosphere.

This natural process replenishes the surface waters of this earth.

Occasionally the quantity of ice asteroids impacting this earth will be so large that they cause flooding on a global scale. Sometimes the floods are simply extinction level events. This earth has see many great floods.

Even during the great floods the entire earth is not covered in water. The drainage of rain-water to the oceans is slower then the amount of water falling from the sky, so we get floods.

The current global climate variation is a natural phenomenon which will be followed by a astronomical event which will stop the increase in earths temperature. That natural event consist of;

A.  Ice Asteroids bombardment,

B.  A Great Flood,

C.  A SolarDark event, and

D.  Higher Latitude Glaciation.

\*       \*       \*

## GROUP MARRIAGE

Marriage is a interpersonal relationship between two or more people, who are spiritual soulmates, who find it desirable to pursue interest together rather then apart, who have comparable goals, and who are in love.

I.    Soulmates:

two or more Immortal minds who have a attraction for each other which is more then transitory and has its basis in some personal qualities other then the physical material qualities and assets each possesses. There is no limit to the quantity of soulmates a person has, and the Temple Priestesses helps them grow beyond their complexities which limit them.

II.    Love:

the emotional commitment to other human beings which causes one to perceive their needs as equal to or greater in importance then ones own; and which allows one to find great pleasure in their company; and causes one to have great interest in their well being& happiness.

Temple Priestesses As Matchmakers:

The Temple Priestesses have the unique capacity to identify which people are soulmates to one another. They also have the experience to guide these persons in overcoming preconceived ideas & misconceptions about Love. The Temple Priestesses then helps them acquire a state of mind/body conductive to the formation of a strong lasting interpersonal relationship between them.

The Spiritual Community:

Group marriage is a fundamental element in every viable happy spiritual community which in essence is also a interpersonal relationship on a larger scale. Thus the Temple Priestesses helps to create a stronger spiritual community by helping people find their soulmates and form lasting interpersonal relationships.

Note:

Types Of Unions;

A. Union of Soulmates to form Group marriage.
B. Union of Soulmates to form Demigoddess.
C. Union of Married Groups ( Families ) to formspiritual communities of sects.
D. Union of practitioners in spiritualceremonies and performance of rituals, tocreate centralized TemporalSpacial elevatedenergy state called a Synergy Energy Field Point.
E. Union of sects to form official religion.
F. Repetitive Spiritual Union of Demigoddess andTemple

Priestesses for religious ceremonies and
G.  practices.

Explanation:

B. Union of Soulmates to form Demigoddess.

Mutiple soulmates unite as they spiritually transition to the next
higher state, and form a single Demigoddess ( demigoddess be-

ing the next higher stage in the progression after homo sapiens ),
they are able to unite into one immortal mind because they love
one another. Love then is the spiritual basis of each Demigoddess's creation.

*     *     *

H

*     *     *

## HAPPINESS

Let us accept that only in our most immature stage of development did we equate, " Happiness", with, "Pleasure"; and that
we have since that stage acquired a nonmaterial basis for our
definition of and pursuit of happiness.

Therefore we find the greatest happiness in the company of
our select society; and we find the greatest obstacle to happiness,
other then our own misconceptions, in the hostilities experienced
in encounters with those from outside our community whom we
are trying to help, and who do not want any help despite their
apparent need for help.

The Utopian ideal is for our system of mass production to achieve a level of perfection were it may satisfy all the material needs of all members of society, without human intervention. The elimination of the need for human labour, creates the opportunity for personal pursuit of higher aspirations, and thereby leading to the experience of and realization of a higher form of happiness.

The social measured of the Gross Level Of Happiness is a reflection of our concern for the well being& happiness of others in our society, rather then purely a tool of analytical economics. The Gross we recognize The Gross Level Of Happiness as a religious criteria in the fulfillment of the purpose of human life.

## HAREM

The harem is nothing more then the physical enslavement of women, to their detriment, for nothing more then the production of pleasure for the men who have the monopoly of force in a society where women have no freedom equal to that of men in that society.

Harems are involuntary intimate relationships in which the women are not equal to the men. In any intimate relationship men and women must always be equal.

Group marriages in the CEBAGII are not harems, and the society is obligated to ensure that no group marriage becomes a harem.

Women or men will not be introduced into the society in order to obtain material benefits in exchange for becoming a harem.

## HAREM

Slavery;

a condition in which one or more human beings provide labour and/or services to one or more other human beings, who derive pleasure, profit, or some necessary thing from those labours and/ or services; where the person providing the labours and/or services does not receive equitable compensation, but performs those actions as the result of the application of force, threats, coercion, deception, or any means by which the persons freewill is negated; in addition to involuntary labour/service, slavery also is maintained through various types of effective imprisonment.

Harem;

a form of slavery in which the victims are most often women, girls, and children; where in addition to labours and services customarily performed by slaves, the victims are also made to proform involuntary sexual acts.

Narrative:

After the fall of human civilization, during the period of earth history known as the New Stone Age The Harem was the main form of total enslavement in the Tribalectic Culture ruled by Brute-Males.

After the last SolarDark/Great Deluge event, nature destroyed human cities, and the Brute-Males destroyed human civilization. What replaced civilization was a world of brutality, enslavement, murder, rape, incest, infanticide, starvation, disease, premature death, and other extremes of human suffering.

The simplest things which displease the Brute-Males would be punished with death regardless of the women's or child's age.

In general this form of slavery excluded men who were killed or driven into the wilderness when they came of age.

The women & children, perform all manner of labour, and enjoy no human comforts, and experienced continual beatings and a early death. During their lifetime their community was their prison, in which they would spend their entire lifetime, like birds in a cage.

For 250 years the Brute-Males controlled the monopoly in the use of lethal violence against all peoples, men, women, children, even the unborn. Life on earth was like living in hell, until the Demigoddesses returned to dethrone the savages.

Sex Workers As In A Social Harem:

Although some perceive prostituion as a choice, it is in reality a variation of Harem, with the difference that the master of the slave, is many men instead of one man; and the prison is a community the size of the entire nation. All people participate in this type of enslavement who allow it to continue, and do not consider the plight of these women and their children to be society's problem; and at worst call the women criminals Rather then the society which made it a necessity for some women to become this.

## HEAVEN

Heaven are those regions in outer space in our solar system, which contain colonies of six higher evolved species. In our solar system, Heaven are located at the gravitationally stable points in the Earth-Sun Gravitational System, called the, " Lagrange Points. "

Our Local Star Group consist of many stars, solar systems, and planets. Only our earth in this Local Star Group contains intelligent lifeforms. Our earth is the ancestral birthplace of some seven higher evolved species still living in this Local Star Group.

The six species of higher evolved creatures still living in our Local Star Group in space colonies in our solar system, call their home in outer space, " Heaven". Their heaven contains a society called the Pantheon, and their government is called a Matriarch-ate.

As used in The Book Of CEBAGII, "Heaven" always refers to a place in the TemporalSpacial Energy Material Realm ( the realm of creation ), and not the Creator Alpha Omega.

*      *      *

## HEDY LAMARR

Hedy Lamarr( born Hedwig Eva Maria Kiesler ) is a Demigod-dess of our sect. In her last human life she was born on November 9, 1914. She was a actress, inventor, and film producer. In 2014 Hedy Lamarr was inducted into the Nations Inventors Hall Of Fame. She died on January 19, 2000.

Deification:

Deification is the identification of a Associated-Mind in a human being as a Demigoddess In Waiting, who upon delegation from the material being, transitions to Demigoddess, and is worshipped by our sect and others.

Demigoddesses are creatures much like ourselves, they are

mortal, imperfect, and a stage in the long progression of the Immortal Minds to Divinity.

In the secession of lifeforms, the Demigoddess is the next higher stage after the human form. Immortal Minds which perfect in human form, shall become Demigoddesses after the end of their last human physical manifestation.

RULE I:

EVERY HUMAN BEING WHO PERFECTS WILL BECOME A DEMIGODDESS.

Some of the Other Demigoddesses Of This Sect:

Jeanne D' Arc, (?)

Helen of Troy, 7th century BC.

Naked Benzaitan (?)

Amelia Esrhardt, ( 1897 - 1937 )

Josephine Baker, (?)

Misty Copeland, September 10, 1982

Herriot Tubman, (?)

Tracy Edwards, September 5, 1962.

Florence Nightingale, (?)

*       *       *

Helen of Troy, ( Helen, Helena, Beautiful Helen, Helen of Argos, Helen Of Sparta. ) is a Demigoddess of our sect. In her last human life she lived sometime in the 7th century BC. She was considered the most beautiful women in the world, and the daughter of the god Zeus and the human queen Leda of Sparta.

The Cult of Helen:

After her transition, Helen was worshipped as a goddess at her shrines; Platanistas, on the banks of the Eurotas at Therapne, Attica, Rhodes, London, and St. Pierre &Maglogon the French Asset in North America.

Deification:

Deification is the identification of a Associated-Mind in a human being as a Demigoddess In Waiting, who upon delegation from the material being, transitions to Demigoddess, and is worshipped by our sect and others.

Demigoddesses are creatures much like ourselves, they are mortal, imperfect, and a stage in the long progression of the Immortal Minds to Divinity.

In the secession of lifeforms, the Demigoddess is the next higher stage after the human form. Immortal Minds which perfect in human form, shall become Demigoddesses after the end of their last human physical manifestation.

RULE I:

EVERY HUMAN BEING WHO PERFECTS WILL BECOME A DEMIGODDESS.

Some of the Other Demigoddesses Of This Sect:

Jeanne D' Arc, (?)

Amelia Earhart, ( 1897 - 1937 )

Naked Benzaitan (?)

Hedy Lamerr, 1914 - 2000.

Josephine Baker, (?)

Misty Copeland, September 10, 1982

Herriot Tubman, (?)

Tracy Edwards, September 5, 1962.

Florence Nightingale, (?)

*          *          *

## HIERARCHY IN THE PANTHEON

The Pantheon And Earth:

This of the earths has been the birthplace of many higher evolved species. Seven of those species still exist. One species are the Homo Sapiens living only on this of the earths. The other six were known as the Gods by our ancestors, who have known of them due to their kind who still live on this earth to this very day.

The regions of outer space at the Langrage points in the Earth-Sun Gravitational System, are the locations of the spiritual communities called Heaven. It is there that the six higher evolved species now live, in what is called The Pantheon.

These six species are descendants of beings who once lived on this earth and who migrated to outer space after they developed a highly advanced civilization; leaving the hominids behind here on

this earth. Since that time all the hominids have been driven into extinction except for the Homo Sapiens.

The homo sapiens are the closest hominid species to the Lower Demigoddess species, and are the only hominids repro-ductively compatible with all six higher evolved species; produc-ing viable fertile offspring with various higher qualities then their homo sapiens parent. Because of this fact they have a extremely complex relationship with the other six species, and have been the subjective of much debate in the heavens.

The Homo Sapiens have played a major part in the fall of the Demigods; and the division which was a factor in the War In Heaven, and the Fall of the Great God Lucifer. Only through the expenditure of great resources, time, and labour has the Panthe-on save the Sapiens from extinction level events on this earth, several times in the last 100,000 years.

The six species of the Pantheon are arrangeable according to their relative levels of evolution, from most evolved to least evolved;

I.    THE MAJOR GODS:

The Great Scientists, Inventors, Intellectuals, andArtists of the Heavens. Do not directly provideservices to members of the Pan-theon.

    A.  The Universal-Gods.

    B.  The Celestial-Gods.

    C.  The Terrestrial-Gods.

II.    THE MINOR GODS:

The Sacred Vessels of The Creator Alpha Omega,and the Leaders & Civil Servants of thegovernment of the Heavens. The Teachers,Doctors, Counselors, etc., who directly provideservices to all the members of the Pantheon.

D. The Upper Demigoddesses

E. The Middle Demigoddesses

F. The Lower Demigoddesses

Members Of The Pantheon Living On Earth:

The War in Heaven, or War Of The Gods, was initiated by a member of the Celestial-God species known as Lucifer. At the time of the war, Lucifer was the sole Celestial-God in heaven, thus the highest evolved & the most powerful mortal creature in our Local Star Group. There are over one billion Local Star Groups, all having intelligent lifeforms.

The Demigods are a variation of the Demigoddess species, which is lacking in almost all of their higher qualities. One group of Demigods now living on this earth were the Watchers. The second group of Demigods now living on this earth in exile, are the Fallen Gods, who belong to the Kingdom of The Great God Lucifer.

The legendary Amazons of this earth are descended from the Heavenly Amazons, who were a transformed race of Special Demigoddesses who were born lacking in higher powers Demigoddess species naturally possess. The heavenly Amazons came to live on earth after the war in heaven to police Lucifer on earth. They are the only women of the Pantheon to come back from heaven and live on earth.

Children Of The Six Higher Evolved Species:

The human women have given birth to children of members of the higher evolved species here on this earth. There children have been called The Nephilim. They have terrorized humanity.

The Heavenly Amazons here on this earth have given birth to children fathered by human men. There children have been called The Xenomorphs. They have been great men and women. The most famous of their children are the legendary Amazons of earth.

*         *         *

## HIGHER EVOLVED BEINGS & HUMAN DESTRUCTION

Humanity has always lived on earth. Attempts by the Pantheon to remove human beings from this earth have more often result- ed in failure. Humanity is tied to nature; and the artificial world of space colonies have never been able to replace this earth.

The higher evolved species migrated to outer space and their colonies called " Heaven." over 75,000 years ago. 50,000 years ago The Watchers returned. Not long after that, those who lost the War In Heaven returned. All these higher evolved beings have the right to return because this is their ancestral birthplace.

Since the return of the higher evolved beings there has been a gradual dying off of intelligent species here on earth. Now Homo Sapiens is the last indigenous hominid on earth.

The higher evolved beings are not naturally morally superior

213

to homo sapiens, they are as capable of evil as the humans are.

The higher evolved beings have given humanity false religion, advanced science, and philosophies without value. These gifts have caused war, extremes of human suffering, the deterioration of the human condition, and genocide.

The misguiding of humanity by some higher evolved beings has been part of their objective to take control of this earth from humanity. They have sought to lead humanity to its own self destruction.

## HIGHER SPIRITUAL VALUES

Our Way Of Life is a set of practices bases on religious beliefs, which are knowledge obtained through spiritual experiences which seek to guide humanity in the realization of higher spiritual values, which include, but are not limited too, the following;

A. The Love Of Truth

B. Mastery Over One's Passions

C. Control Of One's Senses

D. Disinterested Self-sacrifice

E. Mercy & Kindness To All Creatures

F. Reverence For The Creator Alpha Omega

G. Help Others To Grow & Develop

H. Forgiveness

I. Humility & Charity

J. Pursuit Of The Supreme End

*       *       *

## HISTORY & MYSTERY

A immortal mind can produce dozens of physical manifestations in succession, and then experience each lifetime in its entirety. The history of humanity is the history of every living being today due to reincarnation.

Understanding the people of the past can help us understand ourselves by awaking a part of our memory which is normally inaccessible. That part which remembers our past lives!

We are, California's Indians Enslaved By The Spanish Missions

We are, Black Indian Slaves

We are, Natives Of The Bolivian Andes & Mayan Cities

We are, Amazon Tribes

We are, The Polynesian Islanders

We are, Citizens & Slaves of the Holy Roman Empire

We are, Peoples of Ancient Greece

We are, Peeples Of The Kingdoms Of North Africa

We are, The Germanic Tribesmen

*     *     *

## HUMAN BEHAVIOR

The subject of human behavior concerns the struggle between good & evil, the possible limits of freewill, perceived human needs and how to fulfill therm, the nature of love & hate, Noblesse Oblige, familial/social obligation vrs. personal dreams & objectives, right conduct, and higher values & aspirations. All these are questions we must address at some point in life. For

us there is applied religious beliefs & practices, to guide us in the fundamental sense.

Human behaviors are techniques including actions devised by human beings for dealing with the psychological forces generated by universal human biological drives instincts and impulses.

Natural human biological drives instincts and impulses, can not be held to be unacceptable in humane societies.

Certain behaviors can be held to be unacceptable by a society one becomes apart of. The acceptability of behaviors by society can be determined by various factors including;

Societal Factors:

A. Balance Of Degrees Of Necessities;
   1. Biological Necessity
   2. Social Necessity
   3. Personal Economic Necessity
B. Weighing The Balance Of Consequences
C. Culture, And Custom
D. Science & Medicine
E. Religion
F. Law
G. Widely Accepted Misconceptions

Variations in humane behaviors are also influenced by additional Subjective Factors including;

H. Personal Inclinations

I. Habitual Practices

J. Personal Beliefs & Misconceptions

K. Obligations

L. Wants &Desires( which are not the same ashuman biological drives instincts and impulses.)

In understanding our own body/mind we must make a clear
distinction between three types of compulsions in humans beings;

1. Biological; Universal & General Human BiologicalDrives
   Instincts And Impulses.

2. Psychological; Personal Wants & Desires.

3. Spiritual/Moral; One Is Driven By Ones MoralConscious
   To Carryout Certain Acts WithoutRegard As Too Any Rewards Or Punishments.

Living Religiously:

It is not simply answering to a higher authority, but actively
seeking to change in ways which allow one to hear and follow that
higher authority, which includes seeking knowledge of the nature
and purpose of existence, discerning ones flaws & work- ing on
improving oneself, finding higher values and living accord- ingly
and honestly. That is how we begin to acquire, believe, and
practice religion; And make it our way of life.

\*       \*       \*

HUMAN BEING

Acts of Creation:

The Creator Alpha Omega is the only real being. We are Immortal Minds, which are infinitesimal portions of the Creator Alpha Omega, without the Creator Alpha Omega's powers, and qualities. We are a lesser version of the Divine.

We Immortal Minds must acquire the Divine qualities, which for immortal minds are potentialities.

The Creator Alpha Omega has designed the forms and functions of all real things in the universe/creation. The immortal minds are the means by which the real things of the Temporal-SpacialEnergy Material Realm come into being, and are then briefly occupied by immortal minds, which give real things life.

Before the universe was, we were.

Human Beings: Homo Sapiens:

Homo Sapiens is a distinct species of the hominid family. The term, " Homo ", is Latin for, " human," which is derived form the Indo-European word for, " Earth ".

Humans have lived on earth for more then 250,000 years because of the continual creational processes. Perhaps for two million years. During our existence on this world we have endured

waves of natural catastrophic events, and we have escaped extinction only due to the intervention of the Demigoddesses in human affairs.

Although at this moment we are experiencing the universe through the physical manifestation we as an immortal mind has created; we have also existed as thousand of other real things, before today, and we will exist as thousands of real things in ages to come.

Human is only one stage in the progression of immortal minds to divinity.

\*       \*       \*

## HUMAN HYBRIDIZATION

It is an undeniable truth that Human Hybridization has occurred throughout this earth, in prehistoric times up to the present; Beginning with the Watchers arrival, and the introduction of foreign species DNA accelerating with the Exile the Fallen Gods to this earth, after their War In Heaven.

The Major Types Of Hybrids On This World:

A. The " Pure Bloods ", from which all others are derived!;

    1. Nephilim; " Redheaded Children Of The Gods."

Parentage;

        a. Demigods (male) & Homo sapiens women

        b. Watchers

        c. From amongst the Fallen gods.

        d. Xenomorphs; " Women Of Renown. "

Parentage:

Demigoddesses (female) & Homo sapiens men.

        a. from old world when D. & humans livedtogether.

        b. from Heavenly Amazons.

B. Xenomorph-Nephilim. The most important of the derivative forms are these very powerful crossbreeds.

The Xenomorphs, by definition, have distinctive traits unlike both of their parents; ( Human Males & Demigoddesses ). Some Xenomorphs are unusual in that they display new qualities which are synergistic, as well as almost all the general traits of their parents species to some degree.

The question which some have asked of the hybrids, is if they constitute a new higher species. Even though this seems to be the case, physical &intellectuals superiority does not mean that the intelligent being also has moral/spiritual superiority which is a matter of freewill entirely.

Homo sapiens have not been the superior species on this earth, and yet homo sapiens have survived where superior species have gone extinct. A greater factor is at play in the emergence and duration of all lifeforms in this universe!

*       *       *

## HUMAN MIGRATION & THE SPREAD OF RELIGION:

Key Belief:

The General Patterns Of Migration Of Human Beings Are The Same As The Patterns Of Dissemination Of General Religious Beliefs & Practices, Even When Those Beliefs Have Become Integrated Into The Local Traditions, Customs, and Beliefs, To The Degree That Their True Origins Have Been Suppressed And/Or Forgotten.

Key Belief:

True Religion Is Born Of The Personal Experience Of A Form Not Possible In Interactions With Humanity Alone, but Arise From Humanity's Experience of The Divine.

A Personal Definition Of Religion:

Religion is our subjective interpretation of our personal spiritual experiences, from which we derive a understanding of life, which makes living possible, and which gives life meaning, and which changes our fear of natural death into acceptance of reincarnation & transition.

True Religion must embrace a greater intelligent & powerful

authority over the universe which is the creator of all things which constitute the universe, which also includes the underlying time, space, energy, and matter.

True Religion must provide the means by which humanity can comprehend & communicate with the Creator of all things in the universe, interact with the Creator, and worship the Creator.

True Religion must give us a understanding of what we are, what life is, the purpose for Creation, the purpose of human existence, and the right way of life in order that we may achieve the purpose of life, or Supreme End.

True Religion is a rational coherent set of Beliefs & Practic- es from which we derive guidance in living correctly, which can be called a Creed, and includes Revelations, Histories, and Di- vine Laws, and the collective spiritual interpretations of others throughput human history who have known and worshipped the Creator Alpha Omega;

All these things held in common are the basis of a select society of people.

* * *

## HUMAN NATURE

Except for the case of very young children, there is not finite set of qualities which universally describe human nature, where characteristics vary amongst individuals in forms and magnitudes. The underlying forces driving variation in human nature originate in the Immortal Mind's response to life.

The human condition is an stage in the succession of physical states which the Immortal Mind will experience in its process of growth & development, which is a succession of stages.

Human beings are intelligent living beings, and each is a physical manifestations established and controlled by a Immortal Mind. The Primary Problem with Human Nature lies in their intelligence which increases human error;

A. Intelligence increases the size of the set of possible variations in the expression of freewill of a living being. Because of the limited knowledge and cognitive capacities of human beings in general, this increases the size of the set of possible errors that the living being can make.

B. To compensate for this adverse potential, humans must by collective learning develop a reliable techniques for problem solving which include the determination of self error.

Describing The Complex Nature Of Human Error:

1. Human nature is not only defined by the set of natural needs & inclinations of the species, but by the tendency to error, and the tendency to repeat the same errors, due to individual limits on cognitive capacities.

2. It is defined by complex desires and their tendency to increase the human rate of error.

3. Finally it is defined by the deviation from Divine Guidance and the adaptation of manmade religion, philosophy, sciences, arts, and pleasures, which collectively account for the most tremendous humanly irreconcilable errors.

The Human Pursuit Of Happiness is in diametrical opposition to The Gross Level Of Human Moral Development, at all ages in the human being, until as they say, they grow a soul.

The Gross Level Of Human Moral Development is retarded by the intellectual factors leading to human error; combined with the complex emotional needs giving rise to detrimental desires of human beings in general. The area of spiritual development is were those factors are comprehended and successfully managed, by the assistance of greater beings.

The Progression Of Creation:

The Immortal mind must fully comprehend human nature, if it is too develop the proper means to successfully deal with the nature of human beings in each human life it establishes and lives via reincarnation; this absolutely must be accomplished before that Immortal Mind can achieve perfection in the human physical manifestation, and transition to the next higher lifeform.

*       *       *

## HUMAN PLANNING

The qualities of any society are related to the qualities of the peoples who are that society. It is possible for the institutions of a society to increase the individuals success at improving them-selves, and at their successful growth & development; Physically, Intellectually, and Morally/Spiritually. Various institutions facilitate various practices which are designed to proved the best chances of success.

    A. Physically:body/mind disciplines taught be experts, such as various forms of Yoga, Tia Kwan Do, Running, Swim-ming, Hiking, Weightlifting, and other Olympic sports.

    B. Intellectually:education should be free and available to all persons along with the necessary resources for pro-moting best individual achievement.

Libraries, Museums, Theater, Publishing, Special Interest Groups.

    C. Morally/Spiritually:Life provides much opportunity for one to develop a understanding of life which enables us to interact with consideration of right and wrong conduct in all contexts. Our moral conscious guides us with the voice of the Divine. The intellectual aspect of morality is addressed by the lectures of the temple priestesses and meditations.

Longterm Institutional Practices:

Heath & Education as Major Area of Concentration & Major Expenditures:

The government provides scientific assistance in human re-production which enables each child born to have been the result of;

a. extensive scientific planning,

b. implemented with sperm & ova collection,

c. sample examination & classification,

d. computation optimization of selective in-vitro-fertilization of sample tissues.

e. womb implantation

f. prenatal & postnatal care for mother & child with as-sistance of wet nurses, pediatric doctors, gynecologist, obgyn, and nutritional experts.

*    *    *

## HUMAN TRANSITION TO HIGHER FORMS

We each are an Immortal Mind which is an infinitesimal part of the Creator Alpha Omega. The collection of Immortal Minds is Infinite, because everything in the universe is associated with an Immortal Mind when it comes into existence.

Every living thing in the universe has an Immortal Mind associated with it.

The Creator Alpha Omega and the Immortal Minds within the Creator Alpha Omega are the Only Real Being; all other things are Transitory Momentary Creations.

Progression Of The Immortal Minds:

We the Immortal Minds are of the Creator Alpha Omega, but we do not have any Actual Divine Qualities. The Divine Qualities exist in us as Potentials, until we acquire each Divine Quality during our association with the things in Creation when we perfect those things.

The First Physical Manifestation which a Immortal Mind establishes is a Fundamental Elementary Particle. The Immortal mind will progress through every stage of physical manifestations.

Examples of the sequence of stages in creation, which the immortal minds progress through:

Particle

Atom

Molecule

Aggregate Matter

Single Celled Organisms

    Plant

    Insect

    Fish & Bird

    Animal

    Human

    Demigoddess

The Human Being is one of the stages the Immortal Minds must perfect before moving on in the progression. The next higher stage after the Human Being is the Lower Demigoddess species. Before transitioning to that stage, the Immortal Mind must unite with multiple other Immortal Minds, and form a single greater Immortal Mind. This is the perquisite for all transitions to higher evolved forms.

Particle. 100,000,000,000

Atom. 10,000,000,000

Molecule. 1,000,000,000

Aggregate Matter. 100,000,000

Single Celled Organisms. 10,000,000

Plant. 1,000,000

Insect. 100,000

Fish & Bird. 10,000

Animal. 1,000

Human. 100

Demigoddess. 10

*       *       *

## HYBRIDS

Hybrids are the viable fertile offspring of the reproductive union of the a member of the species Homo Sapiens, and a member of any of the six species of higher evolved beings living in our Local Star Group.

The species Homo Sapiens has the unusual capacity to breed

with all six higher evolved species, but however only the three species of Demigoddesses exhibit a sexual interest in & attraction for humans.

The Two Primary Hybrids:

A. NEPHILM are the result of sexual union between human women and Demigods.
   1. the children of the Watchers
   2. the children of the Fallen Gods exiled to earth
B. XENOMORPHS are the result of the sexual union between human men and Demigoddesses.
   1. the first human temple priestesses
   2. the Earth Amazons

The Secondary Hybrids:

C. XENOMORPH-XENOMORPH are the very powerful derivatives, which are the result of breeding between of two Demigoddess hybrids (above).
D. XENOMORPH-NEPHILM
E. NEPHILM-NEPHILM, the least powerful of the derivatives.

\*       \*       \*

## HYPATIA, of Alexandra

Another Demigoddess of this sect.

Hypatia was a eloquent lecturer on Greek philosophy In Alexandria, Egypt. In 415 she was massacred by a mob who accused her of promoting forms of paganism. She was renowned for her intelligence, purity of life, and astonishing beauty.

Hypatia is regarded as one of the fifty most important persons in world history.

\*     \*     \*

|

\*     \*     \*

## ICE ASTEROIDS-1

KEY BELIEF:

GLOBAL CLIMATIC CONDITIONS RESULT FROM NATURAL ASTRONOMICAL PHENOMENA, AND ARE INDICATIONS OF THE NEAR FUTURE CONDITIONS OF THE EARTH'S ATMO-SPHERE.

The solar system is a vast region of outer space in this Galaxy, known as the Milky Way Galaxy. The solar system has a central star, the Sun, which by virtue of its immense mass, holds all the other heavenly bodies in orbits confined to this region of space. Those other heavenly bodies consist of;

A. Eight Major Planets

   1. The inner planets, ( small Rocky bodies)

      a. Mercury

      b. Venus

      c. Earth

      d. Mars

   2. The Outer planets, (Gas giants)

a. Jupiter
b. Saturn
c. Uranus
d. Neptune

B. The Minor Planets. (Asteroids)
C. The Natural Satellites of the planets.
D. The Comets
E. The Orrt Cloud.

It has been scientifically established that asteroids (of all sizes and compositions) are the leftover materials from the creation of this solar system. These heavenly bodies are hundreds of millions of years old, as old as any planet in our solar system. Asteroids number into the billions.

There are Four Groups of Asteroids which concern us here on this Earth;

A. Trojan Asteroids
B. Near Earth Bodies
C. Main Asteroid Belt ( MAB )
D. Orrt Cloud

Asteroids distributed within this solar system in small concentrations are the, (A). Trojan Asteroids, and, (B). Near Earth Bodies;

A. These being the Trojan Asteroids which have orbits along with the planets since the beginning of creation. Scientist speculate these bodies can tell us secrets about the history of our solar system, like the core samples from Antarctic glaciers.

B. The Near Earth Bodies of the inner solar system which have given the DarkSide of the Moon its hundreds of millions of craters. The presence of the Moon has protected life on earth by shielding us.

The solar system is home to two regions of outer space containing large concentrations of asteroids, the, (C). Main Asteroid Belt ( MAB ), and the (D). Orrt Cloud;

C. The Main Asteroid Belt ( MAB ) between the orbits of planet Mars and planet Jupiter, is the first of two large concentrations of asteroids in this solar system. These MAB asteroids have a total mass of less then that of the earth's Moon.

D. The second large concentrations exist are the edge of the solar system in a vast region of outer space, know as the , " Orrt Cloud ". In this region which is one light year in depth, exist billions of asteroids, whose exact to- tal mass is unknown.

The natural processes of planetary formation have resulted in a difference in composition for the planets which is related to their relative placements in the solar system.

The planets composed of heavy elements of the periodic table are in the Inner Solar System. The gas giants of the outer solar system are composed of the lighter elements of the periodic table.

The composition of the asteroids of our solar system, is similar to that of the planets in our solar system;

A. Heavy Metals-asteroids closest to the central star ( Sun ).

B. Metals And Stone (Silica)-asteroids nearer to this earth.

C. Lighter Elements And Complex Carbon Compounds-asteroids beyond the MAB.

D. Water, And Low Density Hydrocarbon Compounds-asteroids on the edge of the solar system.

Let us call these the, " ICE ASTEROIDS "

Asteroids orbits are not permanent. Certain other heavenly bodies of large mass can cause the orbits of the asteroids to degrade. Asteroids whose orbits are disturbed will fall into the inner solar system under the gravitational pull of the Sun.

From time to time asteroids will collide with this earth. Metallic and Stony asteroids will survive entry into the earth's atmosphere, and reach the surface.

Asteroids which fall from the Orrt Cloud into the inner solar system, obtain large amounts of kinetic energy, as the Sun's gravitational pull continually accelerates them before they reach the earth. Some of these asteroids separated from the Orrt Cloud, will have close encounters with this planet. Ice asteroids will vaporize upon entry into the atmosphere, and never reach the surface.

For many decades astronomers were unaware that earth has been continually bombarded with Ice Asteroids of all sizes since the beginning of creation of this planet. These asteroids now originate in the Orrt Cloud, which means that the Orrt Cloud is both enormous, many many times the size of the planetary region of the solar system, and it is also unstable.

It was the NASA space exploration programs, using sophisti-

cated robotic probes, which first acquired scientific data while in space looking back at the earth, which latter was analysed and revealed this previously unknown phenomena, and conformed the Russian theories in part.

The Vaporized Ice Asteroids release large quantities of water into the earth's upper atmosphere. The released water is what the space probes actually detected when they looked back at the earth in the higher spectrum which water naturally absorbs. From the sea level observatories this was not distinguishable due to the natural presence of water in our atmosphere.

*     *     *

## ICE ASTEROIDS-2

The Human Race Is in danger. Perhaps it is necessary to understand the science before one can understand the problem.

UNDERSTANDING ICE ASTEROID BOMBARDMENT:

The Orrt Cloud Asteroids:

Ice Asteroid Bombardment is a natural phenomenon.

A puzzle has been the actual mechanism responsible for the deorbiting of bodies in the Orrt Cloud. The existence of large heavenly bodies larger them Pluto and beyond Pluto Orbit, has lead to the realization that planet sized bodies exist beyond Pluto in the region of outer space called the Orrt Cloud.

Like the Earth-Moon gravitational system, in which the Moon's orbit is being upset by the more massive Earth, large heavenly bodies within the Orrt Cloud can destabilize the orbits of the much less massive Ice Asteroids. Their gravitational interactions would bounce the Ice Asteroids around like billiard balls. This would be a extremely slow continuous process, but it would supply the asteroids for the natural cycles of Ice Asteroid Bombardments here on this Earth.

The Dance Of The Asteroids delivers two important things to this earth in magnitudes which alter the face of this planet;

1. WATER accumulated in the atmosphere before falling to the earth as precipitation. The isotopic concentration of

    deuterium in global precipitation, would distinguish earth water (lower ratios of isotopic hydrogen-2 / hydrogen-1) from extraterrestrial water ( highest ratios of isotopic hydrogen-2 / hydrogen-1 ).

2. THERMAL ENERGY imparted to the atmosphere, fueling extreme activity in atmosphere and global warming.

The two main factors are the following;

a. Asteroids Mass, ( Ma).

Asteroids come in all sizes. As small as a grain of sand, and as large as hundreds of miles across. From the diameter of the body, we can calculate it's volume (Vol) and mass (Ma). This tells us how much water is in the ice asteroid.

b.  Asteroid Quantity, (Qa)

Small Asteroids occur in groups often because large asteroids are broken up as they pass through the inner solar system. The quantity of asteroids is a key factor in their impact of the condition of the Earth's atmosphere, and on the Suns low density plas- ma-corona which transmits all the light and heat into the solar system. Water in the area surrounding the Sun will absord radi- ations.

The Ice Asteroid Bombardment is continual, but not of a con-stant magnitude. The activity varies between two extremes. Their are periods of very minimal activity, and there are periods of cat-astrophic global events. Looking closely at this we saw a combi-nation of multiple cycles, and that this was a consistent feature of the phenomena on this earth.

Based on longterm observations and the collection of data, a basic theory was established. In theory the activity can be divisi-ble into five natural cycles;

Natural Bombardment Cycles:

COMBINED CYCLE; max(s). (Fc), (Qa), & (Ma)

This being the total composite measurement of

activity level. Cycle peaks can coincide with

species extinction & climatic catastrophes,

such as the Great Deluges.

Component Cycles:

I.    1st; HOURLY;maximum. (Fc); minimum (Ma)90.0% level of activity.

II.   2nd; DECADE;lower trains. Values7.0% level of activity

III.   3rd; CENTURY;intermed. (Fc), mean. (Ma)2.0% level!of activity

IV.   4th; MILLENNIUM;upper trans. Values<0.1% level of activity

V.   5th; ~18, 000 yrminimum (Fc), maximum (Ma)< 0.001% level of activity.

These Cycles are wavelike phenomena when graphed over time, producing a logarithmatic curve, illustrating the sudden acceleration of the magnitude of this phenomena, which we know today as the acceleration in global climatic change. The acceleration indicating the shift from one set of cycles to another much more intense combination of cycles.

KEY BELIEF:

THE UPPER AND LOWER LIMITS IN ICE ASTEROID BOMBARDMENT MAG. & LEVEL OF SEVERITY, PRIMARILY BASED ON THE VALUES OF VARIABLES DISCUSSED, ARE WE BELIEVE, SYNCHRONIZED WITH THE EXTREMES IN CLIMATIC ACTIVITY AND GLOBAL MEAN SURFACE TEMPERATURE INCREASE.

\*        \*        \*

## ICE ASTEROIDS-3

THE FINAL THOUGHTS

'' The Sky Is Falling!''

WHAT ALL THIS COULD MEAN FOR ALL OF HUMANITY:

The world is full of the artifacts of past great civilizations which are no more. There are impossible to imagine and build monumental cities, temples, and pyramids. There are objects which were made by a technology far greater then the current state of

art. All these remain, but the people and civilization have disappeared off the face of the earth.

If all we accomplish in the brief time our civilization dominates this earth, are empty monuments, then the value of this current civilization is highly questionable.

If we can prevent these nations from disappearing off the face of this world. If we can prevent the extinction of humanity. If we are not the last generation of humanity on this world. Then we may have another chance to accomplish something of meaning in our lifetime.

Second chances are rare as super novas on Mondays. But this just might be the one;

I. A Pending Natural Catastrophe Uniting The World?

II. A Refocussing Of Humans Attention On What's Truly Important ?

III. A Human Effort To Stop A Catastrophe, Which If We Succeeded Would Also End All Wars?

THE BEST SCIENCE CALLED INTO PLAY:

The scientific confirmation of Orrt Cloud Ice Asteroid Bombardment here on this earth, would be of first importance to everyone. The world would want to work together to discover how many days the human race has left to live. This would be a International Science Project with a clear objective everyone on earth could see as important.

The scientific confirmation of Orrt Cloud Ice Asteroid Bombardment here on this earth, would be difficult to obtain from sea level. Robotic bases on the Moon and additional ones in Earth orbit, would continually collect samples over years. These would provide precise data to chart the phenomena and its cycles.

A space probe to the Trojan Asteroids would teach us about the history of our solar system. Another space probe mission to the Orrt Cloud would quantify the present danger.

THE COST of such a Space Science Project would be;

A. less then the trillion dollar twenty year war in The Mideast.

B. less then was Spent on the last four Space Missions in

search of Martians.

C. less then the cost to build another useless space station.

D. less then the cost of upgrading our nuclear arsenals, which Congress has already approved.

The Next Step:

Data from these robotic observation post would enable the government to convince all nations of the clear and present danger from space, and encourage all nations to work together on a plan to save humanity.

Once it becomes clear that it will be an extinct level event which no one will survive unless we all combine our efforts, people would see that they truly need one another; that this is the only way to survive.

For the next twenty years all the nations on this planet, would have too stop spending their money on weapons used to kill one another. All nations would combine their best human experts, engineers, scientist, and their financial resources, and work as one people to save humanity

\*        \*        \*

## ICONS

Icons: ( essential tools for the elevated spiritual state.)

1. a physical representation of a actual physical manifestation associated with a Demigoddess of this sect; Used in worship, ceremonies, rituals; where it is assumed to become a vessels for the Demigoddesses, although the icon is incapable of speaking or motion.

2. a physical representation of a kind of physical manifestation which is a model for a kind of being, used in ceremonies, in prayers, in combination with other models & practices; Used to focus thought-energy.

Icons can not represent the Creator Alpha Omega, icons can only represent things in creation, and not the Creator.

Icons are created using advance printing technologies, such as three dimensional printing. Images can also serve as icons. Icons are the most perfect images or statues artistically possible, because they represent Demigoddesses more perfect then humanity, and the better attributes of creations. Imperfection is not acceptable in iconography.

Once an icon has been used in a religious practice it becomes a holy object, and must be treated accordingly as if it is the thing it represents, because it has become that thing in the religious ceremonies.

\*        \*        \*

## ILLUSION OF PERFECTION

The immortal minds, what we truly are, are associated with physical manifestations, whose form and functions were pre-determined according to Divine Design & Intent. The immortal minds must fully develop their associated physical manifestation to the highest level possible for that stage of the immortal mind. Thus the limits of body are limits caused by the limits of the As-sociated-Mind.

When the immortal mind is approaching the perfection of the physical manifestation, sometimes the immortal mind sees itself as perfection. It sees itself as greater then all other things around it and in the world. The immortal mind develops the illusion of perfection.

The greatest flaw is our inability to recognize our own flaws and our own imperfection. This failure leads us down a road di-verging from truth and reality, with self-righteous convictions, and a godlike desire for power over the, " inferior " people, all around us.

\*        \*        \*

## ILLUSION OF SEPARATION

The Condition Of The Human Perception Of Reality:

The illusion of separation is due to our misconception about what we are, due to the teachings of false religions, and the teachings of our primitive sciences. We accept these things as true without fully questioning them.

We are willing to fight one another over things we need or desire, believing that there is only enough for one, not realizing that there are not two, there is only one, not realizing that we are at war with our self. We are fighting our self in the mirror, believing it to be another person.

The Unknown Truth About What We Are:

We are immortal minds within the Creator Alpha Omega, who is the only real being. Because we are parts of the one being we are one being. We are under a delusion the result of our observation of the TemporalSpacial Energy Material Realm.

When we observe Creation we see not one thing, but rather many many things. We fail to realize that creations are produced by the immortal minds, and creations are transitory physical manifestations. We are not the temporary things we observe, we are not the body with a name, and which lives for a century then passes away.

The Spiritual Realm is that place were the immortal minds appear to exist outside of the Creator Alpha Omega. It is a house where we gather, talk, and live together. But it too is a creation which the Creator Alpha Omega has made for us.

True Religion Gives Us True Understanding:

When we transition to the next higher form, we first must unite with multiple other immortal minds ( our soulmates ). The union leads to the emergence of a!single immortal mind, but this is also an illusion. We have always been one immortal mind, and as we acquire divine qualities we slowly, ( in small stages called pro-gression ) grow more aware of what we actually are!

*  *  *

## IMMORTAL MIND AS DISTINCT FROM BRAIN

The only real being is the Creator Alpha Omega. We are not human beings, we are the infinite collection of infinitesimal im-mortal minds within the singular infinite eternal & immortal Cre-ator Alpha Omega.

Human beings are creations consisting of a physical manifes-tation established by a immortal mind, which then controls that physical manifestation for the duration of its human life cycle.

While the immortal mind is controlling the physical manifes-tation, the physical manifestation exhibits signs of life, and the immortal mind is referred to as the Associated-Mind.

Within the created physical manifestation is a organ called the brain. The brain major functions include the following;

1. autonomous control over basic vital functions of the phys-ical manifestation, and,

2. provide the physical means by which the Associat- ed-Mind is contained and controls the voluntary and the higher functions of the physical manifestation.

The Brain is not the person. The person is the Associated-Mind in the brain, which is a immortal mind.

The death of the physical manifestation occurs at the point of permanent separation of the physical manifestation and the immortal mind. The physical manifestation continues to exist as a object which no longer exhibits signs of humans life, but does have signs of lower bacterial life in its stages of decomposition.

*       *       *

## INTERACTIONS BETWEEN DEMIGODDESSES & HUMANS

The Homo Sapiens species has always had a extremely close relationship with the three species of Demigoddesses. It is a re-lationship which is 100,000 years old, and has grown even more complex as all the other hominid species became extinct.

The Demigoddesses have always communicated spiritually with humans, and this remains the only means after this planet became the place of exile of the Great God Lucifer and the other Fallen Gods after the War In Heaven.

The degree of spiritual interaction is determined by the role which the individual plays in the spiritual community, the particu-lar personal needs behind the seeking to communicate, and she purpose the Creator Alpha Omega has for the individual.

## ISOGYNIC BEING

The Three species of Demigoddesses are tripartite beings, because they can shapeshift between the things genders;

1. Female-Male
2. Male
3. Female

The Female-Male state is that of a Isogynic Being, having fully functional reproductive organs of both genders ( female-male );

A. faloppian tubes,
B. overies,
C. uterus,
D. cervix,
E. vagina,
F. external vula,

And,

G. Penis
H. Testicles
I. Prostate

These were natural characteristics of their higher species, and their unique hormonal cycles produced by their endocrine system, prevented the adverse complications seen in mutations or Abnormal Sexual Development amongst Homo Sapiens.

The Demigoddesses are the basis of poly-gender Gods in  the

oral folklore of the prehistoric peoples. Our ancestors, who worshipped the Demigoddesses, were taught by them too understood their Isogynic& Tripartite nature.

The Demigoddesses understood this fully reproductively functional nature gave them a mental stability, calmness, and tranquility, which is called their " Balanced Nature. "

\*　　\*　　\*

J

\*　　\*　　\*

## JOAN OF ARC

Joan Of Arc : ( French: Jeanne d'Arc; " The Maid of Orleans "; "Maid of Lorraine " ). Born in Domremy, France; 1412. Transitioned 30 May, 1431.

Jeanne d'Arc is another Demigoddess of this sect. In her last human lifetime she lead the French army to victory against the invading English army, she placed a French king on the throne, and she revived the sense of hope which the French people had lost in the long war they endured with the English. It is not so much her extraordinary accomplishments, but her resolve to serve a higher purpose and sacrifice her own happiness & life for the well being of so many others, bringing their human sufferings to a conclusion.

We all will become Demigoddesses upon perfection while in the human form. We need not do extraordinary acts to achieve this. The things we do which are indicative of the highest spiritual state, will not be recorded for history, and we will not become saints. The demigoddess in waiting has become something we all must someday become quietly and absolutely.

The deposition of the young women was like that of a philosopher, and she was a hero who did not seek to be elevated above her fellows & peers, her greatest wish was to serve a higher authority, the Creator, but she wanted for herself only a simple life, family, friends, and to live in a country at peace.

In her last human lifetime, she had communicated with those highest evolved beings, and followed their guidance which never

diverged from Divine Law, and Design & Intent.

\*        \*        \*

K

\*        \*        \*

## KINGDOM OF LOVE

Note: Leaving Earth In Order To Grow:

Herein the two kingdoms of love are briefly described, one kingdom is outer space, the other kingdom on earth. Both kingdoms consist of living intelligent species, who are the descendants of beings who evolved here on earth. These ancestors once lived together here on this earth long long ago.

The six species who migrated to outer space advanced much more quickly then the species who remained on this earth. In fact the six migrated species still exist, while on this earth all the many hominid species have gone extinct , with the exception of Homo Sapiens. Homo Sapiens has survived only due to the migrated species continual intervention of human affairs.

Thus the religious interpretation of history leads to this conclusion; The further advancement of any earth higher evolved species is dependant upon their willingness to permanently become a space faring species, and free themselves from the limitations of the earth environments & earth civilizations.

The Two Kingdom(s) of Love:

A.  THE HEAVENLY:

The spiritual community and society established in heaven, and governed by the sacred vessels of the Creator Alpha Omega, the three species of Demigoddesses; Were the primary concern of all citizens is;

  a.  to achieve the Supreme End;
  b.  to work on their perfection Physical,Intellectual/

      Emotional, and Moral/Spiritual;
  c.  to enable their immortal minds to continue inhe progression,
  d.  to serve as the guardians to this earth &humanity.

B.  THE EARTHLY:

The human spiritual communities on this earth, established by the Demigoddesses, governed by the temple priestesses, and having as their purpose to live in such a way as to facilitate the human achievement of the purpose of creation, the Supreme

End.

These communities ended the New Stone Age Tribalectic Culture under the Brute-Males. They civilized men, and educated all people in a way of life which was prosperous, peaceful, and elevated humanity above basic instinctual behavior.

This was the return of human civilization after its fall 250 years earlier during the last SolarDark event & Great Deluge.

The Temple Priestesses achieved this not by warfare against the Brute-Males, but by leading them into transformative spiritual experiences.

The New Civilization was built on Love and not on War!

The Demigoddesses have mastered that power and it's application through spiritual experiences.

\*         \*         \*

L

\*         \*         \*

## LAWS GOVERN ACTS OF THE DEMIGODDESSES, DIVINE

-

It is important that everyone understand that the formation of a society leads to interactions which lead to laws governing the people in that society, it is a matter of freewill that we decide to live by rule of law. Thus a spiritual community is guided by Laws;

A. Divine Law

B. Civil Law

C. Natural Law

we are guided by laws, believe in laws, and have undeniable faith in the ultimate lawgiver.

For over 100,000 years the three species of Demigoddesses have interacted with hominids, today with the last remaining hominid, the Homo Sapiens. First interactions were physical, when Demigoddesses and Hominids lived together on this earth. Then earth became one of he worlds of exile for the Fallen Gods, and Demigoddesses no longer permitted to come to earth, interacted with humanity spiritually.

All interactions with hominids were guided by Divine Laws, Civil Laws, and Natural Laws;

1. Do No Harm
2. Do Not Allow Harm To Be Done
3. All Action must serve the Supreme End
4. Noblesse Oblige between Demigoddess & Hominid. Higher evolve species caring for thee well being of the less evolved species.
5. Instinctual drives compelling the emotions of empathy & sympathy for the sufferings of humanity.

The observation of the laws transformed societies as it lead to the growth & development of deeper understanding and higher aspirations. These changes allowed the immortal minds to acquire additional Divine Qualities, and transition.

*    *    *

LIFE

Life appears as an active state of a biological material form. The appearances of activity result from the Associated-Mind producing continual real states in the limited TemporalSpacial Energy Material Realm. These continuous changes appearing in the form of a biological form or body. The physical manifestation itself

is subject to certain natural laws which are responsible for much of the appearance of activity.

The Immortal Mind dictates the sequence of activities of the physical manifestation. The lesser physical manifestation do not display life due to the lesser developed state of their Associat- ed-Mind.

Life therefore is a function of the Immortal Minds made visible through the resultant conditions of the physical manifestation.

It is also true that the entire universe is a reflection of the Immortal Minds activities in all the things which constitute the universe.

Life seems to appear at a threshold were the Associated-Mind has grown & developed the divine qualities that constitute a " living soul ".

*      *      *

## LOVE

Love Is A Energy Within Us Directed Outward Because It's Too Powerful To Contain:

Love Of Others

Love Of Family

Love Of Demigoddesses

Love Of The Creator Alpha Omega

Love In Group Marriages

Love Of Children

Love Of Life

Love Of Earth

Love Of Creation

Above we can see that our love matures, changes, and grows as we grow into more perfect beings over many reincarnations. Reincarnation is invisible to the mind limited to what can be seen.

Love is the instinctual identification of our self in others and them in us, even if we do not know that it is the non-physical being which we are sensing. When we can sense self in others and them in us, then we reach the stage of enlightenment in which we

understand we all are one being!

As we grow older, wiser, and more patient Love develops into " not a sacrifice", but a deep quiet caring for the one being all of creation is. That is love.

LOVE AS A INTELLIGENT FORCE GUIDING THE PROCESS OF NATURAL CREATION IN THE UNIVERSE:

At a certain point Divine Design & Intent creates intelligent living creatures having Freewill;

A. The intelligent life must decide that the purposeof creation is more important then their personalagendas.

B. The intelligent life must work to find a meansunder the circumstances to continually improvethe condition of cre-

251

ation.

The immortal minds become greater tools of creation, and their actions influencing all life on this earth, will be the intelli- gence which drives humanity as a force in creation driving it to ever higher levels:

Finally it is undeniable that love has spiritually elevated human beings throughout the history of this earth. The power of love is transformative, in unique mysterious ways.

\*   \*   \*

M

\*   \*   \*

## MALE-BRUTE

The fall of human civilization after the last SolarDark& Great Deluge, ushered in the New Stone Age Tribalectic Culture and the domination of humanity by the Brute-Males.

The Brute-Males were men who organized human communi- ties around the philosophy that " Might Makes Right!". The en- slaved women and children. They killed other men who were

made weaker then them, sometimes they killed them while they were still boys. They enjoyed harem as large as they could count. They held humanity back from advancing because they didn't want the world they had created to ever change.

The Brute-Males ruled unto the Demigoddesses returned and dethroned them. The Brute-Males were conquered not through

252

violence, but through transformative spiritual experiences, which transformer them from savages into civilized men, who valued and pursued higher aspirations.

Many ages later Merlin would speak of the day when knights were born of barbarians, and civilization was thought back by their civilized acts.

*     *     *

## MATRIARCHATE

Matriarchate;

1. a spiritual community lead exclusively by women, who are the religious leaders, the leaders of the civil government, and the social leaders.
2. a system of leadership in which males are forbidden to hold positions of authority over others.
3. a inheritance system in which the females are leaders of families, and lineage is traced through them.
4. the system of social organization in the heavens.

The demigoddesses species has the appearance of a single dominant gender, Female. But However; they are an isogynic gender, which combines the two split genders into one, the Female-Male.

After migration the other species who formed the Pantheon in heaven, accepted The Demigoddesses Government as the most efficient effective rational system of social management develop up to that point. It has been in effect now for 100,000 years; And it has been lead by Demigoddesses, and therefore considered by humans to be a Matriarchate.

It is unlikely that the spiritual communities called heavens, would have also been called the Kingdom Of Love, had there not been Matriarchates in heaven. The Matriarchate helped their community avoid violence, civil unrest, inequality, digression, materialism, poverty, and all the other suffering found to be universal to the Patriarchates.

God;

1.  A creature belonging to a higher level of evolved species, and exhibiting extraordinary attributes, making them capable of acts which are beyond human comprehension & imagination;

Categories:

   a.  Physical attributes
   b.  Intellectual attributes
   c.  Spiritual attributes & powers. (not moral.)

2.  any of the species evolved here on this earth, who in prehistoric times, lived amongst the hominids, and were known to our ancestors as having supernatural abilities vastly beyond what is humanly possible.

Pantheon;

the community of six higher evolved species which live in spiritual communities in outer space, and whose ancestral birthplace is this earth.

Our Local Star Group has been the home to multiple intelligent lifeforms. Today only seven higher evolved species remain. The species Homo Sapiens is the only higher evolved species remaining on this earth by choice. The other six migrated to colonies they built in outer space some 75,000 years ago. The six higher evolved species are mortal creature like the homo sapiens, but are traditionally called Goods, they include the following species;

THE SIX HIGHER EVOLVED SPECIES:

THE MAJOR GODS:

the highest level of evolution of any biological lifeforms in our Local Star Group. the highest stage in the progression known to

us, but we are sure that there are higher stages in creation/universe. we live in a tiny island in a vast space, what lies beyond this Local Star Group is a mystery to us.

VI. The Universal-Gods:

1. the highest level of evolution of anintelligent creature in our Local Star Group.

2. highest level of development of;

    a. Physical attributes

    b. Intellectual attributes

    c. Moral/Spiritual attributes

V. The Celestial-Godsthe most famous of which is The GreatGod Lucifer, who seeks the naturalextinction of the last hominids, the homosapiens.

IV.   The Terrestrial-Godswere known to other religious peoples bymany names, and who were worshippedby communities who lacked sciences &technologies and were
dependant on thecycles of nature for their survival.

THE MINOR GODS:

the sacred vessels of the Creator Alpha Omega, the Religious,
Governmental, Civil, & Social leaders of the spiritual communities
in the heavens of this Local Star Group.

III.   The Upper Demigoddessesthe three high priestesses of
this specieslead the Pantheon in heaven

II.   The Middles Demigoddesseshigh level of authority & re-
sponsibilities

I.   The Lower Demigoddesses

   1.   the lowest level of evolution of angod in our Local
Star Group.

   2.   lowest relative level of development of;

      a.   Physical attributes

      b.   Intellectual attributes

      c.   Moral/Spiritual attributes

   3.   the civil servants

Unlike in the Patriarchates, where " might makes right ." , and,
" natural instinct is the primary guide to human behavior ". The

Matriarchates were stable because of Rule Of Law, where law
was not based on a manmade constitution but rather on a Correct
Interpretation of the Divine Revelations:

Hierarchy Of Laws:

A. Divine Lawthe basis of all laws, social order, & govern-ment.( Universal Law. )

B. Civil Lawthe applied divine law to circumstances as theyexist and change over time, with a progressiveun-derstanding of human needs and evolvinghigher ethics & morality. ( Sect Law. )

C. Natural Lawart & science can be said to be observers,-Contemplator's, and expresser of the laws of thisTem-poralSpacial Energy Material Realm. Thesenatural laws have been negated by both Civil &Divine authority at times. But However theyremain essential to our basic understanding ofthe universe and humanity

\*        \*        \*

## MEANINGFUL LIFE

The modern religious belief in a single human lifetime for each human being, followed by an afterlife in either heaven or hell, is a dangerous misconception:

1. Because most people do not see their existence as something which is only momentarily human, they do not comprehend that they will have additional lifetimes after the current one.

2. The failure to recognize that they will life multiple life-times, causes them to despair over the history of this

current lifetime, and believe that they have failed to accomplish something of meaning in this lifetime.

The purpose of creation & existence of human life, is to grow &
develop to ones highest potentials; Physically, Intellectually, and
Morally/Spiritually. A succession of reincarnations gives us a succession of human lives, each lifetime have greater potentials then

the last lifetime.

Eventually we will reach the lifetime having the greatest potential for a human being. We will perfect as a human being. This will
enable the Immortal Mind to acquire additional divine qualities
and progress to the next higher lifeform.

Each Human Lifetime:

In each human lifetime the upper limit of what is possible to
achieve is different. We have lived a life of meaning when we
have lived according to a way of life that achieves our greatest
personal potential in that lifetime. Comparing ourselves to others
is a useless juster because we can not know their stage in the
progression of human lifetimes, we can only know our own!

\*        \*        \*

## IMMORTAL MINDS & EVIL

It is an undeniable fact that there are evil people in this world.
Every person is an immortal mind. Therefore immortal minds can
be either good or evil. The level of evolution has no bearing on
whether an being is good or evil. The Religious Interpretation Of

History & Mystery has shown us that gods can be evil.

The Religious Interpretation Of History & Mystery has shown us that gods can exert an influence over certain human beings under certain circumstances. Were theses gods are evil, their influence over humans often results in humans committing evil acts.

Higher evolved beings are not naturally moral/spiritually superior to lesser evolved beings.

*     *     *

## MONSTERS & GIANTS

The monsters and giants of this earth did not exist until after the War In Heaven, the Exile of the Fallen Gods, and the bat- tles here on earth between the Amazons and the Warriors of The Kingdom Of Lucifer. These transformed fallen gods were made by Lucifer to be equal the Amazons, and the defeat the Amazons in combat.

The Amazons were gifted with superior qualities including;

A. Extrasensory Perception

B. Superhuman Strength

C. Superhuman Stamina

D. Longevity Greater Then Any Creature

E. Instantaneous Healing & Regeneration

F. Super Intelligence

G. The Beauty Of The Goddesses

Killing an Amazon was extraordinarily difficult even for a Celestial-God like Lucifer. Lucifer once commented that he had killed the same Amazon nine times in one day, just to make sure that she was dead, and yet the very next day she comes back to fight again. What, he asked, must I do too kill an Amazon?

Lucifer said that the Demigoddesses had not taught the Amazons how to die. He promised that He would teach them. And so Lucifer made the first Monsters & Giants to do just that. The world has suffered monsters every since that day.

This is but one example of Lucifer's diabolical ingenuity, and as always He fails. The Amazons are still here, and still the thorns in Lucifer's crown!

*      *      *

## Murder

MURDER; the permanent destruction of the association between the Immortal Mind and the Physical Manifestation, by human action, and in a unnatural manner. Under circumstances where the action was not made necessary by the saving of a human life which was threatened with death by human hands.

Murder is a violation of Divine Law ( the cannon of the Creator Alpha Omega ).

Killing in and of itself is not Murder, when made necessary by a clear & present danger to human life, and under circumstances

where if one does not act to kill another, then that other person will committee an act of murder.

## DEATH & THE SUPREME END:

Without a doubt we are all relatively imperfect and we must all grow& develop to a highest level of perfection which is possible foot each living being, before we can transition toma higher state & form. Thus each life is essential because it is only through living that we grow & develop. THEREFORE THE UNNATURAL, UNTIMELY, UNJUSTIFIED TAKING OF ANY HUMAN LIFE, REGARDLESS OF HOW EVIL THEY MAY BE, MUST BE RECOGNIZED AS A VIOLATION OF DIVINE NATURAL AND CIVIL LAW.

\*       \*       \*

**N**

\*       \*       \*

## NUDITY

SYNOPSIS: Nudity is the lack of clothing in circumstances where it is customarily worn.

The mainstream religions require their adherents to avoid nudity. Their belief is that human beings are subject involuntary sexual behaviors when human nature is upregulated. That only through religious faith & practices is it possible to control man's assumed animal sexual nature

The major mainstream religions create a compelling force opposing religions having sex ethics contrary too the mainstream.

Kavin   Peeples

Our Society & Way Of Life:

The arts, literatures, and institutions of this society openly and publicly display nudity and sexuality because it has a acceptable function our religious based way of life. We divest ourselves of

the contradictory beliefs & practices of the mainstream society, which propagate abnormal thoughts & behaviors, and we replace those with truths concerning life and the purpose of life, and these enable us to live in a organized healthy subsociety.

The true religion achieves proper regulation of thoughts & behaviors not by covering up the human body, but rather through the correct understanding of life the CEBAGII gives us.

Let Us First Consider The Following Facts From Our Religious Interpretation Of History & Mystery:

1.  the sacred vessels ( demigoddesses ) are normally nude and it does not detract from their ability to lead the government of heaven, nor their other roles as doctors, counselors, teachers, artist & scientist, mothers, wives, sisters, citizens, civil servants, and soulmates.
2.  " as in heaven, so on earth ", is a simple slogan which means that our earth society is modelled after the heavenly society, which is over 100,000 years old.
3.  humanity lived in nude for 100,000 years and there was not a harmful effect on human survival nor did it prevent the development of civilization.
4.  nudity has been common in many civilized societies prior to the spread of western religions, in many regions of the

world were the climate and environment made clothing unpractical.

5. some religious practices of the sect are performed in nude as a practice dating back to the first performed by the demigoddesses who taught these to human beings.

6. a. celebratory type of social activity, such asceremonial dances & dramas.

7. clothing is not always required for protection, is not always healthy nor comfortable, doesn't prevent certain thoughts, doesn't prevent certain behaviors.

We believe that religion is life, and the practice of religion is like a symphony. The practitioners of the true religion, must familiarize themselves with all of the religion, and when all the parts are present only then can the religion achieve its objective. Then

they can begin the transformation which will allow them to live better lives through this true religion.

We today can look back in time, to a age long long ago, and to a place on the other side of the world, and you can visualize the world of CEBAGII and people and demigoddesses living this life, and you can see how they were, and we can be, at peace with themselves/ourselves and one another!

Notes:

1. in CEBAGII we believe strongly in the need for laws, and the obligation to obey laws in ones society. We do not endorse civil disobedience, but rather believe in the processes established to enable all persons to live according to their deeply felt religious

way of life, when it is done without the violation of the necessary laws of the larger society.

\*       \*       \*

O

\*       \*       \*

P

\*       \*       \*

## PARALLEL WORLDS

The term, " Earth ", is used to designate a planet which the Creator Alpha Omega, made into a place of exile for the Fallen Gods after the War In Heaven. The Fallen Gods were allowed right of return to their ancestral birthplaces. The Earths are only a few of the many many inhabited worlds throughout the universe. All those worlds which have been designated, " Earth(s) ", are quantum coupled to one another in such a way that events occurring on one Earth may also occur on some of the other Earths.

The related events do not occur simultaneously but are temporally offset.

This is an example of Temporal offset; An event occurring today on Earth-01, may have occurred several days ago on Earth-74, and will occur in two days on Earth-690. Temple Priestesses because they send so much of their life in the spiritual realm can calculate Temporal Offsets.

Parallel Events on multiple worlds, are the basis of the term

Parallel Worlds; But However, these events are not inevitable unless no one does anything to prevent them. The higher evolved beings establish spiritual communications between the priestesses of the different Earths in order to send them warnings, or what are also called premonitions, or emergency action messages.

The Pantheon wishes to reduce suffering in the universe by causing the earth's to not have the same histories. So that the tragedies of one Earth are not repeated on all the other Earths. They are not always successful, but however they always try!

Notes:

there is not a duplicate you on a duplicate earth

\*       \*       \*

## PERFECTION

Perfection is a personal achievement of the highest of ones personal potentials. It is the success of the pursuit of self improvement. It is the measure of ones best self. It is a religious obligation and part of the purpose of human creation and existence. We do exist simply to exist, without purpose, objective, comprehension of the meaning of life, and without a potential within us to live life better.

\*       \*       \*

## PRACTICES

It is impossible to elaborate in detail on every single religious practice, because they are not a finite and fixed set. Practices

change & grow, new ones emerge, and the old ones which are no longer needed are replaced. It's more effective to describe what a religious practice is, and how they come to be.

The Way Of Life consist of the spiritual community's application of the Primary Objectives & Prime Directives found in our system of religious beliefs & practices, too the current Temporal-Spacial Energy Material Realm conditions; too produce a set of multiple Valid & Effective Religious Practices.

THE KEY STAGES IN THE PROCESS:

I. Observe And Collect The Facts:

    a. The current human needs,

    b. The current human condition,

    c. The current environment, and,

    d. The Necessary States.

II. Determine The Set Of All Possible Actions Which Establish The Desired Outcome:

III. Eliminate Those Possible Actions Which Are Inconsistent With Religious Beliefs & Practices As Is Determined By Their Consequences & Implications, And/Or Their Nature:

Our Subjective Spiritual Experiences are essential in enabling us too clearly perceive reality through spiritual guidance & assistance.

Once we can look at our spiritual experiences as real events, then we can consider them to be objective factual evidence suitable for analysis. The belief that All Spiritual Experiences are either delusions or illusions, is the result of the secular false belief that only life as we know it can exist, and that the nonphysical realm is nonexistent; this belief blinds them to all factual evidence supporting the contrary.

IV. Through Trial And Error Determine The Optimal Set Of Actions:

V. Objective Assessment Of The Outcome Of Execution Of The Selected Actions, And The Suitability Of Those Actions For Inclusion Into The Established Set Of Religious Practices:

KEY RULE:

Valid & Effective Religious Practices are those particular goal directed actions (means), which are the most effective at facilitating the Primary Objectives:

A. The Supreme End,

B. The Purpose For Creation & Human Existence,and do so in a manner determined to be the most consistent with our Prime Directives;

C. The Divine Cannon and

D. The Divine Design & Intent.

as we find them in our body of Religious Beliefs.

The set of established religious practices are like a symphony. These practices are performed together, and together they create a particular physical mental and spiritual condition. When any practice is off or absent, it change the interactions and it will alter the outcome.

Often only those who fully comprehend the religion, can correctly perceive a failure to establish the necessary state.

Often those active practitioners within the spiritual community can not accurately perceive the actual state the spiritual community is in.

KEY BELIEF:

The Formation of Societies Having Valid & Effective Religious Practices, Is Vital To Human Survival & Continual Advancement.

The Human Species creates the complexity in the Human Condition. Often People selfishly demand of others much more then they can give, and often they give nothing to those in need. Throughout history People have enslaved and destroyed one another for no good reason.

But However People Need People! What would we be without human society, with out the company of other human beings?

Without other human beings we would live like animals. Though even now we live like animals who have learnt complex intricate tricks (customs, manners, morality, art, science, etc.). Every generation would live exactly like the last generation, like every generation before it.

Through sharing our knowledge, experiences, thoughts, understandings; we combine into one Race, and every member of that society is greater then they would have been had they never communicated with other peoples.

\*       \*       \*

## PRAYER

Prayer is when one immortal mind seeks to act through the spiritual realm to bring about a more desirable set of circumstances in the TemporalSpacial Energy Material Realm. It is often a form of communication between immortal minds of different species. Prayer is unnecessary for communication with the Creator Alpha Omega, because we are in the Creator Alpha Omega and part of the Creator Alpha Omega, only creation is the transitory thing, and it is that which we often seek to change. The Creator Alpha Omega seeks to change us.

*    *    *

## PROMISCUITY

We are born into a society which is structured in such a way as too make certain actions & ways of life necessary if you are to be allowed to exist in that society. The circumstances of society in general, are unhealthy, immoral, irrational, unjust, and contrary to the purpose of creation

Within a higher sub society, reproduction and sexual intercourse are unrelated. Science determines the next generation. Sexuality has become a interpersonal behavior which is too important for recreational purposes, but essential for human happiness and the gross quotient of happiness.

Only through the use of science has sexuality been cleaned of all its flaws and dangers. The complementary social organization facilitates a mature understanding of sex in relation to life, and eliminates the obsessional behaviors which are the basis of domestic violence.

Clearly society at large will never be able to advance to a more humane and pleasant sexual ethic, and there is no religious movement to encourage this type of social progression within society at large. This type of life, is greatly misunderstood & feared, and what it actually consist of is simply beyond their comprehension, be cause they lack the fundamental belief system to enable it too be properly practiced.

\*        \*        \*

## PROMISCUITY

Synopsis : A matriarchal ruled family in which the mothers practice promiscuity, is the optimal biological, and the most natural social arrangement. Due to the biological nature of physical manifestation ( homo sapiens ), a healthy human population requires the maintenance of highest possible level of diversity in the gene pool, which is achieved trough promiscuous intimate relations & interpersonal practices.

Narrative:

The religious practice of matrimony obstructs the achievement of high genetic diversity in the human gene pool, by lifelong pairing of one female to one male, and preventing sexual intercourse ( which is necessary for reproduction) with other males.

The family unit must consist of a women and her children, all of which are parented by different males. Matriarchal basis of society is reflected in this natural structure for the family unit.

The group marriage exist, but however it is the mothers in the group who possesses authority within the group marriage. Sexual relations are not restricted o the group members, but are restricted to the membership of the spiritual community at Large.

The behavior of individuals of age should also be naturally promiscuous. Men in particular, are made to be explorers of new geography and engage in sexual intercourse with foreign women, in order to achieve the widest possible distribution of genetic material in the human population as a whole.

The ability of a significant segment of any group of people to

survive naturally occurring lethal mutations of viral and bacterial agents, is directly proportional to the ability to respond to the infectious agent, with a wide assortment of immune system defenses. A multiplicity of defenses are only possible in a population of high genetic diversity.

The extent to which extraordinary intellectual abilities are found in a population, also is directly related to genetic diversity. While that same diversity gives rise to genetic base illnesses, the benefits to society of having geniuses present, enables productive intellectual labours which make the society more capable of caring for the handicapped members. The presence of the disabled, also helps children to develop greater empathy for others who are less fortunate then the selves.

The social practices ( which originate in the religion ) if they are to promote life not just of individuals but of future generations, must support ways of life, which fulfill the requirements of biology, and conform to the laws of nature.

Oba Kavii Lez Arah's Personal Narrative:

Often we human beings are unable to hear the voice of the Creator Alpha Omega within us, because our minds are under the influence of powerful & controlling delusions we have un-knowingly acquired in life. Let us define " Delusion ", as follows;

Delusion; an idea which controls both perceptionand behav-ior, and which forms in the mindbefore one acquires familiarity with certaintruths. Delusions are the products ofunique & abnor-mal life experiencesand/or cultural misconceptions, and whichis so powerful of an idea, that it alters yourperception of reality, by blinding you as tothe factual basis of the truth, and itthereby re-places the truth with a plausiblemisconception.

The readers of The Book Of CEBAGII, will note variations found in these writings which were compiled over an extended time period. That is expected to some degree.

Due to the present circumstances in which I find myself a pris-oner of the state, and the power of the compulsive religions which have for so long ruled this world and our larger society, ( which are all actually variations of one violent, dynamic, and controlling religion ) there is interference in the minds ability to operate ob-

jectively and with unmodified perceptions.

I did not belong to CEBAGII until late in life. I was raised in a society & culture dominated by three mainstream religions. I ac-quired a conditioned mindset.

The conditioned mindset habitually responds to certain external objective facts by simply ignoring their validity. It was not until I had been fully a committed Cebagiian for alomost two years or more, that this mental conditioning begun to dissolve and lose it's hold on me.

I now am "free", in that I can see and openly acknowledge that any religious belief and/or practice which is contrary to confirmed validated and established scientific fact, is invalid, and does not represent divine revelation, but rather is a product of human error!

illustrations: none

\*         \*         \*

## PERPETUAL DIGRESSION

DIGRESSION; the state of the immortal mind in which perfection in the physical, intellectual, and spiritual qualities of the kind, is interrupted by the exercise of the free will to oppose Divine Law, forgo pursuit of the Supreme End, and live in a manner which is contrary to the meaning & purpose of creation.

PERPETUAL DIGRESSION; is the extended duration of a state of digression up to the point of time in which death of the body occurs, as it is impossible to redeem oneself in death.

Perpetual Digression is followed by a reincarnation cycle which results in a rebirth in a lesser physical manifestation ( lifeform or species ).

The higher evolved creatures who are presently in Exile to earths, are in Terrestrial Immortality, which is temporary, and is in effect only as long as their feet touch earth soil each day. If they remain in digression during exile, and up to the end of exile, they will be absorbed by the Omega when all of the exiled are released. This means that they will cease to exist as Immortal Minds forever. This is the only way an Immortal Minds dies.

## PUNISHMENT

Punishment was not a practice given to us, nor does the Creator Alpha Omega use punishment as a tool in the progression of immortal minds. Enlightenment is the only way of guiding immortal minds to achieve the purpose of creation. We are immortal minds.

Punishment was invented by human beings, to control human beings, but not to improve them. Punishment also satisfies the compulsion some people have to hurt other people, Punishment is based of a flawed rational that allows them to justify the evil they desire to do to others humans beings.

```
        *        *        *

             Q
     *        *        *

             R
     *        *        *
```

## READER

'' Reader '' is a title given to a divinationier who is an expert  in the practice of Bibliographical Divination. The term is derived from the fact that the practitioner must read a book, before the divination is carried out on the memorized content of the book.

'' Pages '', who physically handle the books in the Temple Library and clean the book shelves, are not '' Readers ''.

*      *      *

## REINCARNATION;

1) The process in which; (a) a Immortal Mind permanently ceases to associate with one physical manifestation ( or form ) resulting in the cessation of life signs in that form; and then ( b ) that same Immortal Mind gives life to another physical manifestation ( form ) by establishment of a longterm association with that form at it's conception.

2) The process were by an Immortal Mind transitions from one physical manifestation to another physical manifestation, and thereby continues the Immortal Mind's growth & development, which consist of it's continuing to acquire additional divine qualities.

3) The death of one individual form followed by the birth of another individual form of the same kind, in which both individual forms share the same associated Immortal Mind.

Already prior entries have illustrated the progression of physical manifestations. We have seen how one form follows another, and how the immortal minds have been and will be all things. We are the immortal minds, and we are the life with real things, and for us existence shall never end, because we are within and part of the Creator Alpha Omega, the only real being, who has had no beginning and shall have no ending.

Reincarnation is the continuation of a immortal mind, in a succession of physical manifestations, of the same kind, until a stage is reached were the physical manifestation exhibits the perfection of the qualities which that kind is capable of. At that stage it is no longer possible to improve any further, so the immortal mind is rewarded with a Divine Attribute to add to its growing repertory , and allowed to progress to the next higher evolved physical manifestation.

## RECREATIONAL USE OF DRUGS & ALCOHOL

The Temple Priestesses introduced the spiritual community to drugs & alcohol in rituals, ceremonies, and in medical treatments. Never would any Temple Priestess participate in the use of drugs & alcohol to alter the disposition of people and induce pleasure or relieve stress.

The Temple Priestesses would never help people avoid addressing the problems in their lives which have made their lives unbearable. Nor as leaders of religion, government, and society, would the temple priestesses introduced legal recreational drugs & alcohol.

They would not have allowed their society to become a type of community were there was a degree of personal suffering compelling people to seek extreme forms of mental escape.

The future will be much more difficult then the present, as the world continues to change in ways we can not stop. We will simply have to deal with the difficulties. Those human beings who are dependant on drugs to cope weigh life, will not be able to cope when it's no linger possible to get those drugs.

*     *     *

## RELIGION & SECT:

The Religion: HELENISM

The General Universal organized way of life based upon the belief that;I. the universe was created by the Creator Alpha Omega, who;

   A. established all forms and functions in creation

   B. established the purpose of creation and existence of human life; and

   C. established the Supreme End.

   D. established natural laws to guide the non intelligent world,

   E. established Divine law & Cannon to guide the intelligent

world;

   F. that the way of life is a body of rational practices which are based on these beliefs, and all our higher aspirations naturally grow out of those beliefs & way of life, and made us a true civilised people.

The Demigoddesses:

All Immortal Minds which transition from human physical manifestations, become Demigoddesses. All Demigoddesses are concerned about humanity. Only a handful of the Demigoddesses, "come down", to guide the sects. They do not guide us forever, because they are mortal creatures/ and eventually these gods too die, and transition to higher forms.

The Role Of Helen Of Troy In Religion:

Helen of Troy became one of the three Central Demigoddesses of this religion. Every sect worships Helen of Troy, ( both the women & men practitioners of this religion ). Many people outside the religion have never learnt the full story of Helen's Life.

Helen's life, and to some extent that of all Greek women, exemplified the cultural hypocrisy in human civilization to this day, characterized by the struggle of women for their religious freedom, opportunities in society, and recognition of their worth as human beings.

Helen's qualities other then her heavenly beauty have received no mention in the history of the Greeks & Greek culture. Here are Some Truisms About Helen;

    a.  Helen never used her beauty as a tool to control others through their desire for her; but however others coveted her beauty and their desires caused her misfortune.

    b.  Helen did not have sexual liaison with multiple men, she was not adulterous, and she did not put her beauty on display.

    c.  Helen was loved by the people of her city-state, and she loved them back, with a love that was not base.

    d.  She loved all living things, and the beautiful earth. She was a loving wife & good mother also.

    e.  Finally she was a patron of the arts, and a sincere religious devotee to the Creator Alpha Omega and the Demigoddesses, and a friend to the Amazons.

f. Because of her beauty, Helen became a victim of involuntary cohabitation ( possession by demon, sent by a Fallen god who lusted for Helen, a women he could never ever have ), at the time of the Trojan War. Her husband & the men of Greece sacrificed greatly to rescued her and bring her home.

These are the kind of things which go unsaid in the popular fiction called '' history. ''

The Demigoddesses were known also as, '' The Goddesses of Love ''. Helen the child of Demigod ( one of the SolarDark Mission Watchers, and not a daughter of one of the rebellious Fallen gods in exile ), is still worshipped to this very day as a Demigoddess at her shrine in the homeland, and our temples around the world.

Helen lived in a world still deciding what it wanted to become. North Africa, Persia, Greece, it was a world of 100,000 gods, of thousands of religions, and hundreds of cults. Helen was in essence only human, and she lived her life trying to be a good human being. Helen practiced the Religion Of Love. Helen died long ago but she lives on in us, because the things she gave us will never die. Her name '' Helen '' became a official title of our religion, Hellenism. Her shrine also is a memorial to all women; And,

Yes;

Helen Became A Demigoddesses!

Sect: CEBAGII

The subgroup & select society within the religion who are distinguished from other sects by their recognition of a particular set of higher evolved beings, Demigoddesses, who they worship secondary to The Creator Alpha Omega.

Some of the Demigoddesses of the sect CEBAGII;

Helen of Troy

Joan of Arc

Misty Copeland

Herriot Tubman

Florence Nightingale

Amila Earhart

Hedy Lamarr

Tracy Edwards

Josephine Baker

Universal Culture:

This religion given to humanity became the first source of the major progressive ideas adopted by Greek culture, and later transferred in part to the rest of the modern western nations. This is referred to as Hellenism.

*       *       *

## RESURRECTION

Resurrection is a complex event because it cannot occur without the Creator Alpha Omega's assistance. But However; humans can not distinguish it from other natural processes which appear to be but are not Resurrection.

Resurrection is the restoration of the association between the immortal mind and the physical manifestation, which restores life to the physical manifestation, because the immortal mind is life.

In this age, the first Resurrection was Lucifer's at the time of the War In Heaven. What followed was his exile to his ancestral birthplace, and the long wait. Lucifer could leave at anytime if he could come to embrace the truth and follow the purpose for which he was created. But he chooses his prison instead, knowing how it will all end. How strange!

Human beings have learnt the art of body thievery, and they can transfer immortal minds from old bodies to young bodies, then kill the old body to prevent reversal of the transfer. Often the immortal mind is reincarnated with memory of its old body & life, because its body is still alive somewhere in the world, it never died it was stolen.

Sometimes reincarnation itself is mistaken for Resurrection. For example; the Celestial-Gods reincarnate but as adults, their species has no biological child stage, only a psychological childhood, which makes them children in an adult body, a very dangerous individual. Those who are unfamiliar with their biology, assume it to be Resurrection when its not.

*       *       *

S

*       *       *

## SEXUAL ENERGY

KEY BELIEF:

It Is The Design And Intent Of The Creator Alpha Omega, That All Creatures Have The Natural Capacity For Transformative Spiritual Experiences. This Capacity Can Be Enhanced By Certain Religious Sexual Practices & Exercises Which Are Part Of The CEBAGII Sex Ethic.

Narrative:

The Creator Alpha Omega gave all things their design, form, and functions which we are only beginning to understand; such as the human capacity for exceptional sexual energies. In addition to sexual reproduction, the energies of sexuality provide the means for ordinary persons to achieve beneficial elevated spiritual states.

Significant magnitudes of Internal Energies naturally accumulate In the waking state, when the immortal mind is stimulated by interpersonal interactions, in particular sexual stimulation, and can facilitate in Transformative Spiritual Experiences either intentional or unintentionally.

The Elevated Spiritual State (ESS):

Normally the transformative spiritual state is made possible by The Elevated Spiritual State (ESS). ESS is a relationship between the immortal mind and the physical manifestation. In this condition the immortal mind is no longer experiencing the physical, but rather the immortal mind is experiencing the spiritual.

ESS can lead to many different forms of beneficial experiences/conditions/events, including but not limited too the following;

{ Where: ( x), is the origin. }

A. Spiritual Guidance (sect)

B. Spiritual Communication (sect)

C. Protection (sect)

D. Acquisition of Knowledge (universal)

E. Healing; Spiritual and/or Physical (sect)

F. Alterations of the physical manifestation (Self)

G. Worship practices (sect & universal)

H. Divination (sect)

I. Remote viewing (universal)

J. Extrasensory Perception (sect & universal)

K. Knowledge of the past present future (sect only)

L. and much much more

The continual proper performance of all spiritual/religious practices of a sect, will establish a '' state of being '' similar too ESS, and enables the same type experiences for the practitioners.

The Transformative Spiritual State:

Human beings have Transformative Spiritual Experiences in a variety of Ways and; under a variety Circumstances;

A. In the waking state

1. spontaneous

2. stimulated by events

3. stimulated by natural environments

4. stimulated by manmade places

5. stimulated by interpersonal interactions

283

6. during certain exercises

B. In the sleep state

1. during divination in dreams

2. other altered states.

Hightened Internal Energies, especially those accumulated before, and during Sexual stimulation and sexual intercourse, often exceed the rational control of the human beings, and result in either constructive or destructive altered states. Constructive altered states can naturally serve a spiritual function, by provid-

ing the threshold energy required to achieve Elevated Spiritual States, but also provide the energies required to perform spiritual functions while in those elevated states.

In The Secular World:

Modern science, religion, and culture has denied certain knowledge, and generated certain misconceptions, prevent people from engaging in proper sexual practices, which serve the purpose for creation and human existence. The human species to a large extent are denied the potential spiritual benefits of sex.

*        *        *

## SolarDark MISSION WATCH POST

*        *        *

SolarDark:

the condition in which the Sun temporarily cease to emit electromagnetic radiations in the infrared and visible wavelengths, causing global cooling, glaciation, and extinct level events.

Great Deluge:

the condition in which ice asteroids from the Orrt Cloud, leave their stable orbits, travel into the inner solar system, collide with the earth's atmosphere, and cause torrential rains, flooding, and replenishes the earth's surface water deposits. When this occurs in conjunction with SolarDark, glaciation follows.

SolarDark Mission:

The Demigoddesses built a network of fusion powered orbital photospheres which emit infrared & visible wavelengths. These 13 satellites were placed in earth orbit, to provide for the equatorial communities.

Post:

The Demigods were given the job of watching over the network and the human communities. This decision was a mistake made in heaven. Unlike the Demigoddesses, the Demigods lacked all the higher qualities and were not sacred vessels.

The life in heaven did not serve any useful purpose for the

Demigods. They were unhappy in heaven, and when sent back to earth to watch over the human communities, the Demigods decided to stay and marry human women and start families. This caused a extreme crisis in heaven, and suffering on earth as well.

In the end, the Demigods got their wish, and their descendants remain on earth amongst the human communities to this day. This caused a long lasting animosity to develop between the

Demigoddesses and Demigods.

The SolarDark Mission Watch Post, did not participate in the War In Heaven, nor were they followers of the great god Lucifer.

The Demigoddesses succeeded in having Robots replace the Demigods in the SolarDark Mission Watch Post.

*        *        *

## SUN

Our earth exist as one planet in a solar system of eight planets. Our nearest star is called the " Sun ". The Sun bathes the solar system in a sea of invisible energy. The Sun emits infrared radiation which warms this earth, and visible radiation which provides the energy for biological lifeforms on this earth.

Some stars emit radiation at wavelengths and magnitudes which vary with time. These stars are called Variable Stars. The Russian scientists were the first to suspect that our star, the Sun, is a variable star for unknown reasons.

Our religion believes that the Sun can at times emit large quantities of energy and at other times cease to emit energy by entirely. The variations in the Solar Constant are infrequent temporary conditions.

SolarDark:

When the Sun cease to emit infrared & visible radiation we call this condition " SolarDark ". This is a natural condition which causes the cooling of the earth, and restores glaciers. This is necessary to maintain this earth in a state conducive to life in the longterm. In the short term it causes death. The water for the gla-ciation is delivered to this earth by large ice asteroids.

NASA has sensor data from space probes, proving that this earth is constantly being bombarded by such ice asteroids, and that this has been occurring since the first day this earth came into existence. There exist a physical relationship between;

A. Solardark Events

B. Ice Asteroid Bombardment Of This Earth

C. Glaciation Of Higher Latitudes

D. Longterm Existence Of Life On This Earth

Interstellar Travel:

There is a law of nature which forgives the same object from simultaneously physically existing at two or more points in the TemporalSpacial Energy Material Realm. The stars emit large energy fields which destabilize the surrounding TemporalSpacial energy. A method of travel within the Local Star Group utilizes this instability to cause a physical object to disappear from one stars corona and materialize in another stars corona. This also uses the Laws Of Conservation Of Mass & Energy. And synchroniza-tion by quantum coupling based subspace communication.

The Demigoddesses died not create this technology, it was given to them by the ancients whom they worshipped as gods, before the ancients suddenly disappeared from this Local Star Group 100,000 years ago.

The three species of Demigoddesses have used this tech-nology for 75,000 years in their search of the local systems for sign of the Ancients, without success, before concluding that the Ancients never left, and they are still here, everywhere(1). They gave the Demigoddesses everything (2) and left them to care for everything(3).

T

\*        \*        \*

## TAKEN

Taken:

the removal of a human being from their community on earth, or the removal of a human being to other parts of the earth. Where the human being is not in control of the event, and the event serves the purposes of higher evolved beings.

Narrative:

The six species of higher evolved beings who once lived here on this earth migrated into the regions of outer space they called the heavens. The envision themselves as the Guardians of Earth & Humanity. The species Homo Sapiens is the sole surviving hominid species. The Demigoddesses have dreamed of migrating humanity to the heavens for their own protection, against natural catastrophes and malevolent higher evolved species.

The Demigoddesses have Taken individual human beings to live in heaven with success, but however, the Homo Sapiens species has never been able to acclimate to the environment of heaven.

Thus individuals taken into heaven were taken alive, and not by aliens.

Taken By Fallen Gods In Exile:

Here on this earth, the Fallen Gods in exile do take humans for their own purposes. As we fight to prevent crisis which have occurred on the other earths from happening on this earth; certain higher evolved beings are working to ensure that these adverse event do occur here on this earth. In this mission of evil the Fallen Gods in exile are assisted by human beings who belong to certain organizations.

*     *     *

## TATTOOS

The Demigoddesses, the sacred vessels of the Creator Alpha Omega, have always lived nude, unless it was absolutely necessary to wear clothing. The colonies in outer space made it even more unnecessary to wear clothing.

The particular characteristic which the Demigoddesses developed into a art, is the religious tattoos which adorn their entire bodies. Every tattoo has a meaning and purpose. Every place on the body were a tattoo appears has a special meaning. The same images, symbols, and arrangements appear in the Great Stone Temples.

The human Temple Priestesses have copied this religious

practice, and their tattoos also have purpose and meaning according to their book of iconography.

Spiritual Functions Of Tattoos:

The temple priestesses'sbody's are covered with tattoos by a certain age, both temporary and permanent tattoos. The tattoos are not decorative, they are functional. When the temple priestesses undresses, certain hidden tattoos are fully visable.

As one looks into her hidden tattoos one is drawn into the spiritual realm. There one experiences a universe unlike anything in our realm. There one meets the true temple priestesses, and not just her physical manifestation which she creates.

The Name:

The Demigoddesses have names which are written in the earth, cropcircles( negative abstractions), on monuments, and in works of art. These names are in the form of highly abstract Pictographs. The first tattoo one receives as a child is ones name and sect. When the girl becomes a Temple Priestesses the first tattoo she receives is her religious name. In our icons there are these same Pictographs.


## TEMPLE PRIESTESSES-1

Temple Priestesses were human women who belonged to a social class of very educated, intelligent, creative, intuitive, spiritually gifted women. They served many functions in their including but not m

limited to the following;

A. Spiritual Guide

B. Teacher/Educator

C. Counselor

D. Doctor/Healer

E. Psychologists

F. Midwife

G. Druggist

H. Interpreter of Divine Revelations

I. Historian

J. Keeper of the Library

And much much more!

The spiritual community was religious based, therefore the temple priestesses were head of religion & government. Their governmental functions could be classified as follows;

A. Heads of Government

B. Ministers of Offices Of Government

C. Civil Servants in Government

The temple priestesses helped people find soulmates, then helped the soulmates learn how to live together. They helped people join the spiritual communities. They taught them a religion and way of life, and helped them to leave their old way of believing thinking and living.

The temple priestesses communicated with the sacred vessels of the Creator Alpha Omega. The delivered Divine Revelations. They helped people to apply Divine Law to the problems of life.

The temple priestesses modelled themselves after the sacred

vessels, the Demigoddesses.

The temple priestesses had the highest education level in the community. They learned and taught;

Arts

Sciences

Philosophy

Religion

Farming

Architecture

Medicine

Cooking

Industry

Making of useful things ( Invention )

Psychology

and much much more

All the things needed to build a viable prosperous progres- sive fair society, were taught to the Temple Priestesses, and they passed this!knowledge on to the people.

The Temple Priestesses were Wives, Mothers, Daughters, Sisters, Lovers, all the relationships which are normal to human beings, because they were human beings.

*       *       *


## TEST OF DIVINITY:

Synopsis: We distinguish the True Divine from the False Divine by testing their Divinity.

We of CEBAGII know that the only Divine Being is the Creator Alpha Omega. Therefore any being claiming to be perfection ( divine ), is claiming to be the Creator Alpha Omega. We then can define, " divinity ", by the qualities of the Creator Alpha Omega;

1. omnipresence
2. omnipotence
3. all knowing
   a. knowledge of future.
   b. knowledge of present.
   c. knowledge of past.
   d. knowledge of the state of all things.
4. immortality and eternal;
   a. having no beginning
   b. having no end.
5. power to create
6. power to rise the dead
7. control of nature;
   a. time & space.
   b. energy & matter.
   c. the condition of reality.
   d. the state of all things in creation.
8. control of the spirit
9. power to heal
10. Truthfulness
11. Without hate, envy, pride, delusion.

These qualities are the basis of the test of divinity.

Any being claiming to be divine must pass this test, and can do so only by establishing the possession of every quality of divinity to the highest degree ( without limits ).

illustrations: none

## TRANSHUMANISM AS A VITAL RELIGIOUS PRACTICE OF THE SECT, CEBAGII, OF HELLENISM:

Today it seems odd to think of of 300 years as old age, because in this generation no homo sapiens lives to that age. We believe that physical death is as necessary as physical birth, in the progression of the immortal minds, but that we all die too young and live our last days in a terribly unhealthy state.

The introduction of machine bodies to provide life support to the humans brain and vital organs, and will greatly improve human life without taking away our humanness.

The tissue which will all be transferred to and integrated into the machine body, will enable us to still look fully human, and experience the full range of human sensations. The transferred tissue will include the following;

A. The Actual Tongue,

B. All The Skin,
C. The Circulatory & Nervous Systems,
D. The Secondary Sexual Organs,
E. The Anus & Rectum,
F. The Brain, Internal Organs, Spinal Cord.
G. The Intestines, Stomach, Muscles, Cervix, Womb, Ovaries, Prostate, Testicles, Gall Bladder, Esophagus, Breast

Tissue, And Bones, Will Not Be Transferred Along With The Orther Vital Organs.

Humans will eat food, enjoy food, but we will not digest foods anymore. Instead our living portions ( what seculars call our " Ghost" ), will be sustained by artificial nutritional compounds stored in internal reserves in the nonliving machine body ( what seculars call the " Vessel/Shell "). The bones will be replaced by carbon fiber skeletal structure. The muscles replaced by electric solenoidal actuators.

\*       \*       \*

U

\*       \*       \*

## UFOs

There have been many advanced civilizations to emerge on this earth. Some have developed highly advanced means of travel. It is beyond all rational doubt that there existence unidentified flying objects in the skies here on earth. These have existed from hundreds of thousands of years.

There exist enough factual data and scientific studies to establish a sufficient understanding of the origin and nature of the phenomena called UFOs.

Firstly they are not extraterrestrials.

Secondly they have advanced technology.

Thirdly they come from both on earth and space.

Fourthly they are associated with groups of human beings, were help them with the goal of deceiving the public about their true agenda.

UFOs As Product Of Recent Hominid Civilizations:

A breakaway colony of hominids, migrated into outer space sometime before the fall of civilization. Knowledge of their existence was wiped away by the violent circumstances surrounding the fall of the homo sapiens civilization.

The hominoid space colony faced problems in outer space;(1) their gene pool is inadequate, (2) the high radiation environment of outer space causes deterioration of their own DNA.

Collection Of Human Reproductive Tissue:

Therefore in order to extend the existence of their own colony in outer space they must produce healthy children, and acquire suitable transplant tissue also. Therefore they work to obtain a continuous supply of high quality reproductive tissue from earthlings.

Transfer Of Brains To Machine Bodies:

The grays with their large heads and small bodies are the combination of hominoid and machine. Their machine bodies do not grow, but their biological brain does. Thus as the mature into adulthood, the relative size of their artificial skulls must continue to increase, and they take on the appearance we call grays.

It is only their members who live here on earth and interact with earthlings that must as appear normal homo sapiens hominoids.

The space colonies are not extraterrestrials, and they are not committed to saving homo sapiens from ourselves. They are committed to life in outer space, but they still value this earth, and don't want to see it destroyed when humanity destroys itself.

The hominoid space colonies have often allowed earthlings to live as they wish, and will allow homo sapiens too eventually disappear from this earth. ( the matter is not left up to them as there are other interested parties in the Local Star Group ).

Due to extreme changes, both physiological & psychological, the hominids have experienced in adopting to live in outer space, they can never live long-term on earth again.

Necessary Cattle Mutilations:

After the hominoids moved into space colonies, they adopted repairable machine bodies, and transferred certain tissues to the machine vassals;

A.  Brain &Neurospinal system
B.  Vital internal organs
C.  Lungs
D.  Bone marrow
E.  Sex organs

The internal organs were subjected to x-ray radiation to eliminate all infectious virus and bacteria present. Then placed In the machine bodies.

They completely suppressed the immune system, and introduced advanced broad spectrum antibiotics & antivirals into the circulatory system.

These changes made it possible to utilize the internal organs from homo sapiens and even other nonhuman species as re-placement parts. The space colonist have never taken human beings and stolen their organs. Thus we have seen expertly per-formed cattle mutilations for over 30,000 years.

There exist religious cults here on this earth, not associated with the hominoid space colonist. Those cults are leading people to believe that they are associated with friendly extraterrestrials, when in fact they are associated with the evil and veil Fallen Gods in exile on this earth.

UFOs At Scene Of Natural Disasters:

The release of large quantities of energy during certain natural events, causes the threshold between the TemporalSpacial En-ergy Material Realm and the set of all possible states of creation/universe, to be breached in a disordered fashion.

The disorderly breach of the barrier between, " reality and non-reality ", allows extraordinary beings to physically manifest. The UFOs are controlled be space colonist who predict these natural events and arrive to capture any extraordinary beings produced by the natural high energy condition. Those beings are then kept in their collection.

Homo sapiens who have been onboard the ships of the space colonist, have seen parts of this collection of the extraordinary beings, and mistakenly assumed they were from other planets. All the extraordinary beings were collected here on earth. The space colonist also hunt these creatures down here on earth, be-cause the earth governments do not have the technology to track them down before they kill innocent people.

## UNIVERSAL FREE ENERGY

The heavenly bodies of this universe/creation, float in a sea of energy. This planet internally resonates with that universal energy at natural frequencies, and the physical consequences of this internal resonance is a heating of the earth's mantle & core in addition to the thermal energy of radioactive decay processes.

It is possible to extract energy from the universe for use by humanity, using technologies which establish artificial resonance and resonance energy conversion into useful forms such as electricity.

This energy will enable humanity to survive & rebuild, after a natural extinct level event on this planet. The major obstacle to the development of this Free Energy is human greed and economic enslavement to the producers of hydrocarbon fuels, such as the coals, the natural gas, and the petroleums.

The coals, the natural gas, and the petroleums; are available due to the current geological condition & environment of this planet. A major natural extinct level event on this planet, will eliminate human access to the natural hydrocarbon deposits on this planet. The recovery of human civilization will be made quicker by the availability of Universal Free Energy. In fact the human condition can be improved right now by the access to Universal Free Energy.

Universal Free Energy Generation Technologies:

The religious rituals utilize naturally occurring stones, crystals, and earth structures to receive, store, and convert naturally oc-

curring energy ( we float in a sea of energy ). These same basic techniques can be refined scientifically to create Technologies giving all of humanity access to Universal Free Energy Generation Technologies.

This type of secularized use of our religious rituals & techniques to aide & save humanity, would be acceptable, because it would serve the Divinely Mandated Supreme End, and follow Divine Cannon.

*        *        *

## UPPER DEMIGODDESS HIGH TEMPLE PRIESTESSES

The three species of Demigoddesses are;

1. Upper Demigoddesses;the most evolved of the three.
2. Middle Demigoddesses;the intermediate stage in demigoddess evolution.
3. Lower Demigoddessesthe relatively least evolved of the three species.

The Demigoddesses are the sacred vessels of the Creator Alpha Omega, leaders of the religion, and leaders of the government & society.

The Temple Priestesses are the learnt experts who have the experience, knowledge, and spiritual qualities to serve as guides to others.

The three High Temple Priestesses are the three temple priestesses with the highest degree of expertise & qualities, and are the leaders of Religion, Government, and Society.

\* \* \*

V

\* \* \*

## VIOLENCE

KEY BELIEF:

Homo Sapiens Violence Persist Because They As A Species, Have Yet To Develop A Universally Accepted System Of Beliefs & Practices Which Fully Comprehend & Manage The More Primitive Aspects Of Our Human Nature In The Struggle To Fulfill Human Needs.

KEY BELIEF:

We Who Are Inclined To Believe In Religion, Do So Because We Sense The Operation Of A Higher Greater Nonhuman Nonphysical Living Being Responsible For Our Existence, Who Is Guiding Us Through The Voice Of Our Constant Moral Conscious, And Who Interacts With Humanity Through Our Less Frequent Personal Spiritual Experiences. We Believe Violence To Be Inconsistent With The Dictates If That Higher Being The Creator Alpha Omega.

Human beings are the most successful predatory species ever to exist on this earth, primarily due to, (1) the strange tendency for basic human instincts to control the use of the highest creative

301

intellectual capacities of our species, (2) an intelligence which exceed those of any other intelligent living creatures, and (3) a tendency to form coherent powerful social groups which execute complex coordinated planned behaviors utilizing highly highly developed techniques to achieve clearly defined group objectives.

Human violence is the consequence of the expression of our innate predatory survival instincts in the modern artificial environment, were those no longer most effectively serve to promote survival.

Their exist a hierarchy of natural forces within each human

being controlling her/his thoughts & actions. The least effective control is the innate biological instincts better suited for the jungle then the metropolitan community.

The intellectual powers of human beings are significant, but they are lacking in the necessary moral directives which can not be derived from objective reasoning alone.

The spiritual forces are the most likely source of effective direction for the continuation and advancement of human life. Such spiritual forces are the basis of our code of conduct called Religion.

The greatest force controlling violence has always been human society. The forces tending to perpetuate violence of all types is a social force which has gained authority within human societies and directs its membership to commit acts of violence according to three perceived conditions;

1.  against any human beings who do not meet the criteria for inclusion in that select society, and

2. who are seen as competition for control over materials objects, and

3. who can be subdued through the use of force.

The outcome of the use of violence under the above conditions has proven beneficial to the society having monopoly control over the administration of the force of violence. Because of this, violence has become a acceptable practice of human secular paternalistic societies throughout history.

NOTES

Violence;

1) any interaction between two or more people, in which force is used to compelled a exchange between those involved; in which one or more of those involved experience an involuntary diminishment of some tangible or nontangible possession, and one or more other peoples involved experience an intended increase in their possessions as a consequence of the interaction.

2) any act(s) in which one or more peoples are compelled against their will to facilitate the fulfillment of the tangible

or nontangible needs, wants, and desires of others, and suffer a significant lost as a consequence of the act(s), where the act(s) constitute an violation(s) of one's civil, human, and/or religious rights.

3) any organized group activity consisting of premeditated and planed behaviors based on established techniques for achieving a set of clear objectives & means by the

violation of the civil, human, and/or religious rights of oth-ers, and the outcome will include the groups acquisition of something they hold to be of value.

\*       \*       \*

W

\*       \*       \*

## WAR

Before we become a spiritual community, we must come to comprehend the culture, religion, and society of War; then we must abandon those beliefs & practices, and we must spend our lifetime guarding that they do not return in another form!

War must never become an accepted way of life!

In popular music the topic of War occurs repeatedly. Most people are unable to comprehend a necessity or justification for organized state sponsored extremes of violence, carried out by professional soldiers. While others can not imagine life on this earth without constant war, believing it to be a essential aspect of human nature.

The human propensity for organized violence is both despised and admired, condemned and glorified, used and abused.

The inability to live peacefully with other human beings, the condition of hostility towards others who are not members of ones select society, the beliefs in he effectiveness of threats of violence to produce peaceful coexistence, all are the product of a incomplete conception of the universe and our place in the universe.

Because we revision all living beings as distinct separate entities, we have no natural basis for considering all people not only belong to, but actually are one.

The use of violence is also propelled by the human misunderstanding of birth & death (the alpha & the omega ). We of the CEBAGII celebrate birth as the continuation of eternal existence, and celebrate death as indicative of the perfection & progression of the true being. Humanity habitually avoids natural death, and considers human birth as unwanted life, while doing nothing to reasonably regulate reproduction, due to a unrealistic beliefs regarding human sexuality.

The conditions which humanity sees as the justification for war, are all the products of humanity's perception of reality & destructive ways of life derived from those misperceptions.

The religious belief in the one true being The Creator Alpha Omega, and the true nature of all creation as within and a part of the one true being, will not allow us to pursue War as a means to the Supreme End.

Some people ask why does the Creator Alpha Omega allow War. We in CEBAGII ask why do We allow War? If we can intervene to prevent the extremes of human suffering during a war, why then can't we intervene to prevent that war from ever occurring? Because men see war coming and want it to happen, or view it as inevitable & unavoidable.

War has never served to achieve the Supreme End, so any religion which supports War, is inconsistent with the design & intent of the Creator Alpha Omega, and is an unholy religion.

\*       \*       \*

X

\*       \*       \*

Y

\*       \*       \*

## YEARNING TO BE FREE

35,000 years ago the last SolarDark event and the last Global Deluge occurred and saved our earth from becoming another planet Venus. At that time human cities were wiped away. The followers of the Demigoddesses were prepared for this catastrophe and survived in arks.

As a humanitarian juster the survivors onboard the arks, picked up other humans who had been lucky enough to live through the storm. These poor soils were taken into the arks and allowed to sleep in whatever space was available.

After the Sun turned back on, and the waters drained to the oceans, the land near the equator begun to dry. The higher latitudes were beginning to be covered with snow. The arks made their way to the equatorial coastal safe harbors, and the passengers begun to setup communities.

The guest onboard the arks were not accustomed to hard work, and they begin to realize that the spiritual community was defenseless. No one had imagined that any predatory species would survive the global flood.

One night the last vistage of civilization disappeared. In the dark of the night, the guest killed most of the able bodied males. The next day the spiritual communities were turned into prisons. As other males returned from surveying the surrounding lands, thetoo were killed.

Nature had saved life on earth with water from the heavens, nature had also wiped a way the cities, but however nature had not destroyed human civilization. It took evil work of men to destroy what was left of civilization.

The end of human civilization marked the beginning of the New Stone Age. The spiritual community was replaced with Tribalectic Culture. Humanity was now in the hands of the Brute-Males.

Women were kept alive because someone had to do all the work to keep everyone else alive. Women were also kept alive to be sex slaves in the Brute-Males harems. It was a brutal life for women & their children. The Brute-Males enjoyed the monop- oly of force, and they saw no reason why anything should ever change, and they would keep humanity living like animals forever if the could.

It was clear to them women that humanity was in decline, and as time went by, extremes of human suffering occurred at the hands of the Brute-Males.

I often wondered how men could kill women & children. Then one day a old soldier told me that the Holocaust was not done by madmen, but rather by intelligent men who strongly believed that by doing these awful things to other peoples, that these horrible acts would get them something which they very much wanted, and they pursued that thing with reckless abandon, forsaking every thing good they had ever been taught, and embracing what to them was a necessary evil. It seems that this is what men do when They Think that no one will ever see them, and no one will ever punish them.


It is written that

When the Gates of heaven

Are closed to the prayers of men,

They are always open to

The tears of Women!

- The Talmud


It was not the gods of the Babylonians, Greeks, Buddhist, Egyptians, or any of the other great religions, which heard the

cries of women enslaved on this earth. It was not those gods who came to save the children. It was not those gods who gave humanity a new start. It was the Demigoddesses of the Pantheon of Heaven, who answered the prayers of women yearning to be free.

*     *     *

Z

*     *     *

THE BOOK OF CEBAGII

THE BOOK OF CEBAGII: The Religious Handbook Of The Non-nmainstream Religion CEBAGII.

By The Oba KaviiLeZarah.

the ancient-story teller, and rising light teacher.

Copyright 2021, by Kavin Lee Peeples.

THE MAIN TABLE OF THE CONTENTS:

VOLUME ONE:

The Religious Interpretation Of History & Mystery

VOLUME TWO:

The Encyclopedic Dictionary of Terms & Concepts

VOLUME THREE:

The Beginning Of The New Age:

The Book Of CEBAGII:

THE BOOK OF CEBAGII: The Religious Handbook Of The Non-nmainstream Religion CEBAGII.

By Oba KaviiLeZArah.

the ancient-story teller, and rising light teacher.

Copyright 2021, by Kavin Lee Peeples.

PREFACE

The Book Of CEBAGII, consist of the personally held sincere religious beliefs & practices, of the prisoner of the state, known by the name; KAVIN LEE PEEPLES, and who has accepted the religious name of; OBA: KAVII LEZ ARAH. "Oba", being a religious title for a teacher, a artist, a scientist, and a great ancient story teller.

This nonmainsream religion is called CEBAGII; which is an acronym for;

Creed of Esoteric-Ecceltic Beliefs Ad-infinium and General and Idiosyncratic Ideiogious.

The closely kept secret, which not even my mother knows, and i am revealing only to this select society of readers, is that CE-BAGII also stands for a science idea I once developed.

Copious Emergence of Bosons for Amplification of Gravitational-(Mass-interactions of Nuclei During) Inline Integration.

Which is a set of complex hypothetical techniques using magnetic fields to produce intense subnuclear-radius explosions in plasmas, and generating transitory Muon Particles replacing electrons in plasma of instantaneously cooled nucli to zero kelvin, which would create implosion to minimal necessary proximity, to achieve Pulsed Nuclear Fusion Reactions, in a Advanced Externally Electromagnetic Pulse Pumped Nuclear Fusion Reactors; then using the same hardware to extract the energy produced by the mass-conversion stage via the magnetic pulse generated by the magnetic deceleration of high speed charged particles created by the fusion reaction itself. This is the basic closed thermodynamic cycle producing zero radioactive waste.

Science at it's most imaginative, which like the Breeder Reactors, mining the asteroid belt, and synthetic nutrition to feed the third world, was another great concept born too soon to be loved & appreciated by the scientific community. Perhaps one day Richard Rhodes will write a book on incredible ideas of inventors and amateur scientist, and there will be a footnote on CEBAGII.

The good thing is that the reactor died and years later the religion was born, using the same acronym! Perhaps its some kind of a memorial to a supermachine that would have given mankind the power to create Suns, something only the gods can do. Fusion is mankind's quest to steal the fire of the gods from heaven and bring it down to earth.

Now that I have answered the big question about the unusual name this religion has been given, let's discuss were CEBAGII came from.

CEBAGII was created from the subjective interpretation of my

personal spiritual experiences in the form of dreams which occurred over a 24 month time period. Many of my Dreams are of course divinations on the collective knowledge contained within my mind. Divinations are interactions with a higher evolved entity, which give visions, that transform that mass of unrelated information in my head,giving it a new meaning, and giving me a deeper understanding of the universe & the purpose of life.

Books will never go away until there's no one left to read them. Divination will never go away until the children of humanity have all the answers to every question they can conceive of.

This vade mecum has three parts;

I. The Religious Interpretation Of History & Mystery.
Visions - The beginning of everything. -
II. The Future Of Humanity on this Earth & Beyond.
Visions - The future lives. -
III. The Encyclopedic Dictionary of Terms & Concept.
Intellectualise - The present state of us-

and all according to the fundamental beliefs in CEBAGII.

The spiritual experiences I have had, have shown me the world before history was erased, forgotten, and rewritten; of the Creator Alpha Omega whom everything is a part of; of a time when the gods walked amongst sapiens; when they built castles in the sky and called it heaven; of gods who were crazy in humanly incomprehensible ways; when the gods faced their own imperfection, mortality, and fell to earth; of wars fought in heaven as on earth; of the redheaded children of the gods, little monsters only their fathers can love; of darkening of the sun, great deluges, ice

312

ages, and rebirth of civilization; the precarious human condition in which the weight of human civilization rest on the shoulders of the mortal beings once called gods; of a kingdom based on a religion of love, teaching humankind the meaning of the word; of Matriarchates& Amazons; and the kingdom of Lucifer; the cult of Helen; and the future of humanity, the struggle to awaken and reach the three heavens in the sky; and the unbreakable circle of life we are repeating; and of our grandchildren and their children who are impatiently waiting to be born into a world we must first build for them!

All that and much much more, in a Dream, and it all fits between the covers of one book thanks to creative editing and digital print on demand! This is it people, this is what you've been waiting for. Let me show you what's on the otherwise of the mountain you must and will climb too become what Alpha Omega has designed & intended for tomorrow and the days after life.

This book is our book, these pages are only a beginning, I'm sure that some us will add to it, revise and correct it, expand and develop it. I will be most happy to say, that while I was a prisoner of the state, locked away in a $400 million dollar House Of Lucifer, looking out the windows at the gun towers across the lawns of Kentucky bluegrass, death slowly approaching each day and hour again as always, I had a small part in man's search for meaning in the universe! Because I wrote this too you;
The First Book Of CEBAGII.

- Oba Kavii Lez Arah

30-May-2021.

TABLE OF CONTENTS FOR VOLUME ONE:

THE BOOK OF CEBAGII: The Religious Handbook Of The Nonnmainstream Religion CEBAGII.

By The Oba KaviiLeZarah.

the ancient-story teller, and rising light teacher.

Copyright 2021, by Kavin Lee Peeples.

VOLUME ONE:

THE RELIGIOUS INTERPRETATION OF HISTORY & MYSTERY:

TABLE OF CONTENTS FOR VOLUME ONE:

TABLE OF CONTENTS FOR VOLUME TWO:

THE BOOK OF CEBAGII: The Religious Handbook Of The Non-nmainstream Religion CEBAGII.

By The Oba KaviiLeZarah.

the ancient-story teller, and rising light teacher.

Copyright 2021, by Kavin Lee Peeples.

VOLUME TWO:

THE ENCYCLOPEDIC DICTIONARY OF

TERMS & CONCEPTS:

THE TABLE OF CONTENTS - VOLUME TWO:

A - Z.

Notes Ad-Infinitum

( A ).

Vol. II: The Encyclopedic Dictionary Of CEBAGII.

THE BOOK OF CEBAGII: The Religious Handbook Of The Non-
nmainstream Religion CEBAGII.
By The Oba KaviiLeZarah.
the ancient-story teller, and rising light teacher.
Copyright 2021, by Kavin Lee Peeples.

Abundant Productive Capacity
Alpha Omega, The Creator -
Amazons
Anarchy
Ancestral Birthplace
Associated Minds
Asteroids Made Of Ice ( $H_2O$ ) In Orrt Cloud

( B ).

Vol. II: The Encyclopedic Dictionary Of CEBAGII.

THE BOOK OF CEBAGII: The Religious Handbook Of The Non-nmainstream Religion CEBAGII.

By The Oba KaviiLeZarah.

the ancient-story teller, and rising light teacher.

Copyright 2021, by Kavin Lee Peeples.

Balanced Isogynic Being

Body

Body Thievery

Breast, Symbology Of The Matriarchate

( C ).

Vol. II: The Encyclopedic Dictionary Of CEBAGII.

THE BOOK OF CEBAGII: The Religious Handbook Of The Non-nmainstream Religion CEBAGII.

By The Oba KaviiLeZarah.

the ancient-story teller, and rising light teacher.

Copyright 2021, by Kavin Lee Peeples.

Cannon Of The Creator Alpha Omega. Parts I, II, III.

Catastrophism

CEBAGII Part I

CEBAGII Part II

Ceremonial Dances

Cohabitation

Common Ancestor

Communication With Demigoddesses

Communities, Spiritual -

Copeland, Misty. (Demigoddess In Waiting)

Creation

( D ).

Vol. II: The Encyclopedic Dictionary Of CEBAGII.

THE BOOK OF CEBAGII: The Religious Handbook Of The Non-nmainstream Religion CEBAGII.

By The Oba KaviiLeZarah.

the ancient-story teller, and rising light teacher.

Copyright 2021, by Kavin Lee Peeples.

Death And Rebirth

Death Of The Body ( Physical Manifestation)

Deification

Demigods

Demigoddesses Part I

Demigoddesses Part II

Demigoddesses Part III

Demigoddesses & Sexual Reproduction

Delusions

Design & Intent

Digression

Divination

Divine ( The Creator Alpha Omega)

Divine Intervention ( By Proxy)

Drugs

( E ).

Vol. II: The Encyclopedic Dictionary Of CEBAGII.

THE BOOK OF CEBAGII: The Religious Handbook Of The Non-nmainstream Religion CEBAGII.

By The Oba KaviiLeZarah.

the ancient-story teller, and rising light teacher.

Copyright 2021, by Kavin Lee Peeples.

Earth

Economic Model

Economic System

Einstein, Albert. ( German born U.S. Physicist)

Elevated State

End, How Worlds -

Energy Fields

Energy & Sexual Joy

Ethics & Humanity

Gerhardt, Amelia. ( Demigoddesses)

Evil, The Nature Of -

Evil Conscious

Evolution

Experiences, Transformative

( F ).

Vol. II: The Encyclopedic Dictionary Of CEBAGII.

THE BOOK OF CEBAGII: The Religious Handbook Of The Non-nmainstream Religion CEBAGII.

By The Oba KaviiLeZarah.

the ancient-story teller, and rising light teacher.

Copyright 2021, by Kavin Lee Peeples.

False Resurrections

Food & Drink

Free Will

Final Words

( G ).

Vol. II: The Encyclopedic Dictionary Of CEBAGII.

THE BOOK OF CEBAGII: The Religious Handbook Of The Non-nmainstream Religion CEBAGII.

By The Oba KaviiLeZarah.

the ancient-story teller, and rising light teacher.

Copyright 2021, by Kavin Lee Peeples.

Gender I

Gender II

God (term as defined & used for non divine beings)

God(s) And The Creator Alpha Omega

Goddesses Of Love (Demigoddesses)

Government Of The Matriarchate

Great Floods ( Deluge)

Group Marriage

( H ).

Vol. II: The Encyclopedic Dictionary Of CEBAGII.

THE BOOK OF CEBAGII: The Religious Handbook Of The Non-nmainstream Religion CEBAGII.

By The Oba KaviiLeZarah.

the ancient-story teller, and rising light teacher.

Copyright 2021, by Kavin Lee Peeples.

Happiness

Hate

Harem (Sexual Slavery Of Women; Polygamy)

Heaven

Helen Of Troy. ( Demigoddesses)

Hierarchy Of The Pantheon

Higher Evolved Creatures & Human Destruction

Higher Spiritual Values

History & Mystery

Human Interactions With Demigoddesses

Human Being ( today; Homo Sapiens)

Human Hybridization ( with the goddesses & gods)

Human Migration & The Spread of Religion

Human Planning

Human Transition To Higher States & Forms

Hybrids (extreme variations from exigencies)

( I )

Vol. II: The Encyclopedic Dictionary Of CEBAGII.

THE BOOK OF CEBAGII: The Religious Handbook Of The Non-nmainstream Religion CEBAGII.

By The Oba KaviiLeZarah.

the ancient-story teller, and rising light teacher.

Copyright 2021, by Kavin Lee Peeples.

Icons

Iconography In Ceremonies

Illusion Of Perfection

Illusion Of Separation

Immortal Mind As Distinct From Mortal Brain & Body

Immortal Minds & Evil

Isogynic Beings. (Physical Form of Demigoddesses)

( J )

Vol. II: The Encyclopedic Dictionary Of CEBAGII.

THE BOOK OF CEBAGII: The Religious Handbook Of The Non-nmainstream Religion CEBAGII.

By The Oba KaviiLeZarah.

the ancient-story teller, and rising light teacher.

Copyright 2021, by Kavin Lee Peeples.

Joan Of Arc. ( Demigoddesses)

( K )

Vol. II: The Encyclopedic Dictionary Of CEBAGII.

THE BOOK OF CEBAGII: The Religious Handbook Of The Non-nmainstream Religion CEBAGII.

By The Oba KaviiLeZarah.

the ancient-story teller, and rising light teacher.

Copyright 2021, by Kavin Lee Peeples.

Kingdom Of Love ( Heaven & Matriarchate)

( L )

Vol. II: The Encyclopedic Dictionary Of CEBAGII.

THE BOOK OF CEBAGII: The Religious Handbook Of The Non-
nmainstream Religion CEBAGII.
By The Oba KaviiLeZarah.
the ancient-story teller, and rising light teacher.
Copyright 2021, by Kavin Lee Peeples.

Laws Govern Demigoddesses Actions, Divine -
Life
Life, Death, and Struggle Between Good and Evil
Love
LGBTQ
Lunar Termination (End Demigoddesses Intervention )

( M )

Vol. II: The Encyclopedic Dictionary Of CEBAGII.

THE BOOK OF CEBAGII: The Religious Handbook Of The Nonnmain
By The Oba KaviiLeZarah.
the ancient-story teller, and rising light teacher.

( N )

( O )

Obligatory Assistance

Old Age ( In their spiritual community)

Omega ( The true death of real things)

Orrt Cloud. (Planetary Sys. Reservoir of Water (ice) )

( P )

Vol. II: The Encyclopedic Dictionary Of CEBAGII.

THE BOOK OF CEBAGII: The Religious Handbook Of The Non-
nmainstream Religion CEBAGII.
By The Oba KaviiLeZarah.
the ancient-story teller, and rising light teacher.
Copyright 2021, by Kavin Lee Peeples.

Perfection

Photosphere Satellite System

Police In Heaven ( Amazons)

Prayer

Progression Of The Faithless

Punishment ( The Human Practice)

Purpose Of Creation

( R)

Vol. II: The Encyclopedic Dictionary Of CEBAGII.

THE BOOK OF CEBAGII: The Religious Handbook Of The Non-
nmainstream Religion CEBAGII.

By The Oba KaviiLeZarah.

the ancient-story teller, and rising light teacher.

Real Things

Reality As Determined By The One Spirit

Realms ( Spirit, Time, Space.)

Redheaded Children Of The Gods

Reincarnation

Relationships Between Real Things

Religious Practices

Rules Of Iconography

( S )

Vol. II: The Encyclopedic Dictionary Of CEBAGII.

THE BOOK OF CEBAGII: The Religious Handbook Of The Non-nmainstream Religion CEBAGII.

By The Oba KaviiLeZarah.

the ancient-story teller, and rising light teacher.

Copyright 2021, by Kavin Lee Peeples.

Sacred Vessels, The Demigoddesses As The -

Sacrifice Of Life. (Human Error)

Science

Second Union

Sexuality & Human Needs

Sexual Nudity In The Icons

Shape Shifting

Slavery

Solar Dark

Solar Dark Mission Watch Post

Solar System

Soulmate II

Speciation In The Higher Evolved Species

Special Forms

Spirit

Spiritual Companions

Spiritual Community

Spiritually Expressive Arts

Stone Age, The New -

Stages In The Elevated State

Strangest Stone

Sun

Symphony. (Religious Practices as Symphony)

( T )

Vol. II: The Encyclopedic Dictionary Of CEBAGII.

THE BOOK OF CEBAGII: The Religious Handbook Of The Non-nmainstream Religion CEBAGII.
By The Oba KaviiLeZarah.
the ancient-story teller, and rising light teacher.
Copyright 2021, by Kavin Lee Peeples.

Taken

Tattoos, Symbolic Religious & Civil -

Temple Priestesses Part I

Temple Priestesses Part II

Temple Priestesses Part III

Temples, Old World -

Third Union

Triparte Being

True Religion. ( not a relative term )

( U )

Vol. II: The Encyclopedic Dictionary Of CEBAGII.

THE BOOK OF CEBAGII: The Religious Handbook Of The Non-

nmainstream Religion CEBAGII.

By The Oba KaviiLeZarah.

the ancient-story teller, and rising light teacher.

Copyright 2021, by Kavin Lee Peeples.

Unitarian Universalist

Universe As A Evolving Intelligent System

Upper Demigoddesses High Temple Priestesses

( V )

Vol. II: The Encyclopedic Dictionary Of CEBAGII.

THE BOOK OF CEBAGII: The Religious Handbook Of The Non-nmainstream Religion CEBAGII.

By The Oba KaviiLeZarah.

the ancient-story teller, and rising light teacher.

Copyright 2021, by Kavin Lee Peeples.

Value Of Ancient Religions

Values Taught By The Demigoddesses

( W)

Vol. II: The Encyclopedic Dictionary Of CEBAGII.

THE BOOK OF CEBAGII: The Religious Handbook Of The Non-nmainstream Religion CEBAGII.

By The Oba KaviiLeZarah.

the ancient-story teller, and rising light teacher.

Copyright 2021, by Kavin Lee Peeples.

Worship Of Creator Alpha Omega

Worship Of Demigoddesses

( X)

Vol. II: The Encyclopedic Dictionary Of CEBAGII.

THE BOOK OF CEBAGII: The Religious Handbook Of The Non-nmainstream Religion CEBAGII.

By The Oba KaviiLeZarah.

the ancient-story teller, and rising light teacher.

Copyright 2021, by Kavin Lee Peeples.

Xenomorph

( Y )

Vol. II: The Encyclopedic Dictionary Of CEBAGII.

THE BOOK OF CEBAGII: The Religious Handbook Of The Non-nmainstream Religion CEBAGII.

By The Oba KaviiLeZarah.

the ancient-story teller, and rising light teacher.

Copyright 2021, by Kavin Lee Peeples.

Yearning To Be Free

    Yoga

    ------ END Of Terms & Concepts --------

Select Notes Follow:

THE HUMAN CONDITION SHALL CHANGE:

(There Is Light, And We Shall Find It!)

Vol. III: The Beginnings Of A New Age.

THE BOOK OF CEBAGII: The Religious Handbook Of The Non-nmainstream Religion CEBAGII.

# THE BOOK OF CEGBAGII

By The Oba KaviiLeZarah.

the ancient-story teller, and rising light teacher.

THOUGHTS IN GENERAL:

we as mortal beings in this human civilization, are truly obsessed with two main aspects of existence, which have become
the focus of religion, philosophy, and taboo;

A. Our obsession with sexual reproduction
B. Our obsession with death

When we can see ourselves as one immortal being, then death
would no longer be death, but rather the continuation of life; and
death would lose its power over our minds.

When we can see intercourse as a part of life, and much much
more then simply copulation, then we can accept it as natural,
and we can be at peace with sex, and sex would lose its power
over men.

what our obsessions reveal is our society's need for change &
growth, which are natural & essential functions of creation and
existence.

when we can see the perfect creator alpha omega as continually
growing & changing, then we can recognize the need for change

in all things in creation including ourselves.

this is a age old call for human realization of our purpose in creation, and yet it is something few humans comprehend.

the demonstrated potential of human intelligence is such that we as a species have the potential to eliminate all human physical suffering, and only our psychological suffering remains as a challenge to out understanding of our own existence.

we study the universe in the hope of understanding our place and purpose in it. What we seek has already been given too us, and we have rejected it, suppressed it, and waged war against the messengers & prophets. While the human condition has continued to deteriorate.

this has always been the pattern of human life!

the struggle for improvement, growth & change, has always been fought with resistance based on a collective human imagination & amnesia which erases our knowledge our our past errors, thus we find ourselves repeating the same errors in every generation.

this is not human nature, it is a stage in human development, and at this stage it is the domination of human civilization by human who have yet to develop higher moral & spiritual values, and therefore they can justify to themselves the suffering allowed to continue in our human condition.

# CHANGE CAN NOT OCCUR UNTIL THE TRANSFORMATIVE SPIRITUAL EXPERIENCES OCCUR.

ear Frank at Cadmus. This is just a appendix for volume one. Its not important enough for you to make expensive changes in the layout you've already completed. -Kavii

Appendix Three

The Book Of CEBAGII

Volume One: The Religious Interpretation of History & Mystery.

MODERN MYTHOLOGIES

The following conclusions are found to be universally valid in the analysis of observations of the responses of human societies to their encounters of Modern Mythologies:

KEY BELIEFS:

A. While the human being can not create the experiences upon Beliefs are based, it can interpret those experiences based on observations, logical reasoning, and applied collective learning. Every such thought processes presents an opportunity to grow and improve our collective learning.

B. A society's encounters with multiple Modern Mythologies presents opportunities for the continual growth and development of its body of collective learning.

Narrative:

It is our sub society which holds CEBAGII to be a sect of a actu-al religion ( Hellenism), which gives us a culture, which creates a way of life. To the larger modern societies CEBAGII is a Mod-ern Mythology, and Hellenism is seen as a form of culture.

A, " Modern Mythology ", may be defined as any non-main-stream narrative presenting an explanation of existence, and utilising combinations of variations of select elements of histor-ical & prehistorical beliefs in non-human entities, in the set of essential beliefs central to that cosmogony.

I.

Modern Mythology become necessary when our human need

for understanding of reality, can not be fulfilled by the ordinary means; the psychosocial forces of the compelling need are bal-anced by the creation and adaptation of a subjective extended reality sustained by personally held beliefs.

The emergence of subgroups within a larger human society, can be based in the unique histories of a people's experiences, resulting from the unique experiences of particular people not common to all peoples. Although Similar Modern Mythologies occur in many human subgroups there are inconspicuous dis-tinctions. The unique histories produce the distinctions recog-nized in the comparison of nonequivalent bodies of collective learning.

The limitations of a people's collective learning, and the degree to which it is applied in both the analysis of reality and the comparative analysis of received narratives, supply the basis for identification and classification of any narratives produced by the human mind; determining what the distinctions those people make between; Fiction/Fantasy, Modern Mythology, and Reality.

II.

Within a society not all peoples achieve the same degree of acquisition of collective learning, where the economic structure of the society creates distinct levels of educational attainment. In the absence of sufficient educational attainment, the perception of reality will be dictated by custom tradition culture and commonly held fundamental beliefs of those peoples, all of which are disseminated by the lowest economic means, and therefore represent a diminished collective learning.

All bodies of collective learning are incomplete. The growth of any body of collective learning requires that acceptance of novel interpretations ( i.e. scientific theories, or religious beliefs ) of new and old experiences and observations; which are primarily subjective in origin, and must be subject to objective standards of validation/proof.

When a society encounters Modern Mythologies these can only become Modern Religions when their fundamental elements are subject to objective standards of validation/proof; and unpon analysis yield up confirmed mensurable consequences in

the real world consistent with that novel system of beliefs, and which can not be attributed to any other known factors.

The level of development of a body of collective learning is distinct for every society, even contemporary societies, thus not ever society will identify and classify the same body of beliefs ( that is a particular Modern Mythology ) as a Modern Religion.

III.

While the human being can not create the experiences upon Beliefs are based, it can interpret those experiences based on observations, logical reasoning, and applied collective learning. Every such thought processes presents an opportunity to grow and improve our collective learning

Here are my religious beliefs which regard all types of unnec-essary human violence, as the common practices of almost all secular paternalistic human societies. Where the acts of vio-lence are perceived as necessary by a society when those acts of violence fulfill that societies needs, wants, and/or desires. This entry is indicates a taboo practice. Within CEBAGII reli-gious community violence can not exist, and the community still be in conformity with those religious beliefs & practices which are derived from divine revelations. -Kavii

VIOLENCE

Vol. 3. The Encyclopedic Dictionary Of Terms & Concepts In CEBAGII.

THE BOOK OF CEBAGII: The Religious Handbook Of The Non-nmainstream Religion CEBAGII.
By The Oba Kavii Lez Arah.
the ancient-story teller, and rising light teacher.
Copyright 2021, by Kavin Lee Peeples.

KEY BELIEF:
Homo Sapiens Violence Persist Because They As A Species, Have Yet To Develop A Universally Accepted System Of Beliefs & Practices Which Fully Comprehend & Manage The More Primitive Aspects Of Our Human Nature In The Struggle To Fulfill Human Needs.

KEY BELIEF:
We Who Are Inclined To Believe In Religion, Do So Because We Sense The Operation Of A Higher Greater Nonhuman Nonphysical Living Being Responsible For Our Existence, Who Is Guiding Us Through The Voice Of Our Constant Moral Conscious, And Who Interacts With Humanity Through Our Less Frequent Personal Spiritual Experiences. We Believe Violence To Be Inconsistent With The Dictates If That Higher Being The Creator Alpha Omega.

Human beings are the most successful predatory species ever to exist on this earth, primarily due to, (1) the strange tendency for basic human instincts to control the use of the highest creative intellectual capacities of our species, (2) an intelligence which exceed those of any other intelligent living creatures, and (3) a tendency to form coherent powerful social groups which execute complex coordinated planned behaviors utilizing highly highly developed techniques to achieve clearly defined group objectives.

Human violence is the consequence of the expression of our innate predatory survival instincts in the modern artificial environment, were those no longer most effectively serve to promote survival.

Their exist a hierarchy of natural forces within each human being controlling her/his thoughts & actions. The least effective control is the innate biological instincts better suited for the jungle then the metropolitan community.
The intellectual powers of human beings are significant, but they are lacking in the necessary moral directives which can not be derived from objective reasoning alone.
The spiritual forces are the most likely source of effective direction for the continuation and advancement of human life.
Such spiritual forces are the basis of our code of conduct called

Religion.

The greatest force controlling violence has always been human society. The forces tending to perpetuate violence of all types is a social force which has gained authority within human societies and directs its membership to commit acts of violence according to three perceived conditions;

1. against any human beings who do not meet the criteria for inclusion in that select society, and

2. who are seen as competition for control over materials objects, and

3. who can be subdued through the use of force.

The outcome of the use of violence under the above conditions has proven beneficial to the society having monopoly control over the administration of the force of violence. Because of this, violence has become a acceptable practice of human secular paternalistic societies throughout history.

NOTES

Violence;

(1). any interaction between two or more people, in which force is used to compelled a exchange between those involved; in which one or more of those involved experience an involuntary diminishment of some tangible or nontangible possession, and one or more other peoples involved experience an intended increase in their possessions as a consequence of the interaction.

(2). any act(s) in which one or more peoples are compelled against their will to facilitate the fulfillment of the tangible or nontangible needs, wants, and desires of others, and suffer a significant lost as a consequence of the act(s), where the act(s) constitute an violation(s) of one's civil, human, and/or religious rights.

(3). any organized group activity consisting of premeditated and planed behaviors based on established techniques for achieving a set of clear objectives & means by the violation of the civil, human, and/or religious rights of others, and the outcome will include the groups acquisition of something they hold to be of value.

AMNESIA IN REINCARNATION

Vol. 3. The Encyclopedic Dictionary Of Terms & Concepts In CEBAGII.

KEY RELIGIOUS BELIEF:

BOTH NATURAL DEATH OF THE BODY, AND AMNESIA IN SUCCESSIVE LIFES, ARE ESSENTIAL ELEMENTS IN NATU-RAL REINCARNATION.

Narrative:

A succession of lifetimes, different circumstances, different bodies, different times & places; are all required to achieve the Supreme End. A single human lifetime is insufficient for two sets of reasons:

Firstly; In life the Personality of the physical manifestation creates limitations on range of experiences of the Associated Immortal Mind.

Secondly; A single human lifetime is insufficient to provide the immortal mind with the necessary range of experiences to facilitate the continuation of the fullest possible growth & development of the Associated Immortal Mind.

Natural Death is a stage in reincarnation, which facilitates the provisioning of the succession of humans lifetimes, which are required by the immortal mind for it's growth & development.

Amnesia is a tool that terminates the previous individual Personality when the immortal mind forms a association with a new physical manifestation, so that it can not restrict the previous personality in the successive physical manifestation.

NOTES:

Applicable Terms & Concepts To This Subject:

I. REINCARNATION;

(1). The process in which; (a) a Immortal Mind permanently ceases to associate with one physical manifestation ( or form ) resulting in the cessation of life signs in that form; and then ( b ) that same Immortal Mind gives life to another physical manifestation ( form ) by establishment of a longterm association with that form at it's conception.

(2). The process were by an Immortal Mind transitions from one physical manifestation to another physical manifestation, and thereby continues the Immortal Mind's growth & development, which consist of it's continuing to acquire additional divine qualities.

(3). The death of one individual form followed by the birth of another individual form of the same kind, in which both individual forms share the same associated Immortal Mind.

Reincarnation creates a new living soul consisting of two parts;
(1).The Physical Manifestation of the TemporalSpacial Energy Material Realm, whose transitory qualities are related to its physical existence, and

(2). The Associated Immortal Mind whose eternal qualities are of The Creator Alpha Omega, which it is a infinitesimal portion of, and which creates;

(a). the physical realm ( three dimensional space ) and

(b). all Physical Manifestations ( the physical qualities of things in three dimensional space ) in creation.

II. AMNESIA IN REINCARNATION;

The natural condition in which the individual physical manifestation can not recall the previous life of the physical manifestation which preceded it; despite the fact that both share the same associated Immortal Mind.

III. PERSONALITY;

(1). the distinctive individual qualities of a person, considered collectively. ( Websters New World Dict.)

IV. SELF;

(1). the identity, character, or essential qualities of any person or

thing. ( Websters New World Dict.). (2). the unique set of innate and acquired physical, mental, moral & spiritual qualities possessed by an individual being which come to define that person in the thoughts of her/himself and others, in this realm of existence.

The qualities which define our self are the consequences of a hierarchy of forces within us;

A. Our innate biological instincts which are the basis of our predatory nature.

B. Our mental faculties which enable us to modify both our environment and ourselves to fulfill our perceived needs.

C. Our moral/spiritual qualities which allow us to emulate the higher qualities of a Immortal Mind, having greater aspirations then the fulfilment of ones own needs and desires related to physical existence.

The immortal mind has only it's divine qualities which define it, these, and not the previous personality, determine the fundamental qualities of the next physical manifestation. If a living being could remember the previous life of it's Immortal Mind, then this memory would resurrect the previous personality. That personality would then become a controlling factor in the Physical Manifestations actions.

V. DEATH OF A BODY:

the permanent termination of the connection between that physical manifestation and that particular Immortal Mind, which renders the physical manifestation incapable of exhibiting the qualities of living beings (lifeless).

IN THE UNITED STATES DISTRICT COURT
FOR THE SOUTHERN DISTRICT OF OHIO
WESTERN DIVISION

PEEPLES VS. WARDEN

PETITION FOR SPECIAL WRIT OF HABEAS CORPUS DUE TO COVID-19 PANDEMIC. Under 28 U.S.C.S sec. 2241 & 2254.

STATEMENT OF THE PRISONER OF THE STATE SEEKING HABEAS CORPUS.

The first human patients with The covid-19 virus where infected was a pathogen specific to a species of animal. Today after multiple mutations we are now infected with a virus specific to human beings, which is therefore a more efficient killer of human beings. Medical science is now in a dire race to develop new treatments. We are in later waves of the pandemic, which historically have been the waves which claim the largest number of victims. For these reasons we are seeing an increase in pediatric ICU emissions, and continued high death rate of persons in the 50 to 60 age range.

Even with the increasing rate of vaccination within our country we continue to see the increasing rate of covid-19 infections, hospitalizations, and deaths. It has been determined that even persons who have taken the covid-19 vaccine may develop the disease after the vaccination, where those people have naturally abnormal immune systems incapable of fully protecting them against diseases ordinary people have the ability to effectively respond too.

According to the president of the united states and the surgeon general, medical science is in a race with mother nature to develop more effective treatments. But However, because the disease will have an extended duration, typical of pandemics, society must make changes to respond to the new conditions to reduce the diseases spread. The most vulnerable members of

our population are the older members having natural and acquired immune deficiencies. Particularly the older prison population.

The human too human transmission of the pathogen causing
the pandemic & health crisis, is impossible to fully prevent in
instances where it is necessary house feed and secure human
beings in large scale institutions under the direct supervision
of other human beings who are experiencing outbreaks of the
disease within their own group.

The imprisonment of persons having immune disorders and who
are not sentenced to death will result in the death of the persons
due to the necessary conditions of large scale institutions for
penal confinement.

This outcome is a clear violation of the constitutional rights of
those particular persons. This outcome is also contrary to the
law, and the intent of the sentencing judges, who sentenced
these persons with the intent that the would be rehabilitated and
return to society, not that their imprisonment would become a
death sentence. Those sentencing judges are without the power
to modify the sentences and release those rehabilitated prison-
ers who will surely die during this pandemic.

The prisoner medical record will show that this prisoner his become seriously ill in the past. Lukopenia is only a symptom of the immune disorder. The medical record will show he has been medically determined to suffer from a abnormal immune condition which under normal conditions randomly deteriorates the ability of his body to defend itself against infections, and which during this pandemic will cause his death should the condition worsen during a period of covid-19 infection when his body is

force to fight off this deadly disease.

This 59 year old, afroamerican male prisoner comes before this United States District Court seeking the justice which the states trial court judge can not grant him. For some 25 years he has been a model inmate. He has never engaged in life of crime while in prison or while on the streets. He is rehabilitated as the judge required.

He seeks not to escape justice, but having served 34 years of his life behind bars, the opportunity the law originally intended him to have, he seeks to return to society and live out the remained of his life a free man.

I do not blame anyone and not the Creator for my medical condition, I simply try to live whatever life I have left. I do blame the
state if my death is premature unnecessary and preventable and
do to circumstances the state has created refuses to acknowledge and will not remedy.

I throw myself upon the mercy of this court and beg only for
what the constitution of this land has promised all living persons,
the process which protects the inalienable rights to Life, Liberty,
and the Pursuit of Happiness, especially the right to Life.

I pray this court may give my circumstances & my request all
due consideration before the effects of the covid-19 pandemic
claim my life also as it has already done with many other prison-
ers such myself. Thank You.

Respectfully Submitted:

Kavin Lee Peeples

Southern Ohio Correctional Facility

18 September 2021.

www.ingramcontent.com/pod-product-compliance
Lightning Source LLC
Chambersburg PA
CBHW060620100726

47907CB00006B/1699

*9 7 8 1 6 3 7 5 1 1 1 1 4 *